THE
LEAGUE
OF
SHARKS

THE LEAGUE OF SHARKS

DAVID LOGAN

Quercus

First published in Great Britain in 2014 by Quercus Editions Ltd.

55 Baker Street
7th Floor, South Block
London W1U 8EW

A CIP catalogue reference for this book is available
from the British Library

ISBN 978 1 78087 577 4

1 3 5 7 9 10 8 6 4 2

Printed and bound in Great Britain by Clays Ltd, St Ives plc.

For Lisa, Joseph, Grace and Gabriel.

For my best friend's brood:
Marley, my godson, who was born while I was writing this,
his big sisters, Naomi and Emma, and big brother, Josh.

Glossaries of Jansian and H'rtu
can be found on pages 307–311.

1

Junk Doyle was twelve years old when his mother stopped loving him.

That wasn't supposed to happen. Not ever. It did, of course. All the time, all over the world. Some kids weren't lucky enough to be loved in the first place. Junk was. Very much so. For twelve years anyway. He had a mother and father, Janice and Dominic, and he was the apple of their eye. A chip off the old block. A mummy's boy. A daddy's boy.

He was big for his age. Took after his dad. Dominic Doyle was a carpenter and a good one. He was an artist. He married an American, Janice Truszewski. She had been travelling around Europe with her friend, Esther Creigh. Both from Milwaukee. Nineteen years old. Their first time out of the state of Wisconsin, let alone outside of the continental United States.

Esther wanted to trace her roots. Americans love to trace their roots. Their ancestors struggled to escape only for the offspring of their offspring of their offspring to come back again. Esther and Janice arrived in Ireland and Esther instantly understood why her great-grandfather had decided to leave. Janice, however, fell in love. First with Ireland and shortly after with Dominic. While Esther went back home and married a humourless orthodontist called Steven, Janice stayed and married Dominic. They lived in a tiny village called Murroughtoohy, on top of a cliff looking out over the Atlantic, in a grand old house that Dominic had inherited from his grandmother and spent the next several years rebuilding.

A little over a year after they married, they had a son. Junk. Of course his name wasn't really Junk. It was Colin. Colin Itzhak Eugene Doyle. However, from a very early age, before he could even walk, he had a habit of grabbing anything and everything within his grasp and hoarding it. When he was a toddler he was like a little waddling tramp. His pockets were always bulging with twigs and buttons and biros and springs and toys and stickers and sweet wrappers and all forms of . . . junk. The nickname started off as a joke. It was just a joke that never ended and at some point it became his name. When he started school, he was Colin for less than a week. By the first Thursday, even the teachers addressed him as Junk. He had long outgrown his habit of hoarding, but the name never went away.

And Junk was a happy boy. Why shouldn't he be? He lived on the beautiful west coast of Ireland with lots of room to run around inside and out. And he had loving, doting parents. Everything was perfect until he was six years old. Then, she came.

Ambeline.

Born in the middle of a storm-ravaged night, she was a squalling bundle of wrinkled pink skin. And the noise. The noises she made were the first thing Junk didn't like about her. He woke to hear his mother screaming in pain. He leaped out of bed, stumbling as he raced out of the room to see what was wrong.

His mother, father and two women, a midwife and a doula, were in the living room. His mother was naked, leaning against the sofa, the floor underneath her plastered with layers of newspaper, bin bags, sheets and finally towels. No one noticed Junk hidden in the shadows by the doorway, watching as that creature forced its way out from between his mother's legs. Junk's eyes were wide, tears sputtering in the corners as he saw the blood smeared down his mother's thighs. His precious mother. She screamed. The pain was too much for her to take. Junk could see that. No one could go through such an ordeal and survive. The slowly emerging parasite was killing her.

Junk covered his ears and closed his eyes tightly as his mother screamed again. Junk knew he had to do something. It was up to him. Everyone else, his father included, was just standing around and letting this horror transpire. His father was rubbing the base of his mother's back, trying to convince her it would all be OK for God's sake. *How could this torment ever be OK?* His mother was small, that monster was huge. Junk looked around. His eyes settled on a doorstop by his foot. It was in the shape of a rearing elephant and heavy, made from cast iron. He picked it up; it wasn't easy, it took both hands, and he was all ready to run in and batter that creature into oblivion when his mother started laughing. Everyone was laughing. His father was kissing his mother and saying, 'That's my girl, Janey, that's my girl.'

Junk craned his head and saw that the creature was out. It had burrowed its way out. Still attached by a long, white vein. It was not too late to smash its head in.

'Junk.'

Junk looked up as he heard his name. His father was coming towards him.

'How long have you been standing there?' Junk could only shrug and shake his head. Words were still a way off. He put the elephant-shaped doorstop down and his big father knelt in front of him and ran his vast, plate-sized hand through Junk's mane of dark hair. 'Come on. There's someone you should meet.'

His father stood up. It was like that old TV footage of the Apollo 11 rocket taking off. When his father stood, he just kept going up and up. He took Junk by the hand and led him over to where his mother was now lying on her back, covered with her favourite quilt. The creature was lying on her belly, snuffling. Junk was wary, knowing this demon could attack at any second. He was ready for it though.

'Hey, Poodle.' His mother often called him that.

'Ma!' Junk let out a half-hearted protest, mostly out of habit. He hated it when she called him that, especially in front of other people.

'Meet your little sister. This is Ambeline.' His mother rotated her body slightly so that the small, brown-stained goblin was looking at Junk. It was twisted and grotesque.

'What's wrong with it?' asked Junk.

'Nothing.' His mother laughed. He looked up and his father and the midwife and the doula were all laughing too. 'That's what babies look like. You looked like that once.' Junk frowned. He doubted that very much. 'Now you're a big brother, Junk, it's your job to look after her, make sure no harm ever comes to her. You're her knight.'

As the years passed, Junk proved himself to be a poor knight. His jealousy towards Ambeline was plain for all to see. His perfect little world had been changed, ruined in his mind. Barely a day went by when his father or his mother didn't have to reprimand him for shouting at his little sister, or pushing her, or punching her, if he thought he could get away with it. He blamed her for everything that went wrong. A toy got broken or lost: Ambeline broke it or hid it somewhere on purpose just to spite him. He was constantly trying to get her into trouble.

One grey, wet morning in the third October of Ambeline's young life, Junk was sitting on a window seat in their shared playroom, staring out at the clamorous drizzle that was peppering the glass and making it rattle in its frame. Beyond, the Atlantic fumed, almost black, complementing Junk's mood perfectly.

The door behind him opened and Ambeline slunk in dragging Hup, a tattered old blanket that went everywhere with her.

'What you doin', Jungy?' asked Ambeline, her voice muffled from behind the yellow blanket.

Junk wanted to be left alone. A hot breath of anger flashed through him. His ears darkened to a snarling maroon. 'Go away,' he grumbled, hardly bothering to open his lips.

'Why? What you doin'?' She gazed up at her big brother with huge blue eyes that seduced everyone she met. Everyone but Junk.

Why won't she just go away? thought Junk.

'You wanna play with me?' she asked.

Both of Junk's fists shrank slowly into a tight clench. The sound was like leather being twisted and then one curled hand shot out and struck. Ambeline gasped in surprise, but not pain, for it wasn't her who was hit. It was Junk. He had hit himself across his right cheekbone and dragged his nails down towards his mouth. He screamed at the top of his lungs and fell to the floor, clutching his face. Footsteps came pounding up the staircase and the door flew open. His mother exploded into the room.

'What is it?' she demanded. 'What's happened?' She saw Junk cowering on the floor, a little blood glistening under his eye. 'Oh my God! What happened?' She dropped to his side.

'She hit me!' cried Junk, forcing little anguished sobs between the words.

'Ambeline! You horrible girl! That's very bad!'

Ambeline didn't respond. She just looked at her mother and brother, frowning, a little bemused. She wasn't sure if this was a game. If it was, it wasn't much fun. She would rather play shops.

Janice snaked her arms around Junk and held him lovingly, shaking her head at Ambeline.

That time it worked just the way Junk wanted it to. Ambeline was kept away from him for the rest of the day and even put to bed earlier than usual. Every few weeks after that Junk would try it on again, but soon his parents grew wise to this pantomime and eventually Junk would get punished for trying to get his sister into trouble.

Then, one day, when Ambeline was a little older, some synapses in her brain joined together and she realized, with relish, that she had great power over her brother. She took to walking past him and slapping him or kicking him or poking him, causing him to cry out. Then she would sit by, looking innocent, while her parents reprimanded Junk for yet another ruse. Junk's resentment towards his little sister grew and grew.

This is not an unusual situation. For centuries

siblings have been warring with one another as they grow up. What makes it unusual and warrants this story being told is what happened next. What happened in the early hours of a stormy December night.

By this time Ambeline was six years old and had blossomed into a beautiful little girl with huge almond-shaped blue eyes and long fair hair. Junk was twelve and, though handsome, with dark green eyes and a mop of chaotic black hair, was just not cute any more. Friends and relatives and people in the street would always comment on Ambeline's angelic beauty, and mention would be made of how she was the absolute spitting image of her mother at that age. Usually as an afterthought they would say something about how big Junk was getting.

On 14 December, hailstones pelted the walls and windows, thunder roared across the heavens and lightning lit up the ocean, which could be seen from the Doyle house perched, as it was, on a high cliff looking westward.

Despite their hostile relationship, Ambeline was still just a little girl and looked to her parents and her big brother for comfort and protection. For some reason, that night, it was Junk's bed she crawled into when the storm scared her. Junk half woke as Ambeline shook his shoulder.

'Can I get in your bed?' she asked in a jittery little voice. Junk didn't answer. He just moved a few inches to the left, giving her room to climb in next to him. Ambeline fidgeted and turned as she snuggled in next to her brother and went back to sleep. She could feel his warm breath on the back of her head and it made her feel safe.

Some hours later, Junk was woken by a draught. His nose and ears were icy cold. He glanced up, eyes fighting not to open but being forced to give in. He saw that his window was wide open. The storm had eased some, but it was still raining hard and water was coming in. His plum-coloured curtains were drenched, making them look black. Junk looked down at Ambeline, fast asleep next to him, clutching Hup with a thumb in her mouth. He climbed over her and padded to the window. The wind was strong and it took all his strength to force it closed.

As he turned to get back into bed, he registered a movement out of the corner of his eye. His brain was still computing the information, only just managing to reach the conclusion that someone else was in the room, when he was hit from behind and went down hard, striking his head on the wooden corner of his bed. A cut opened up and blood haemorrhaged into his eyes. He pressed his hand against his eyebrow, stemming the flow. The room was moving, spinning. Someone stepped over him. Someone big. Very, very big.

It was a man, but he was an unusual shape. His head almost reached the ceiling. That meant he was nearly three metres tall. His shoulders were massively broad. In fact, it was hard to say where his shoulders ended and his neck began. His body was top-heavy. His legs were skinny in comparison. As he stood over the bed, looking down at Ambeline, lying there, still asleep and oblivious, a prolonged burst of lightning flashed outside and Junk saw the man in fleshed-out detail. Man might have been the wrong word. His mouth was wide and thin: a red slit stretching around the bottom part of his smooth face. His brow ran into his wide nose. His eyes were very large and set further back than was normal. The one on the left was milky and useless. A deep, jagged X-shaped scar criss-crossed it. His skin had a silver hue, though possibly that was from the lightning. There wasn't one hair visible on his body and he was soaking wet, presumably from the storm outside. Rivulets of water ran down his smooth skin.

His clothes seemed to be fashioned from a farrago of threadbare animal skins held in place by leather straps. It made Junk think of a Viking.

The man's arms were just a little too short for his huge body. His hands were wide and flat. He had five fingers and a thumb on each and when he stretched them out they slotted together leaving almost no gaps.

His chest was covered but his arms were bare. There were tattoos all over his skin and one in particular caught Junk's eye. It was on the upper portion of his left arm. It was black and stood out in relief: five stars circling a shark's fin cutting through the sea.

The man turned his head to look at Junk with his

good eye, which was black and reflective like polished onyx. He grinned. His wide mouth curled into an unnerving rictus and he hissed. Junk's head cleared and he pulled back. He wanted to cry out but his vocal cords weren't working.

The man turned his attention to Ambeline. He scooped her up in one of his paddle-like hands. This wrenched her from sleep and she looked around, getting her bearings. Her gaze settled on the stranger holding her and she screamed.

Dominic Doyle was awake in a second and out of bed. He raced out of his room and hurried to his daughter's room. He expected to have to soothe his young child back to sleep after a bad dream. He entered Ambeline's princess-themed boudoir and sat on the bed, moving stuffed toys and dolls. It took him a moment to realize that his daughter was not in her bed.

In Junk's room the giant silver man reached the window in three large ungainly strides. Ambeline was struggling in his grasp. With his free hand he slammed the window open.

Junk struggled to his feet and ran at the intruder. The giant batted him away with a flick of his wrist. His very touch opened up a series of small cuts on Junk's cheek. He watched as the stranger jumped from the window.

Not thinking, just moving on instinct, Junk pulled himself up and followed. The thing, the creature, the giant with Ambeline in its grasp was running towards the cliff-top. Without hesitation, Junk threw himself out of the window.

His bedroom was on the second floor. He landed on a small pitched roof, which was wet from the rain, and slid down it, picking up speed until he was spat off the edge, landing hard on the waterlogged ground below. Immediately he was on his feet, staggering and slipping but in pursuit.

Half a minute after Junk went out of the window, the door to his bedroom burst open and Dominic charged in. He saw instantly that the room was empty. He rushed to the open window in time to catch a shadowy glimpse of Junk rushing away.

'JUNK!' Dominic yelled at the top of his lungs. The storm was too dense for him to see the giant carrying Ambeline. He turned just as Janice entered the room.

'What's going on?' she asked. She looked at the vacant bed. 'Where are the children?'

On the cliff-top, Junk was running as hard as he could. He was frozen to the bone but ignored the pain coursing through him. He ran after the giant whose long legs were carrying Ambeline away at twice the speed Junk could go. Ambeline was screaming. She could see Junk behind her in the distance.

'JUNK! NO! I WANT MUMMY!' she cried.

*

At the house, Janice and Dominic came out of the front door. Their daughter's terrified screams were carried to them on the wind.

'JUNK! STOP!' Dominic ran as fast as he could; Janice too, trying to keep up.

The giant, hairless, silver-skinned man reached the edge of the cliff and stopped. Ambeline was struggling in his arms, desperate to get away. The man looked back and saw Junk drawing closer. Junk stopped. He held out his hand.

'Ambeline!'

The little girl, her wet hair matted against her scalp, reached out to her big brother, her knight.

'Junk! Help me!'

Junk charged at the man. 'Give her to me!' he shouted. The man kicked at him, knocking him to the ground. He stood over him, one of his massive feet stomping down on Junk's chest, pushing him into the mud and pinning him there.

'Fatoocha mammacoola charla,' he said, and grinned. Junk saw rows of small triangular teeth in his thin, wide mouth. And with that, the giant turned and started running.

'NO!' shouted Junk, but he was powerless. He watched as the man sailed out over the cliff-edge, still clutching Ambeline. She was screaming and reaching out for Junk. He scrambled after them in time to see Ambeline and her abductor enter the tumultuous waters thirty metres below. They disappeared below the surface. Junk watched but they didn't come up again.

'JUNK!' He turned to see his father appearing out of the thick grey rain, his mother close behind. Junk pointed over the cliff.

'He took her! He took her, Da! They went over!'

Dominic Doyle looked down at the waves crashing against the rocks below and let out a horrendous roar of anguish. Janice Doyle caught up and Dominic had to hold her back from the edge.

'Where is she?' wailed Janice. 'WHERE'S MY BABY?' She followed her husband's gaze down to the angry water below. Then, slowly, they both turned to look at Junk. 'What have you done?' said his mother.

Junk started to shake his head. 'What? No! There was a man. A giant. He took her.' But the words might as well have been snatched by the wind. As long as he lived, Junk would never forget that moment. His mother looked at him, looked back over the cliff and then back at him, her eyes boring into him with hatred.

Junk Doyle was twelve years old when his mother stopped loving him.

2

In the days that followed, Junk was interviewed and questioned by a succession of men and women in suits and uniforms. He could tell they all thought he had thrown Ambeline off the cliff. No one believed his story. Sure there were things that didn't quite add up, the strange cuts on Junk's cheek for one thing, but no one believed in the existence of a giant, silver, hairless child-snatcher. Clearly there was another explanation: maybe Ambeline's tiny little fingernails, desperately trying to defend herself against him, he overheard one of them saying to his colleague.

He didn't care about any of them or what they thought. There was only one person whose opinion mattered. His mother hadn't spoken to him apart from a few cursory, strained words here and there. She made sure they were never alone together. Every time she left a room as Junk entered, his stomach would twist itself round and round and he could feel the tears gurgling up in his throat, desperate to burst out in a burning wail of anguish. But he stopped himself. Choked them back. Swallowed them down. Into that black pit deep inside him. Sometimes the blackness would seep out and it would fill his body with emptiness. It was torture. Like he was drowning from the inside out, until that moment when he was completely empty or completely full, depending on your point of view. And then, he was nothing. Everything was blank. He was sure this was what death would be like.

It never lasted long enough. Sound would be the first thing to invade the emptiness. The ticking of a clock. Rain against the windowpane. His father hammering in his workshop. Or his mother crying, the door to her bedroom closed and locked or, even if it was wide open, closed and locked to him.

His father blamed him just as much as anyone else did but forced himself not to show it. He tried to be normal with Junk. Not like nothing had happened, but he would hold him a lot. His big hands on Junk's shoulders. Ruffling his son's hair. Just like he always had. Except it was completely different, and Junk knew it. It was a pantomime. A show. He knew his father was just going through the motions. Mimicking actions he had done hundreds, thousands of times before. He loved him for doing it, but hated it every time he touched him. Every touch was agony. Junk smothered that pain too. 'Com-part-mental-ized it,' as one of the suits had said. Not to him, of course. Very few people said anything directly to him, apart from the endless questions that they didn't want the real answers to.

Murroughtoohy was a small enough town that by the very next day absolutely everyone knew what had happened. Whatever friends Junk thought he had before didn't call. He knew it was probably their parents rather than them, but as time passed he felt more and more alone. He didn't know a single person on the face of the planet who didn't think he was a murderer.

It all came to an end eleven days after Ambeline's death. Christmas Day. Junk woke to the sound of his mother crying. This was no longer unusual. She was in a rage again, he could hear. She was breaking things. It didn't seem to matter what any more. She would vent her fury on anything. A few days earlier he had seen her attack the Christmas tree. It was a bizarre sight. A grown woman wrestling on the ground with a massive tree covered in red and gold decorations. The tree fought back. Its needles scratched and cut her, as did the jagged edges of the shattered baubles, but she didn't even seem to notice the blood. She ripped and pulled and kicked at that tree until its spine was broken and it was suffering in sap-stained agony, thinking, What did I do? I'm just a tree!

Junk got out of bed and edged out on to the landing. The noise was louder out here. He could see lights on downstairs. The sounds were coming from the kitchen. He thought his mother was probably going twelve rounds with the turkey: knocking the stuffing out of it. Literally.

As he descended the intricately carved staircase, built by his father, he glanced out of the window and saw lights on in the workshop in the back garden. He hesitated. His father was in there, not downstairs, not somewhere in the house, somewhere where he could help. Junk looked back up the stairs and knew he should turn round and go back to bed, even if he wasn't going to be able to sleep. Whatever he did, he should not even contemplate going down to the kitchen. His mother didn't want to see him, and it would only make things worse.

Slowly he continued to descend. The commotion coming from the kitchen stopped as Junk reached the foot of the stairs and he wondered if his mother had heard him coming.

The hallway was in darkness. The rectangle of light coming from the kitchen seemed somehow brighter than usual. *Go back now,* Junk said to himself in his head. *Turn round. Go through that door and everything changes.* He wanted so badly to stop and turn round and go back to his bedroom, but for some reason he didn't. He drew closer and closer to the kitchen. Until he stepped through the doorway, into the light.

Everything was broken. Everything. Plates and cups and glasses and dishes were smashed. Cutlery was bent. The shade covering the fluorescent strip light had been bashed free, which was why the light seemed brighter than usual.

All the cupboards had been wrenched from the walls. The tall, wide fridge-freezer had been tipped forward, snagging against the overhang opposite. The doors hung open and all the contents had rained out from within and collected in a large jammy, milky, chutney-y mishmash on the ground.

Junk's mother was sitting, head bowed, in the middle of the room. She was covered from head to toe in flour. It looked as if she had been baking and the bread had fought back. Rivulets of ketchup spread out around her. There was an unopened tin of peaches embedded in the partition wall leading to the utility room. A variety of cereals littered the floor: Weetabix oozed Marmite next to bran flakes peppered with pasta shapes.

Junk stared. Taking in the devastation all around him. His mouth was dry. He stared at the top of his mother's head. 'Ma,' he said in a small voice, unsure if he should speak at all but unable not to say something.

Janice Doyle didn't move for several long, awful moments. Then, slowly, infinitesimally slowly, she raised her head and for the first time in days she looked into her son's eyes. He held her gaze, desperately hoping that she would reach out to him and be his mother again. Then, like film of a raindrop hitting a leaf in extreme slow motion, a tear, a single fat tear, grew in the corner of his mother's eye. Junk couldn't look anywhere else. He was fixated on that tear. He watched it grow and swell until it had no choice but to submit to the laws of nature and gravity and it fell. It slid down Janice Doyle's cheek, cutting a path through the white of the flour until it reached her chin and fell to the ground. His mother's lips parted ever so slightly. He could hardly hear her voice but it was deafening:

'I wish *you* were dead.'

Junk swallowed that, banished it to the black pit within, and then he turned and he walked away.

He went to his room and grabbed his hurling kitbag. It used to be his father's and his grandfather's before that. He hesitated. Maybe he didn't deserve it now. Then he remembered he hadn't done anything except try to save his sister. He grabbed clothes from drawers and stuffed them into the bag. He crouched by the skirting board in the corner and prised a section loose. Behind it he kept his precious things in a green metal lock box, including eighty-seven euros and change. He threw that in the bag too and hefted it on to his shoulder.

He paused in the doorway and looked back one last time. He knew he'd never see this room again. Bitter tears streamed down his cheeks and he scraped them away with his sleeve.

He went back downstairs but avoided going anywhere near the kitchen. He turned back on himself at the foot of the stairs and lifted the latch on the pale green door that led into the boot room. He threw on his coat and his boots and left through the side entrance. Outside it was raining hard. He put up his hood and crossed a patch of sodden earth to his father's workshop, where he stood on tiptoes so he could see inside.

His father had his back to the window. It was warm in his workshop. Music was playing. Tom Waits. His father would always play that when he was feeling doleful. Junk saw that his father was working on a small ornate box of walnut with pearl inlay. This was going to be Ambeline's Christmas present. A beautiful box for all the cheap pieces of tacky, crappy jewellery she collected from the front of magazines, like any girl her age. That was so like his father. Always had to finish what he had begun. Even though there was no point. Now the recipient of the box was gone. Junk knew that in a day or so that box would be in Ambeline's bedroom, sitting on the shelves her father had made for her before she was born. Junk's eyes were red, but the tears were lost to the rain now.

Inside the workshop, Dominic heard or sensed something and turned to the window. But there was no one there. Junk had already left.

Junk walked east from Murroughtoohy until he reached the main road. He walked for three hours in the blackest of black nights. The rain was so hard he could feel every individual drop as they struck his face like a million pinpricks. He came across an articulated lorry parked up at the side of the road. He climbed up to take a peek through a slit in the cab's interior curtains and saw the driver asleep in a cot inside.

Junk found a shallow nook at the front of the trailer

behind the cab. It was just deep enough for him to shelter inside and get out of the rain. He pulled his sodden coat around himself and fell asleep.

He was woken a few hours later as the lorry's engine roared to life with a shudder. Junk was numb with cold but his little nook gave him some protection from the elements as the lorry pulled away, the driver oblivious to his stowaway.

The lorry drove to Galway, to the docks there, arriving just before first light. Junk pulled back deeper into the recesses of his little nook as a small, doughy man wearing a high-vis tabard and carrying an official-looking clipboard in an officious sort of way approached the driver. The man sported a comb-over that twirled and danced in the early-morning breeze and would not stay in place no matter how many times he patted it down.

The wind carried the voices of the two men away from Junk so he couldn't really hear what was being said apart from the occasional word. One thing he did hear was that the lorry was bound for somewhere called 'Kroona'. He didn't know where that was, but it sounded as good a place as any.

3

Kroona turned out to be A Coruña in northern Spain. Junk managed to stow away successfully. Many illegal immigrants try to sneak into Ireland. Very few people try to smuggle themselves out.

Even though he had left Murroughtoohy without any sort of plan other than to get far, far away, on the journey across the Channel an idea started to form in his mind. He would find him. He would find the giant who took his sister and he would bring him home to Murroughtoohy, dead or alive, and he would lay him down in front of his mother and say:

'This is who killed Ambeline. You see – I was telling the truth.'

When he reached Spain and got off the boat, he realized he didn't have the first idea how to find the man, but how many hairless silver tattooed giants with massive scars across their faces could there be in the world? He found an Internet cafe and stared at a search page for several minutes, trying to work out how to start. He typed in 'scars' and got some interesting results. Interesting as in sick and demented. The woman at the next terminal glanced at his screen, glanced at him and then quickly moved away. After searching for scars, giants and hairlessness, he spent the best part of two hours looking for references to the tattoo. He found nothing helpful and in the end decided that he wouldn't find the answers via a keyboard, in a book or by staying in one place. He figured the answers were out there somewhere in the world and he would have to go to them.

He decided that the tattoo of the shark fin and five stars suggested some connection to the sea, so that was where he would concentrate his search. He went to the harbour and hung around, trying to make friends with the local fishermen. This wasn't easy, seeing as he spoke absolutely no Spanish. But gradually he picked up a few words here and there and there were enough Spaniards about who spoke English.

His eighty-seven euros and change lasted long enough for him to start picking up some casual work. Usually cleaning out the boats after their return from sea. It was dirty, stinking work that paid little, but Junk was a hard worker and that was a virtue that was appreciated here.

To begin with his lack of age raised a few eyebrows and the odd direct question, but Junk sidestepped the realm of direct answers as much as he could. When he came across someone who was too interested in why he was there and seemingly parentless, he would just move somewhere else.

He moved from one port to another and worked

every sort of boat going. Over the next three years he travelled the globe, working on fishing boats, trawlers, dredgers, ferries, cruise ships and tugs. In that time Junk grew taller, broader and stronger, looking more like his father every day. By the time he was fifteen, Junk could pass for eighteen without raising a single questioning eyebrow. His skin had become darker from working in the elements. Day after day of intense sunlight burning down on him and the continual spray of seawater had roughened his skin, aging him. His verdant green eyes stood out even more because of his tanned face. He was an intense and serious-looking young man though still crowned by an explosion of wild black hair, which was forever flopping over his eyes.

He had been all around the Mediterranean, North Africa, the Caribbean, Australia and New Zealand, and spent most of a year in South America. Now he spoke eight languages, not one of them fluently, not even English any more. Sometimes he would go for months without talking to another English speaker, but he would get by in pidgin French or strangled Russian or a smattering of Arabic. Somehow the multinational seafarers could always find some common ground when it came to language.

For a long time, he found no trace of the scarred giant. No one he met had heard of such a man or recognized the tattoo that Junk would reproduce quickly and expertly on a napkin or the back of a menu or beer mat when the moment called for it. Then one night in Valparaíso, Chile, in a rundown waterfront bar, he met a grizzled sea dog by the name of Salvador de Valdivia, who took a shine to Junk when he discovered he was Irish and swore blind that he himself was descended from Bernardo O'Higgins Riquelme, Irish–Chilean hero of the nineteenth-century Chilean War of Independence. Salvador was an old drunk with his best seafaring years far behind him, but he and Junk got talking nonetheless. Salvador's English wasn't bad, but his attempts at mimicking Junk's admittedly fading Irish accent made him sound Jamaican. He didn't recognize the description of the giant and pointed out that it was unlikely he would ever forget such an individual, but when Junk drew the tattoo for him the old man gasped, muttered to himself in Spanish and started nodding excitedly. This he had seen.

'Where?' asked Junk, his heart pounding violently in his chest. Frustratingly the old man couldn't remember immediately. He squeezed his rheumy eyes shut and tapped his rough sandpapery fingertips against his leathery, corrugated forehead as if he could jar the memory loose, and maybe he could because after a moment he sat up, arms raised triumphantly.

'*La Liga de los Tiburones!*' he shouted.

It took Junk a moment to translate: 'The League of the Sharks?' he said.

'*Sí*, the League of Sharks,' said Salvador. 'This is their symbol.'

Junk couldn't believe it. After all this time, at last, a

lead. Something. He looked at the old man. 'What is it? What is the League of Sharks?'

Salvador shrugged. 'I don't know.'

'What d'you mean you don't know?' asked Junk petulantly.

'La Liga de los Tiburones is older than me. Is ancient. My grandfather told me about it when I was a child. His grandfather told him.'

'So it's Chilean?'

'No.' The old man shook his head.

Junk sighed with frustration and forced a level tone into his voice. 'So where does it come from?'

'I don't know. Nobody knows.'

'Somebody must know.'

'No,' said Salvador. 'It's a legend as old as the sea. A myth lost in time.'

Junk sighed. He didn't understand.

The old man went on. 'The stories my grand-father would tell me were about sharks who walked like men . . . who stepped out from the sea and walked on land.' The old man stuck out his lower lip apologetic-ally and shrugged. 'But they are just stories. Nothing more.'

'Where would I go to find out more about La Liga de los Tiburones?'

The old man shook his head. He didn't have an answer.

As Junk walked away from the waterfront bar that night he was filled with a bleak sense of failure. After

27

all this time he finally had a lead, but one that led nowhere.

No!

Junk rejected his negativity. He had a lead. Slight as it was, it was more than he had when he woke up that morning. More than he'd had for a thousand mornings. He had something. He had La Liga de los Tiburones.

In each country he visited from then on he would find a bar or a cafe or any place where people congregated and he would find an old-timer like Salvador, who loved to talk for the price of a bottle of aquavit in Göteborg, cheap wine in Marseilles or Metaxa in Kerkyra. He would let them do the drinking and the talking. He would refill their glass and listen. He would ask about La Liga de los Tiburones and legends of the sea. Especially ones that involved strange creatures. Most times he would get nothing, but every now and again he would hear a story about fish who could walk on land like men, talk like men. He would hear stories about whale-men who were thirty metres tall or women with tentacles instead of legs. The majority of these stories were embellished half-truths, their genesis lost to time and imagination.

But eventually Junk realized there were elements that kept being repeated, whether the story was told in Valparaíso or Saint Petersburg or Bangkok.

He met an old British merchant navy man called Ian in Tampico on the Gulf Coast of Mexico. Ian had heard of La Liga de los Tiburones. He said it had many names:

De Bond van de Haaien in Dutch; sha yu tuan dui in Mandarin; O Adelfóthta tou Karcarión in Greek; Shaark Ki Sangha in Hindi, but all of them meant the same thing: the League of Sharks.

Junk sighed. He had heard these before. 'I know what I'm looking for now,' he said. 'But I'm no closer to finding it. Every country seems to have some connection to the League of Sharks. They don't seem to come from anywhere in particular.'

'Which is odd, if you stop to think about it,' observed Ian. 'Lots of countries or religions share myths. Jesus and Mohammed are basically the same person, but they all adapt the stories to suit their own proclivities.' It wasn't quite the right word but Junk chose not to correct him and Ian carried on. 'But the stories about the shark league are all the same, whether you hear them from a Turk or a Chinaman.'

Junk thought about this for a moment and it was true, though he wasn't sure if that meant anything.

'There's one place you could try, if you haven't already,' said Ian.

Junk listened eagerly.

'Ionian Sea . . . south of Corfu. I've never stopped to count them up, but if you poked me with a stick and made me, I'd guess I've heard more stories connected to that part of the world than anywhere else.'

Junk frowned. Could that be true?

That night when he got back to his bunk on the cargo ship he was currently crewing on, he took out a small leather-bound notebook from his hurling bag. He had made a note of all the stories he had heard in connection with the League of Sharks. Close to a hundred by now. He was angry with himself that he had never thought to do this before. It was so simple. He went through all the stories, one by one, to see which part of the world they mentioned. The result wasn't overwhelming, but Ian was right. The Ionian Sea cropped up more than anywhere else.

Junk left the cargo ship when they docked in Miami and found work below decks on the *Adventuress*, a bargain-basement cruise ship crossing the Atlantic to North Africa. The passengers were mostly retired Americans who had saved for decades to be able to afford this once-in-a-lifetime trip, but when it came to it all their years of thriftiness didn't amount to quite enough and they were stuck on an old ship that should have been decommissioned long ago and where the headline entertainment on board was someone who had come second on the Armenian version of *The X Factor*.

On arriving in Casablanca, Junk left the *Adventuress* and worked his way north up Morocco's western coast to Tangier. From there he was able to find employment on a salvage ship, the *Pandora*, with a Russian diver called Timur, whose crew consisted of himself and his small, permanently angry Chinese wife, Kit-Yee, who was supposed to be the ship's cook but couldn't cook anything edible if her life depended on it. By the end of Junk's second day on board, he had taken over galley duties as well as assisting Timur when he would dive down to wrecked ships looking for anything remotely valuable.

For the next few months, the *Pandora* sailed around the Mediterranean and the Ionian Sea. Junk used all his spare time to look for traces of the League of Sharks, but disappointingly found nothing.

Timur turned out to be a hopeless drunk. He was as useless a diver as his wife was a cook. With a hangover would come debilitating claustrophobia, which would mean he couldn't dive without bringing on a panic attack. Within a relatively short space of time, Timur had trained Junk to dive for him. Timur was supposed to stay on board and monitor Junk's progress, but usually he would get drunk and sing along to ABBA songs of which he was a fanatic.

Junk woke to the sounds of Timur's heavy Vladivostok brogue strangling the lyrics of 'The Winner Takes It All' and knew that Timur and Kit-Yee had been arguing.

'Vinner take it all, Loser standing small, Beside victory, That's *HIS* destiny . . . !'

Then Junk heard Kit-Yee throwing pans in the galley and knew the row was a bad one. Junk just hoped Timur hadn't called Kit-Yee by the wrong name again. Timur had been married five times, each time to a small, fiery Chinese woman, and he wasn't very good at remembering their names. Especially when drunk. It didn't help that they all had quite similar names. Timur had a very specific type, it seemed. His fourth wife, Ming-Yee, had duct-taped him to his bed and set the *Pandora* heading out to sea with no one at the helm. Timur travelled across the Indian Ocean for three days until the fuel ran out and then drifted for another four until he was miraculously rescued by a Chinese fishing boat. He married the skipper's daughter, Kit-Yee, after she nursed him back to health. When Timur had told Junk this story it was never clear if Timur was still married to Ming-Yee or in fact to any other of his previous wives.

Junk lay in his bunk, listening to the end of the song. It restarted almost immediately. Again not a good sign. Junk knew he should get up and get the day started but he wanted to postpone his involvement in Timur and Kit-Yee's domestics for just a little longer. He turned his eyes to the wall next to him. It was papered with drawings, mostly his own amateurish doodles of the tattoo, interspersed with a few more professional offerings he had picked up on his travels from people with an artistic flair, whose imaginations had been ignited by Junk's description of the man (creature?) who had killed his sister. Junk had taken to calling his quarry the 'Sharlem'. He had met an elderly Jew in Buenos Aires, who told him stories from Hebrew myth about golems: monsters made from clay and brought to life to avenge wrongs. Junk decided that whatever had taken Ambeline was not of this world. It was a monster, like a golem but from the shark side of the family. Hence Sharlem. Though that didn't quite work as a moniker, not nearly scary enough, it was better than Golark, which sounded quite sweet.

'The Winner Takes It All' came to an end again and Junk lay and listened. After a few moments of silence, 'Lay All Your Love on Me' started to play. That was promising. Not as good as 'Honey, Honey', but better than 'The Name of the Game'. It meant Timur was calming down.

Junk got up and threw on a pair of shorts and a T-shirt and left his cabin.

The *Pandora* was a fifteen-metre former albacore jig boat. As it was no longer a fishing boat it had been modified for a new exciting life as a diving support vessel. Gone were the six-metre outriggers to which two dozen fishing lines would have been attached to troll for tuna, though part of the support for these was still visible on the port side because Timur had never got round to dismantling it properly.

The *Pandora* was anchored off the north-east coast of Corfu. The green and rocky island sat to the starboard and across the Notio Steno Kerkyras sea channel sat Albania, all dusty brown and uninviting.

Junk came up from below and found Timur stretched out on the *Pandora*'s foredeck wearing a pair of crusty boxer shorts and a tatty silk dressing gown that hung open, revealing his unnaturally hairy torso. Timur Nikolayev was a slovenly, bearded man who farted and belched more than anyone else Junk had ever met. His personal hygiene habits were abysmal. He rarely washed.

He preferred to stand naked on deck during a wild storm and let the angry spray clean him.

Timur was resting his head on the capstan, a bottle in one hand and a remote control for the stereo, stored up in the deckhouse, in the other. 'Lay All Your Love On Me' finished and Timur held up the remote. He pressed the pause button as he looked up at Junk. His eyes were red from crying and there were crumbs of cheese and a glob of taramasalata sitting in his bushy salt-and-pepper beard.

'She's goin' to leave me, Junk!' He pronounced Junk's name as *Yunk*.

Junk nodded. 'Probably. What did you do wrong this time?'

'NOTHING! Nothing . . . nothing . . . nothing did I do wrong!'

'Did you call her by the wrong name again?'

Timur growled and stuck his little finger in his ear, wiggled it violently and pulled out a small ball of wax, which he proceeded to smell and then wipe on his robe. 'I might have done.'

'Well, that does tend to annoy her.'

'I say to her, call me any . . .' He paused momentarily and belched loudly. 'Any name you want – I don't care. A name is unimportant.'

'And what did she say to that?'

'She threw bottle at my head!' Timur lifted his shaggy fringe to reveal a bloody welt. Junk made an ambiguous sound and set about organizing the diving equipment. 'And look what she does when I'm *a-sleeping*.' Timur rose to his feet unsteadily and pulled off the silk robe, twisting at the waist to show Junk his back. Like his front, it was covered in a thick, bushy layer of black hair. Three Chinese symbols had been shaved into it.

'What does it say?' asked Junk.

'I don't know. She won't tell me,' said Timur. Five Chinese wives and he had never bothered to learn the language. 'But I think she is insulting my mother. In my back hair! Have you ever heard anything like it?'

'It's original,' said Junk, and turned back to the equipment.

'If she leave me, I will kill myself.' Junk was not concerned. Timur threatened to kill himself with some regularity. The wind was too strong or not strong enough; he would threaten to kill himself. They were out of the crackers he liked; he would threaten to kill himself. A seagull looked at him funny and he would threaten to kill himself. 'When I'm gone, I want you to have the *Pandora*. Continue my legacy, like son I never have.'

'You have eight sons, Timur, and six daughters. That you know of.'

'But not one is Russian.'

'More Russian than me.'

'You are Russian in your heart. Plus you have Russian thumbs.'

Junk stopped what he was doing and looked at him, frowning. 'Russian thumbs?'

'Strong. Russian thumbs are strong.' Junk looked at

his thumbs. His hands were rough and weathered from three years of hard physical work, from pulling coarse ropes and tying knots.

'Are you diving today?' Junk looked at Timur, already knowing what the answer would be.

Timur screwed up his face and shifted uncomfortably. 'I have pain behind my eye.'

'Do you want me to go?' asked Junk, already pulling on a wetsuit.

Timur clamped a big hand on Junk's shoulder and smiled paternally. 'You are good boy, Junk.'

Junk tipped off the side of the *Pandora* and entered the water. He liked to dive. He found the silence soothing, like the first morning after heavy snow. Everything was muffled and calm, his own breath the only clear sound. He got his bearings quickly and started to descend, following a guide rope he had set up on his first dive at this particular site three days earlier. It led him down thirty metres to a sunken wreck. It was a forty-metre Dutch three-mast schooner called the *Pegasus*. It had been down here since the 1920s, when it belonged to friends of the Rothschild family who owned a villa on the island.

Even after some ninety years sitting in its watery grave and covered with a thick husk of barnacles, the *Pegasus* was still a magnificent-looking vessel. Junk could easily imagine how it would have appeared in its heyday: its ebony hull cutting through the cerulean water, brass railings glinting in the blinding afternoon sun. The deck had been walnut, inlaid with ivory and mother-of-pearl. To this day, no one knows how the *Pegasus* sank. There was a dirty great hole in its hull, but whatever caused the fissure came from within rather than from something colliding with the boat.

Still, Junk wasn't down here to find out what had happened. He was here for salvage. Of course, after this long there was unlikely to be anything of value remaining, but sometimes you'd get lucky.

Junk approached the *Pegasus* from the stern and swam three-quarters of its length to an open hatch. The beam of his torch cut through the turbid water. Crabs scuttled away to hide and small fish darted in and out of rusty holes peppering the bulkhead. Junk swam inside.

A long corridor stretched ahead. The *Pegasus* had come to rest at a forty-five-degree angle, bow down, so it felt to Junk like he was descending further into pitch-blackness. He passed five bloated wooden doors, each marked with a cross scratched into the grain: Junk's marks to tell himself which cabins he had investigated already. He entered the sixth.

It was a small state room. He stopped in the doorway and shone the torch around. Its light picked out a large ebonized chest of twelve drawers. He swam over to it and tried each drawer in turn. Most were empty. One held the remnants of a pair of gloves, now more holes than fabric and worthless. Timur wasn't an archaeologist. Junk's remit was not to preserve the past but to profit from it.

Junk opened the eighth drawer and something small

and metallic fell out and sank quickly. He trained the torch on the floor and crouched down. He found an old key. He glanced around looking for a lock it might fit but saw nothing. Frowning, he checked his watch. His air was getting low. He'd have to think about surfacing.

Just then something caught his attention. Thin fingers of green light were seeping in through a rusty hole in the hull. Junk frowned and lowered himself for a closer look. Through a hole about the size of a tennis ball, he could see a bright rectangle of green luminescence some twenty metres away from the boat, just sitting there on the dark, silty seabed. It was taller than it was wide and shimmering as if beams of emerald light were criss-crossing. The centre was brightest and solid, the light becoming more translucent at the unnaturally straight edges. Suddenly something large swam past his viewing hole. Junk pulled back, startled. He steadied his nerves and looked again.

At first he didn't see anything. Then he saw a shadow approaching the green light. As it drew closer, Junk gasped. It stopped a few feet away and then walked on two legs. Junk could tell straight away that it wasn't the creature that took Ambeline, but it was one of his kind. He was shorter, skinnier. Maybe a little more than two metres tall. He had a tattoo of a fish on the top of his hairless head. He stopped in front of the green rectangle of light and glanced back over his shoulder at the *Pegasus*, looking straight at Junk. On his left bicep he sported another tattoo: five stars and a shark's fin. The symbol of The League of Sharks. Junk froze and held his breath. Then the shark-man walked into the light and vanished. The light was a portal, a door. Slightly ajar. It started to fade. Junk realized the door was closing. What to do? No time to decide. He looked at his watch. He only had a few minutes of air left. He had to go up, but after three years he knew he couldn't.

He turned and swam as fast as he could out of the stateroom and back into the corridor beyond. He kicked his legs, powering through the water. In seconds he was out of the hatch. The green light was almost gone, and he was still several metres away. He didn't see how he could make it before it vanished completely, but he had to try. His legs kicked and his arms pumped. His chest burned with the exertion and the dwindling air supply. Moving like this was wrong. It was using up precious oxygen. It was now touch-and-go if he could get back to the surface at all, but Junk wasn't thinking about that. He wasn't thinking about anything except getting to the green light before it was gone.

Three metres. Two. The light kept reducing. It was possibly now too small for him to pass through, but he kicked harder. No time to hesitate. With one last surge of effort, he went through. He could feel the opening constrict around him like a solid aperture closing.

Finally the light disappeared completely and Junk with it. All that remained was the tip of one of his fins. Sliced clean through, it floated slowly to the seabed. Junk was gone.

4

Junk squeezed his eyes shut. His head was pounding. He ripped off his mask, spat out his mouthpiece and filled his lungs. He opened his eyes but found it hard to focus so he closed them again. Closed out the spinning room.

Room . . . ?

He opened his eyes again. There was a cold, hard, reflective floor beneath him. It was metallic, green-black. It made Junk think of a picture of a scarab beetle he had once seen in a book. He was disorientated.

His head didn't hurt so much now. He sat up and looked around, pulling the neoprene cowl off. He had no idea where he was. He was in a cavernous chamber so large that he couldn't see the ceiling or the walls. The distance just dissolved into shadow. But all around him were portals of green light, just like the one he had come through. Thousands of them. Thousands of doors. A room of doors.

The doorways weren't set into walls. They were

free-standing. They were arranged in ordered rows and columns. Junk pulled off his one and a half swim fins and stood up. He walked around the door he had passed through. He was able to view it from three-hundred-and-sixty degrees and it looked the same from all angles. The green hue was deeper in here. It pulsed at regular intervals like a heartbeat.

Only now did Junk notice that all the doors were pulsing softly, in unison, and if he trained his ear on the sound he could feel a sonorous thrum reverberate through him every ten seconds or so. It entered the soles of his feet and moved upwards. The room felt like it was inside a living organism, a vast whale maybe. The sensation had soporific qualities and Junk found his eyelids growing heavy. He sucked in a sharp bubble of air. It was cold, like air in a meat locker, and it made Junk feel alert.

He remembered what he was doing here. The creature. Where had he gone? He looked around but there was no sign of him. He listened but couldn't hear anything other than the low drone of the doors. Now what? Then he noticed footprints. A trail of wet tracks leading away from him. He followed them.

The tracks moved away to the right for about a hundred metres and then stopped at one of the many doorways. Evidently the creature had gone through. Without hesitation, Junk followed. As the light from the doorway touched his skin, he could feel a tugging sensation as if some invisible force was pulling him in. For a moment he started to pull back, but the force was growing stronger and he was unable to stop himself being drawn in.

For a second or two Junk felt as if he was moving so quickly that the molecules of his body were being sucked apart, but before he had time to panic they were all slammed back together and he was spat out.

He found himself on a narrow ledge still in the Room of Doors but much higher up. He was a good fifty metres or more off the ground. He could judge this by the fact that there were twenty or so levels of doors beneath him now, whereas before they had been only above him. He looked down and spotted his air tank, mask and swim fins a long way down. A surge of vertigo-induced dizziness fluttered through him. He groped for a wall but there was nothing to hold on to. The only solid thing was the tiny ledge beneath his feet. It was made of the same cold, hard, metallic green-black substance as the ground level and was about a metre wide. After a moment Junk got his balance. He looked around and saw that the trail of wet footprints carried on to his left. Gingerly he started to follow them, walking sideways to maintain the most secure balance.

After he had gone thirty metres or so, the footprints started to evaporate and Junk felt a flicker of panic at the prospect of losing his only clue as to the creature's path. Then he reached two doorways that stood side by side, with only about half a metre's gap between them. Here the footprints, or the little that was left of them, stopped. The only problem was that it wasn't clear which of the two doors the creature had gone through. The two portals were so close that the shallow film of seawater was in front of both. Junk could see nothing to do but choose one and hope for the best.

He looked back the way he had come and counted the number of doorways he had passed on the ledge: eighteen. Then he turned and looked down, searching for the first doorway, the one he had initially come through. His empty air tank, mask and discarded swim fins were sitting on its threshold. He counted the doorways he had passed on the ground level: thirty-nine. Now that he felt confident that he knew the way back, he turned to the two doors in front of him and pointed at the one on the left and recited a rhyme from the deep recesses of his mind:

'Eenie, meenie, tipsy, toe, Olla, bolla, domino, Okka, pokka, dominocha, Hy! Pon! Tush!'

The left door. He took a deep breath and then stepped forward. He felt the pull take hold of him and suddenly he was yanked into the portal.

Once again he felt himself travelling at great speed, this time for a little longer than before. He felt his molecules being pulled apart and circling around one another, before being slammed unceremoniously back together in more or less the right order as he was spat out.

For a few moments he was encased in a shroud of air bubbles, but these slowly disappeared and Junk realized he had not come out in another part of the Room of Doors this time. This time he was underwater once again. It took him only a moment to realize that he didn't have his air tank or mask with him. Another moment to realize he didn't know which way was up and which way was down, and what was worse he didn't know how far down he was. The only light was the light of the doorway, but the momentum with which he had passed through it meant he was moving rapidly away from it.

Junk opened his mouth for a split second to allow a single bubble of air to emerge. It chose a direction and rose quickly. This told Junk which way was up. He made a decision and spun round. He started swimming, chasing his air bubble as if he was trying to get it back. His arms reached up and pushed the water down, causing him to ascend swiftly. His lungs were starting to burn and the spent air bubbled out from his nose as he swam upwards in a panic. His oxygen was running out, this time much faster than before and with no doorway to pass through. The portal was shrinking many metres below him, but Junk wasn't even aware of it. All his focus was aimed straight up as he scrambled madly to reach the surface. His lungs were empty. Utterly depleted. His instinct was to inhale, but he fought the urge as hard as he could. He knew if he breathed in he would drown. He wasn't going to let that happen. He ploughed on, racing upwards, but still he couldn't see an end. No sunlight or moonlight from above. Nothing but darkness all around him. His head was beginning to pound mercilessly as his brain protested at the lack of oxygen. His vision started to blur and black tentacles of unconsciousness started to creep in from the peripheries. Still he kept his jaw clamped tightly shut and still he continued upwards.

Then it was too late and the unconsciousness beat him. And as his body went limp, his jaw opened and the cold seawater gushed inside him. He started to thrash about as he drowned, the water entering his lungs. Fortunately Junk had lost consciousness altogether. The thrashing was nothing more than a mechanical response of his body. He was not aware of his own death.

Garvan Fiske lay in his boat, staring up at the clouds above him. He liked this time of day. The cool, salty breeze that danced over the top of the calm, still water moved the thick hairs on his powerful forearms and he could feel his skin pimple. It made him think of his home so far from here. He remembered lying on the old jetty, trailing a hand in the water as he was doing now and looking up at the sky. It was the same sky. The same shade of pale blue. But the sounds were different. Back there he would hear the insects and animals in the nearby forests and the sound of his brothers and sisters playing. Here there was none of that. A few gulls floating nearby squawked occasionally and he could hear the waves breaking on the distant shore. The sea thumped against the side of his boat and the oar moved in its cup, creaking softly. Now he thought about it, he realized how quiet it was. How different the sounds were. Back home, laughter, song and labour. Here, emptiness and solitude. He remembered how alone he was and he felt a spike in his throat. He sat up and shook those thoughts away. He started humming in a vague approximation of the song he had enjoyed hearing his mother singing. He made tuneless guttural sounds from the depths of his windpipe and he knew he sounded like a constipated cow, but there was no one here to object apart from the gulls. One of them flew away but the others stayed. He reached behind and grabbed his net. He checked the areas he had spent the previous evening repairing and saw, in the cold light of day, that he had done a good job. The only way one could tell they were new was by the difference in colour. The mended sections were lighter than the old, but after half a dozen fishing trips it would all look the same.

Garvan stood up and his little boat rocked under his immense frame. He wore nothing but a pair of old shorts cut down from a pair of trousers that once belonged to his father. They were patched so often now that there was more new material than the original. Everything he possessed now was patched, mended and repaired. His net, his boat, his cabin, his shorts. How different from his early years. Maybe one day he would once again be the first to own something. Before anyone else. Something new. Actually new and not just new to him. He paused to wonder what it might be, but nothing came readily to mind.

He loosened his broad shoulders and started to spin the fishing net above his head, getting faster and faster and raising it higher and higher until, just at the perfect moment, he let it go and it sailed out to sea, spreading wide as it went. Landing the optimum distance from the boat, the small weights attached to the edges started to sink and in moments the net vanished from view. Garvan wrapped a trailing rope around his arm and waited. He was perfectly still. The rope twisted around his forearm tightened as the net filled with fish. Then, all of a sudden, something much heavier and much bigger than his usual catch was scooped up below the water. Garvan knew this because he was yanked forward. His reactions were quick. His muscles tensed and he brought his powerful leg up, slamming the four toes of his right foot against the bow. He grunted and started to bring the net up, drawing it in hand over hand.

It was too heavy and he wasn't sure he was going to be able to land it. That would be a disaster. He would have no alternative but to cut the net away and all his fine work repairing it would have been for nothing. He was determined not to let that happen. He growled with exertion and pulled harder. He could see the net coming up. Only a few more metres. He paused, breathing heavily. He took a moment to brace himself and then with an almighty tug he hauled the net into the boat.

Garvan's feet slipped out from under him and he fell backwards. He lay there for a few moments panting. Then he looked up. What had he snagged? What had weighed down his net? Could it be one of the big gaper fish? They still came round here, though he hadn't caught one for a long time. He saw a black and grey shape in the middle of the net, covered with a hundred silver-green mackies flapping and writhing.

Garvan grabbed an oar and used it to open up the net, staying a safe distance away. As the net unfurled, the fish parted and there was Junk, lying in a twisted heap. Garvan frowned and poked the lump with the end of his oar, causing Junk's arm to slip to the side. Junk was lying on his back, but not moving and apparently not breathing. Garvan poked him again with the oar, a little harder this time. He was debating what to do. Should he throw it back in the sea? It looked dead. He poked it one last time and suddenly Junk started to cough and vomit up a huge amount of water. Garvan held up the oar as a weapon, ready to bring it down if Junk attacked.

Junk didn't. After all the water had evacuated his body, he opened his eyes and tried to focus. He saw Garvan looming over him. To Junk, Garvan was immense. He was easily four metres tall and about half as wide. His skin was somewhere between light brown and grey. His shoulders were broad and muscular. His hands were twice the size of Junk's head and he had only four digits on each. Same as his toes. He had a strong chin but a weak mouth. His nose was broad and little more than nostrils. It was almost snout-like. He had long unkempt brown hair. For a fleeting moment the thought started to bloom in Junk's mind that he should panic, but before it could amount to anything substantial unconsciousness overtook him once more and he passed out.

Garvan looked down at Junk, who looked as unusual

to him as he did to Junk. He prodded him with the oar again but Junk didn't move. Then, feeling brave, Garvan crouched down and poked him roughly in the chest with his index finger. Junk didn't react. Garvan tossed the oar down on the deck and stood contemplating his unusual catch. What was he supposed to do? The fish were all still by now and he had to get them out of the sun before they spoiled. He knew he should throw Junk back. It would be the sensible thing to do. A little voice inside his head was telling him that if he didn't, he would live to regret it. No good would come from this. However, on the other hand, by the rules of the sea, he had landed him so he belonged to him, and Garvan never threw anything away unless he knew it wasn't going to be useful. He wasn't sure how or if Junk would turn out to be useful, but he didn't know that he wouldn't be, so he made a decision, locked the oar back into place and headed for shore.

5

When Junk next woke, he was lying on a bed of soft silver fur. It was so plush that he sank into it and the fur closed around him, enveloping him in its delicate embrace. It was probably the most luxurious bed he had ever slept on.

He sat up and looked around. He was in a cabin made of wood. The ceilings were at least eight metres high. The craftsmanship that had constructed it was stunning. Junk knew about wood because of his father. Without consciously seeking them out, Junk was drawn to the joints in the elaborate roof. A mix of mortise and tenon joints and comb joints, all cut to perfection. Even though he recognized the style, there was something different about how it was put together. He couldn't quite work out what it was. Maybe it was the wood itself. The grain was extremely tight. Its colour was a rich burnt coppery orange.

Half the room was in darkness even though it was light outside. Sunlight streamed through the windows. Something caught Junk's attention and he frowned as he stared at the nearest window. The glass looked different from normal glass. It was slightly translucent, thickening the light as it entered. Nothing was sharp.

All the furniture was wooden, handmade and huge. The table was as tall as Junk himself. In fact, he would probably have to stand on tiptoe to see over it.

He threw off the blanket that had been covering him and discovered two things. The first was that he was wearing a shirt that was vast. The sleeves were three times the length of his arms. He pulled and pulled and pulled some more to roll one of them up enough to free his hand. He managed to tuck the ends inside, but it meant there was a lot of bunched-up material hanging from his arm. He did the same thing with the other sleeve. The shirt went down past his feet and the second thing he discovered when he hoicked it up was that he was tethered to the bed with an intricately woven leather manacle. A criss-cross of thinner strips of leather, almost like laces, seemed to secure it, and as Junk tried to undo them, all he managed to do was tighten them even more. The way the strips of leather were arranged seemed to offer the chance of freedom just by loosening the correct strand. Unfortunately loosening one strand tightened another and after several long, frustrating moments, Junk gave up.

He looked around some more. Where was he? Whose cabin was this?

'Hello?' he called. No reply. 'HEY!' he called louder. '*HELLO!*' Louder still. Nothing.

He sat up as tall as he could and saw a belt hanging

over the back of one of the chairs by the giant table. The belt was made from woven strands of leather and looked a lot like the manacle around his ankle. Attached to the belt was a leather scabbard and sticking out of the scabbard was the hilt of a knife. Junk rolled over on to his hands and knees and crawled forward. The material of his voluminous shirt gathered around him, hobbling his progress.

He crawled as far as he could, until the leather strap around his ankle became taut, and then he stretched out his arm, reaching for the knife. Infuriatingly it was still beyond his grasp. He pulled forward, causing the straps to tighten around his ankle. They started to cut into his skin and cause him pain. When he pulled back, they didn't then loosen. Once tightened they stayed that way. They were cutting off the flow of blood to his foot which was now turning a rather alarming shade of purple.

However, Junk knew that if he could reach the knife then he could cut himself free so he persisted and stretched further. The leather around his ankle constricted even more. The pain increased. Junk was becoming desperate. If he didn't get the knife, there was a good possibility that he would pass out from the pain and maybe lose the foot. He wasn't sure, but he thought if the circulation was cut off from an extremity such as a foot then it would wither and die. He was pretty sure that was true. He was pretty sure he'd seen it on a documentary once, though there was a possibility it was in a horror film. He turned his attention back to the knife.

He dug his fingernails into the seam at the top of his baggy shirt sleeve and ripped. It came apart with relative ease and he was able to pull it free. He tied a hefty knot in one end to give it a bit of weight and then took aim and launched it at the belt hanging from the chair, keeping hold of the other end. First time, he missed. It bounced off the belt and hit the floor. He reeled it back in and tried again. Second time, the knot looped through the belt and came back around a little. By incremental flicks of his wrist, he was able to coax the knotted end of the shirt sleeve closer and closer to him until at last he was able to grab hold of it. A rush of euphoria shot through him. Holding both ends of the sleeve, he pulled at the belt but it was hooked over the top of the chair. He tried his wrist-flicking again to get the belt off. On the third try, it worked. The belt was dislodged and it fell to the floor.

'Yes!' he said triumphantly and started to reel it in. Suddenly a hand came out of the shadow, followed by a face. Garvan's face. Garvan's enormous face. Terror and panic raced through Junk. He screamed and shot backwards. The sudden movement caused the leather strap on his ankle to tighten even more and he cried out in pain.

Garvan had been sitting in the shadows watching Junk all along. He picked up the belt with the knife and placed it on the table, well out of Junk's reach. Then he stood over him like a passing oak tree. Junk was both terrorized and in agony. Instinctively he yanked at the manacle but only managed to make it tighter still. He was desperate to get away from this terrifying giant looking down at him.

'Jesus! Jesus! Jesus!' Junk said in panicked prayer. Garvan lowered himself down and grabbed hold of Junk's foot. It was almost black by now. He held it still and with more finesse than one would expect possible from his huge fingers, he loosened the bindings so that the constricting pressure was alleviated, though Junk was still restrained. The pain ebbed away almost at once. Junk lay still, breathing hard, but his pounding heart was calming down. He stared at Garvan's colossal features.

'Who are ya?' Junk managed to say on the end of a breath, but Garvan didn't answer. He made no response at all. He just put Junk's foot down gently and rose to his feet. Junk had never seen anyone so big. He was easily half the height of the very high room.

Junk tried again. 'What do you want from me?' Garvan didn't react. 'Are you going to hurt me?' Nothing. 'Where am I?' Garvan turned and walked away. 'My friends are looking for me.' Junk always thought it was phoney when kidnap victims said that in movies, but here he was saying it himself. It was because he couldn't think of anything else to say and he really felt like he should have something to say. It never did any good. The kidnappers never went, 'Oh, I'd better let you go then.'

He watched Garvan as he moved around the cabin. Junk's head was spinning. He didn't know what to think.

Garvan looked human but not. Junk had never seen such a big person. He was a giant. A proper giant. His face was different too. His nose lacked cartilage. It was wide and soft. His mouth was weak, as if he'd had a stroke. The old priest back in Murroughtoohy, Father Austin, he'd had a stroke and the left corner of his mouth hung lower than the right. However, there the similarity ended. Father Austin's whole left side was affected. He dragged his left foot, his left arm hung uselessly and his double chins gathered in a fleshy pleat on that side of his face. Garvan, however, had a firm, strong jaw. He stood straight, walked cleanly. His shoulders were broad and powerful. Each of his arms was wider than Junk's torso.

Garvan returned holding a plate made from a flat piece of slate. On it was a selection of berries, some fruit Junk didn't recognize and what looked like bread. Garvan set it down in front of Junk and backed away to the table. He grabbed a chair, turned it round and sat, watching. Junk suddenly realized how hungry he was and wasn't sure how long it had been since he last ate. He grabbed a piece of the unknown fruit and bit into it. Its flesh was orange in colour but its texture was like that of a banana. It was sweet. A little like vanilla custard. He scoffed it all down quickly. He couldn't stop. The first bite had awakened the hunger pangs in him and they were demanding satisfaction.

'This is good. Thank you,' said Junk, biting into the bread-like substance. It was close to bread but it wasn't quite bread. It was delicious though. Crisp on the outside, sweet on the inside. The texture was like an Italian Christmas cake that he'd tried once. Panettone, it was called. 'My name's Junk,' he said. He looked Garvan in the eye, wanting to make a connection, see some sort of reaction. But there was nothing. 'Can you tell me where I am?' That was the second time he had asked that question and the second time that it garnered no response. 'Do you understand me? Do you speak English?' Nothing. *'Ellinika?'* Greek? *'Milate Ellinika?'* Do you speak Greek? After all, when he went diving he was off the coast of Corfu. It made sense. Junk went through the languages he knew in his head, then looked at Garvan and listed them: *'Français? Italiano? Deutsch? Español? Português? Svenska? Arabi? Russki? Zhongwen?'* The list could have gone on, though conversation would have become increasingly limited. For example, the only thing he could say in Urdu was 'my donkey likes your tree'. So far it had never come in handy. As it was there was no conversation at all. Nothing Junk said elicited anything vaguely resembling a response from Garvan, and after about twenty minutes Garvan got up and left the room.

Junk didn't see him again that day. The light faded gradually as day turned to night. There were no lamps or candles within view and so Junk sat in the darkness on his fur-lined bed until fatigue overcame him and he fell asleep.

At dawn, Garvan came back and sat watching the boy as he slept. His mind was racing with the thought that this might be the one he'd been waiting for. He didn't look like he expected him to look, but he spoke in a strange alien language that Garvan didn't understand. That was the first marker. The first sign. He had played the sequence of events that were due to unfold over and over in his head a thousand times. Ten thousand. A hundred thousand. But he shouldn't get carried away, he told himself. This might not be the one. He would test him and see. If he passed, it still wouldn't mean he was the one, but it would be another step in the right direction. The boy started to stir.

When Junk woke he felt refreshed, having had one of the best sleeps in memory. He opened his eyes and looked around. Garvan was sitting watching him again.

'Morning,' said Junk, sitting up. No reaction from Garvan as always. 'What sort of fur is this?' Junk asked, running his hand through the luxurious pelt beneath him. 'This is the softest bed I've ever slept on. Spent most of the last few years sleeping in bunks on ships and boats. They're pretty much the same wherever you are. Thin mattress, thin blanket. Can't remember the last time I was this still. Got used to rooms swaying around me.'

Junk wasn't sure why, but he didn't feel scared around Garvan any more. There was something serene about the big man. At that moment he thought about the monster in *Frankenstein*. He'd read the book when he was about nine and found it again a year ago on board a fishing boat he had crewed on out of Gdansk. Of course that ended badly. The book, not the Polish fishing boat.

Maybe because Garvan said nothing, Junk felt compelled to speak. He didn't expect a response and left less and less opportunity between sentences for Garvan to say anything.

'So what can I call ya? Got to call you something. You got a name?' He did pause then but got no reaction. 'How about Frank?' he said, thinking about the book again. 'So I'm Junk, you're Frank. How's things, Frank? Looks like a nice sunny day out there.' He craned his head to look out of the misted window. 'Any chance I could go for a walk? I won't go far. Just stretch my legs. Get a breath of fresh air. That sort of thing.' No reaction. 'No? Fair enough. It was worth asking though, wasn't it?'

There was a moment of silence as Junk considered what to say next. His stomach rumbled and he realized he was starving.

'Any chance of some breakfast? That fruit you had yesterday or the bread or anything really. What was that fruit? What's it called? Don't know why I keep asking questions. Seems like a waste of words. I mean what if I found out everyone was allotted a finite number of words and I was using mine up willy-nilly talking to you. Like a man in a desert having a bath. A good, long, hot soak. I suppose I could always borrow some of your words quota. You don't seem to have any need for them. I wonder what the hell I'm talking about. Strange things pop into your head sometimes, don't they?'

Junk stopped talking. The two of them sat in silence. Junk's stomach rumbled again. This time Garvan got up and crossed to his kitchen. He started putting some more food together. He brought a plate over to Junk and set it down in front of him. Junk looked at him when he was close.

'So you can understand me?' No reaction from Garvan. 'Or maybe you just heard me stomach. Thank you anyway.'

Junk dug into the food. There was more of the bread that wasn't bread, some more berries, a different type of fruit. It was crunchy like an apple but bitter like grapefruit. Junk didn't enjoy his first bite, but the taste grew on him and by the third he was loving it. There was also something in a small wooden bowl that resembled cottage cheese. It had a sharp oaky, nutty taste.

'This is lovely. What's this? It's kind of cheesy. Doesn't look that appetizing but tastes gorgeous.'

Garvan returned to the kitchen area and came back with a plate of food for himself and two clay beakers full of water. The beakers had been made with great skill, the same craftsmanship that was evident in the architecture of the cabin, the furniture and the plates. Junk drank deeply, emptying the beaker in one go. Only then did he realize how thirsty he had been.

'Oh man-oh-man, I needed that! Read somewhere that when you get really thirsty, like dying-of-thirst-type thirsty, your body shuts down the bit of you that feels thirsty so you don't know you're thirsty. Crazy, huh?'

Garvan didn't reply. He just stared at Junk as if he was the most fascinating creature he'd ever seen.

'So where am I?' asked Junk. 'Am I still in Corfu?' No response. A thought occurred to him. 'Wait. Is this Albania? I was diving in the Corfu strait so I guess I could've come up on the Albanian side. What language do you speak in Albania? Albanian? I don't know any Albanian.' He looked Garvan in the eye and pointed with both index fingers straight down. 'Albania? Is this Albania? Albania?' Nothing. No response.

The day continued in much the same way. Junk would talk and Garvan would not. Sometimes Garvan would go out and come back with food and water. Day became night and Junk slept.

The following day was pretty much the same, as was the day after that and the day after that and the day after that. Junk lost track of time. He was certain he'd been here more than a week, but he wasn't sure if it had been two weeks yet.

At some point, while he was asleep, Garvan had extended the length of the strap connected to the leather manacle around his ankle. It meant Junk could walk around a little. Not far – a metre or so, and Garvan made sure there were never any knives or other tools left within his reach.

To fill the time, Junk started telling Garvan all about himself. About his home back in Murroughtoohy, about his mother and father and about Ambeline. He spoke a lot about Ambeline. He told the story of that night. Told him that he was looking for the man who killed her. He told him about La Liga de Los Tiburones . . . the League of Sharks.

As time went on, Garvan would do more than just sit and stare at Junk. He had a fat book covered in animal hide, stained dark brown, in which he would write or sketch as Junk spoke. Often Junk would ask what he was writing or sketching, but Garvan never showed him or responded to anything he said.

One morning Junk woke to find Garvan was nowhere to be seen. A moment of panic rose in him. He had grown used to his captor being the first thing he saw every morning.

'Frank,' he shouted. 'You around?' But there was only silence. Then he noticed a small wooden box next to his bed. It was a cube with sides about fifteen centimetres long. A dozen types of wood had been used in its construction. They were naturally different colours. It was highly polished. There was no hinge or obvious opening, but there was something inside. Junk could hear it rattle when he shook the box.

He spent the best part of an hour examining it before deciding that it didn't open and putting it down. Still there was no sign of Garvan, and after boredom took hold again Junk returned to pushing, prodding and poking the box. Then, suddenly, a corner clicked out. Junk tried the other corners but they didn't move. He realized it was a puzzle box. There was a way to open it; the way just wasn't very obvious. He'd come across something similar in a market in Shanghai. This realization fired his imagination and he spent the next several hours attempting to figure out the box's secret.

Eventually Garvan appeared. Junk held the box out to him.

'So come on then, show me. How do you open it?' Garvan placed some food and water next to Junk and left.

It took Junk four days to open the box. In that time he hardly saw Garvan. The big man would come in with food and leave again. When Junk finally worked out how to open the box (the corners had to be turned a quarter, half or three-quarters rotation, and in the correct sequence) he found an intricately carved model of some sort of animal that looked a little like a wild boar.

The next morning Garvan was sitting and watching him when he woke. Garvan spent the whole day with him. They spoke. Well, Junk spoke. He told him more about his life, his family, his travels. Garvan scribbled in his book. They ate together and Junk was happy for the company.

The next morning there was no Garvan but there was another box. This one took him five days to open. Inside there was another intricate carving. This time of a mushroom. Junk thought it an odd subject to choose to carve but he couldn't deny the beauty of the workmanship.

The morning after that, there was no Garvan and no box. Except there was. A few hours passed before Junk noticed it. During the night Garvan had come in and cut the tether leading from the manacle. Then he had reattached the two ends inside another puzzle box. Junk considered this and he thought he understood. He hoped he understood. This box was his freedom. If he solved this puzzle, he could leave.

6

This box was the most intricate one yet. How Garvan had managed to make it was a mystery. It seemed to defy all laws of logic. It was spherical in shape, about the size of a cricket ball. Its surface was made up of a hundred or more small polished interconnected wooden blocks. It took Junk two days just to work out how to manipulate them. Press one block and nothing would happen. However, press a specific combination of blocks simultaneously, sometimes as many as ten blocks at once, which was like playing Twister just with your fingers, and Junk could feel and hear some sort of mechanism moving inside. He could then twist the different hemispheres and rotate them. If he did it slowly he could feel the two halves clicking over internal ridges. If he pressed in the right selection of blocks, the northern and southern hemispheres would move but so too would the eastern and western as well as the diagonal, both south-east to north-west and south-west to north-east.

Working out how to manipulate the object was only the first task. Then he had to work out the sequence of turns needed to 'unlock' it. It was a code with no cipher and therefore impossible. There were so many possible combinations that Junk could spend years trying them all.

After a week he gave up. He was angry and frustrated. When Garvan came in with food and water, Junk would turn away from him, displaying his annoyance with these silly games through childish petulance. When that provoked no reaction from Garvan, Junk tried another tack and begged.

'Frank, this is killing me. My head's just gonna explode. Please, just give me a clue, show me how to start, anything. Nudge me in the right direction. Please.'

Garvan just looked blankly at him. Then he left. He returned a few moments later with a clay bowl, about the size of a dog's bowl. The inside was glazed in a dark green colour. It was full of water and Garvan set it down next to Junk.

'What's this supposed to be? I'm not a dog.' But all Garvan did was leave. Junk stared down into the bowl of water and saw his own reflection staring back at him. Exasperated, he fell back on to his fur bed and looked up at the ceiling. He would probably never leave this place.

Hours passed. Junk tried to sleep but he couldn't. He curled up into different positions until he found himself staring directly at the spherical puzzle box. He gazed at it for a long time, hardly blinking.

And then he saw it.

*

The individual blocks were different colours, various shades of light and dark. A small group of them had lined up perfectly and the areas of light, dark and in-between all matched. There was an image there. This wasn't just a puzzle box, it was also one of those games that kids play where you have to slide tiles around a grid until they form a coherent picture.

Reinvigorated, Junk sat up and started to manipulate the sphere, looking to match similar areas of hue to see if he could work out what it depicted.

Then he remembered the bowl Garvan had brought him. What did it mean? It was a clue. He was sure it was a clue. Garvan was helping him. But how? It was just a bowl of water. There was nothing else to it. He lifted the bowl carefully and looked underneath. Nothing. It was a bowl. Terracotta on the outside, Lincoln green on the inside and holding nothing but water. He took a sip. Yep, just water. He put the bowl down again and the movement caused the water to ripple. He stared into it as it settled. There was nothing else. It was empty. Nothing inside. Just water and . . .

In a flash of inspiration, he suddenly knew what the picture on the spherical puzzle box was. Now he just had to recreate it.

It took him another three days of trial and error. Moving the hemispheres of the box this way and that until his own face was staring back at him from one side of the globe. The only other thing that had been in the bowl of water was his own reflection.

When Junk made the final turn, the sphere made a resounding last click and simply came apart in his hands. He unwound the leather strands from the top half and he was free.

Junk stood up and stretched his legs. He had been sitting for hours, desperately trying to solve the conundrum. He edged over to the door but stopped as he reached it. What if it was a trick? What if Garvan was waiting outside for him with a gun or a knife or whatever?

He moved to the window nearest the door, but it was too high. He grabbed a chair from the table and, with difficulty, because of its size, he shunted it over to the window. He scrambled up on to the chair and looked out. His view was blurred by the translucence of the glass. As Junk touched it he realized that it wasn't glass. It wasn't cold to the touch like glass would be. It was more like plastic. He could make out vague shapes. Trees. There were a lot of trees. Bushes. General greenery. Blue sky. Nothing seemed to be moving. And nothing resembling the distinctive size and shape of Garvan.

He jumped down from the chair and looked around for a weapon. He couldn't see anything so he riffled through cupboards and drawers. There was a small chest that had been just out of his reach while he was tethered. He opened it up and was puzzled by what he found inside. Clothes. Thing was, they were all far too small for his host and just the right size for him. He pulled out a pair of trousers and a pair of thick boots made from light brown animal hide. Then there was a grey shirt, similar to the one he was wearing but a fraction of the size. Finally there was a jacket, also made from animal hide but a darker brown than the trousers and boots. Junk got dressed. Everything fitted him perfectly. Had Garvan made these for him? He must have done. That caused a dilemma for Junk: should he play to his captor's game? Should he wear the clothes, which was clearly Garvan's intention, or cast them aside and refuse to be manipulated like that? It occurred to him that the only alternative was to stay in the massive shirt, which was ridiculous; he could hardly walk in it without tripping up. This one time, he decided, he would do as his jailer wanted, but he wouldn't like it. Though the jacket did look cool. It looked like the sort of thing Clint Eastwood would wear in a spaghetti western. Junk's dad was a huge Sergio Leone fan and together they had seen them all.

Once changed, Junk moved to the door. He reached out and took a hold of the handle and turned it. The door unlocked with a satisfying thunk and Junk pulled it back.

Sunlight spilled in, blinding him momentarily. He closed his eyes and saw a collection of nebulous shapes floating through his field of vision. One of them was a silhouette that resembled his captor. When he opened them again and blinked half a dozen times until the world outside came into focus, there was no one there. Just a veranda leading to three wide steps down to the green and brown earth.

Junk moved forward, outside, down the high steps to where the grass started to grow. Another step to where it became thicker, healthier. The scent of the flora around him and the warmth from the sun brought with them a feeling of calm and for a moment he remembered running, barefoot, through the grass behind his house back in Murroughtoohy. Just then, he heard a snort from behind him and he was ripped from his reverie. He turned to see Garvan sitting on a sort of chair-swing back up on the veranda. Junk had walked right past him. How had he missed him?

Junk and Garvan stared at one another. Garvan made no attempt to get up and come after Junk. He sat and looked from under heavy-lidded eyes, but Junk was still scared. In his head, he was sure Garvan was about to pounce on him, pin him down and then drag him back inside and shackle him up once more. Junk backed away slowly until he was a good distance from the cabin and then he turned and ran as fast as he could.

Garvan reached over to a beaker of cool water, lifted it to his lips and drank deeply. It was a hot day.

The boy had passed the tests. He was intelligent and resourceful. It was a good sign. He'd worn the clothes. Garvan was pleased about that. He was proud of his handiwork. He had never made anything so small and fiddly before. For a moment the pit of his stomach twisted as the skeleton of a thought flitted through his mind about what was coming next. He wasn't looking forward to it, but there was no way to avoid it.

*

Junk ran and ran. The terrain was ever-changing. One minute he was running on lush, moist grass that felt like velvet underfoot and the next the grass vanished, replaced by dusty, dry brown earth, pitted with small, sharp stones.

The further he moved from the cabin, the heavier the foliage became. The cabin was in the middle of a dense forest of impossibly tall trees. It reminded Junk of the redwood forests of northern California. His parents had taken him on holiday to America when he was very young, barely three years old. The only thing he could recall from that whole seven weeks was one solitary moment when he was all alone in a forest, surrounded by giant trees. It was like being in prehistoric times. Junk wasn't sure if he had made that connection at three. That might have come later, at around six, when his fixation on dinosaurs kicked in.

And now, as he ran, he made that same connection. He stopped to catch his breath. He listened for sounds of Garvan pursuing him but heard nothing. In fact, he realized, he heard nothing at all. No wind rustling through the leaves. No animals scurrying in the undergrowth. Nothing. Then somewhere, a long way away, he heard the screech of some sort of bird and it startled him into running again.

He ran as fast as he could for as long as he could. After several weeks of incarceration that wasn't very far. The muscles in his legs soon started to burn and his chest grew tighter. Breathing became increasingly difficult and he started to feel dizzy. He slowed down until he had to stop, slumping against a tree. He listened again for any indication that he was being followed, but still he heard nothing. Gradually he realized that wasn't quite true. He could hear something. Not the screech of that far-off bird this time but water crashing against rocks. The sea. The sea was his domain. The sea meant ships, and ships meant escape.

He pushed on, having to kick his way through wide leaves and thick bracken that hampered his progress, but the sound of the sea grew louder with every step and this spurred him on.

Finally he pushed through a clump of tall ferns and found himself at the top of a high cliff, looking out at an expanse of ocean. The cliff-face beneath him was almost vertical and impassable. Black volcanic rocks reached down sixty metres or more to where waves crashed angrily against them. He looked left and right and the cliffs continued in both directions for as far as he could make out. He couldn't see any way down.

He looked out to sea, hoping for some sort of landmark so he could figure out where he was, but there was nothing. Just miles and miles of open water in every direction.

Every direction? A flash of inspiration raced through him and he started back the way he had come. He stopped at the first of the impossibly tall trees he reached and started to climb. The tree was old and gnarled and therefore covered in thick protruding knots and welts.

To begin with, it was easy to climb. However, as he got higher the bark started to smooth out and there were fewer handholds. Fortunately for Junk, in the last few years, he had crewed many a sailing ship, replica topsail schooners with masts forty metres high and brigantines and barques converted into luxury cruise ships. He had become a bona fide rigging monkey, able to scamper to the top of the highest mast faster than anyone else. This tree was no different to Junk than a mast on a ship.

Within minutes he made it to the very top. Admittedly it was more than three times as high as any mast he'd ever climbed, and when he emerged through the canopy the view took his breath away. He felt light-headed from the altitude and the exertion of the climb and took a moment to steady himself. He looked around, turning to his left and then swivelling to his right to take in as much of a three-hundred-and-sixty-degree view as was possible. His heart sank. Two things were readily apparent. One, he was on an island, and two, there was almost nothing but ocean in every direction. The only other land he could see was a smaller island about two kilometres away. It had high black cliffs on the side facing him and tall trees much like the one he was at the top of right now. There were some curious-looking large birds circling it. Maybe if he could find a way down to the sea, he could swim to it. It wouldn't be easy. The water was choppy. And even if he got there, then what? It didn't look inhabited. No more than this island. Maybe there was just another Garvan over there.

Junk hooked his leg around the branch he was on and leaned back against the trunk of the tree. Garvan must have a boat somewhere. He must. He couldn't just stay on this island forever. Junk decided his only hope was to find it.

7

Junk followed a path that took him to the edge of the cliff, looking out to sea. In the distance he saw the black rock thronged with birds. He noticed one of the birds out on its own, circling high in the sky. It turned and started gliding towards him. As it drew closer he saw how big it actually was. He had thought it was the size of an eagle, but now he knew it was much bigger. The size of a man.

At first Junk couldn't comprehend what he was seeing. The bird *was* a man. Half a man at least. Its torso looked almost human. Its legs were thin but muscular and tucked up beneath him as he flew. Its wingspan was easily four metres, maybe more. The lower half of its body was covered in dark brown feathers. The upper part of its chest, neck and head were bare and pink, like a plucked chicken. Where its wings joined its body they were thick and muscular, almost like human arms, and they ended in hands. Much like human hands but with only three digits. Two of these ended in long, sharp talons. Its face was owl-like: flat and round with bulbous, lucent orange eyes and a fierce scowl etched on it. Its beak looked like a hard, shiny nose, half-buried in the mottled flesh of its face, sharp and pointed at the end.

By the time he realized that the birdman was coming straight for him, it was too late to react. The birdman swooped. His long, sinewy legs uncurled from beneath him and his vice-like talons latched violently on to Junk's shoulder. Junk howled as the birdman pumped his massive wings and started to rise.

As Junk's feet lifted off the ground, something flashed past him. Something big, moving fast. Garvan. He must have been following him since he escaped the cabin. Junk had never been free at all.

Garvan jumped into the air and wrapped one of his great hands around Junk's ankle. The birdman let out a wail that was pitched somewhere between a squawk and a furious roar as Garvan's immense weight pulled Junk downwards. Snorting with exertion, the birdman flapped his wings even harder and rose a little. Garvan strained, his back expanded as his muscles tensed. Junk cried out in pain as the birdman's claws sank further into the flesh of his shoulder.

They were getting dangerously close to the edge of the cliff. If they went over, Garvan would have to let go of Junk or risk snapping him in two. His feet just touching the ground, Garvan started to pull back. He got a hand on to the birdman's leg. Bellowing from the depths of his throat, the birdman let go of Junk instantly, deciding escape was the better option at this point, but Garvan reached up further still, burying his hand in the feathers around the creature's abdomen, and brought him crashing to the ground. Junk was thrown aside and went skidding across the loose dry soil. He noticed Garvan's bow and a quiver full of arrows nearby. The thought occurred to him that he could try shooting the creature, but he dismissed that idea almost immediately. The bow was designed to Garvan's proportions, not his. He looked up to see Garvan and the birdman wrestling, rolling over and over. The birdman emitted a furious hiss and its razor-sharp beak snapped at the dusty air around Garvan's face. They were getting closer to the cliff edge.

'Frank!' Junk called. It wasn't clear if Garvan had heard him, but he suddenly twisted his body savagely around, away from the drop. In one swift movement, Garvan was on his feet and, holding the birdman by the ankles, he slammed him down on the ground repeatedly until the creature didn't move any more. Its human-looking mouth was twisted open and a long, rasping gurgle dribbled out. Garvan kicked the dead birdman over the edge of the cliff and looked out to sea.

Junk lay on the ground and stared up at the sky. He was shaking with fear and pain. His shoulder was throbbing and bleeding, but he saw that the jacket Garvan had made for him had taken the brunt of the birdman's grip and only the very tip of one claw had got through. He knew he should probably be running right now, putting distance between himself and Garvan before the latter could take him captive again, but that just didn't seem important any more. The thought occupying the forefront of his mind was that he quite clearly was not on Earth any more. Maybe he should have realized earlier when confronted with a four-metre-tall behemoth like Garvan, but he had honestly just thought he was some sort of freak of human nature. Human being the pivotal word. He couldn't think that about the birdman. There was no way that was human. That was most definitely alien, and alien meant another planet. Junk was on another planet.

The only thing was, he would have expected an alien world to be, well, more alien. OK, flying birdmen is pretty alien, but the sky was blue, the sea was wet, the ground was dusty, the trees looked like trees. Part of him would have been less surprised to see green clouds and purple grass.

Junk was ripped from his thoughts by Garvan pulling him sharply to his feet by his collar.

'Hey! Take it easy, will ya?' Junk snapped without thinking. He regretted it immediately. 'I just mean I could've done with sitting a while longer. It's . . .'

He noticed that Garvan wasn't paying any attention to him but was staring over his shoulder with a disconcerting little nervous tic playing havoc with his left eye. Junk turned to see what had the giant's attention.

'Oh,' was all he could think to say. Other than that his mind was a total blank. Or possibly so active that all the different synapses that were firing off simultaneously had just merged every thought into one huge jumbled featureless whole. More birdmen had taken to the skies from the black rock. Thirty or more. Probably drawn by their recently deceased brother's dying shrieks. They were flying this way and at speed. In the few scant seconds that Junk was looking at them, the sky darkened as they became all he could see.

Garvan stabbed his toe under his bow and propelled it into his waiting hand, nocked an arrow in one smooth and fluid movement, aimed as he turned and fired. The arrow snatched one of the advancing birdmen out of the sky. Garvan nocked and fired again and again and again. Every arrow hit its target true, but too quickly the quiver was empty and there were too many birdmen still coming.

Junk cried out in surprise as he was lifted off his feet once more but this time by Garvan, who tucked him under his arm as if Junk was a ball in a rugby match. Garvan shielded Junk's head with one hand and set off into the foliage. Junk screamed, vocalizing the cocktail of adrenalin and panic that was coursing around his whole body. He could feel branches whipping at his legs.

The trees were dense around them but there were pockets of light that broke in, and as they were running, Junk could see shadows cutting across the sunbeams and he knew the birdmen were overhead now, looking for a way through.

Garvan skidded to a stop and Junk found himself twisting in the air as Garvan set him down roughly on his feet, positioning him behind his own fortress-like girth. Junk heard throaty calls ahead. He peered slowly out from behind Garvan and shuddered as he saw a dozen of the birdmen were blocking their path. He heard movement from behind. Garvan and Junk turned together and saw more closing in on them. They were surrounded, the birdmen walking on their spindly human legs. Their feet looked vaguely human too, apart from the fact that they were split down the middle, making two wide toes, each tipped with a talon.

The birdmen were emitting strange, repetitive calls from the back of their throats. En masse, it sounded to Junk's ears almost as if they were talking to one another. It was rhythmic. Like Australian aborigines playing a didgeridoo. Junk thought he could hear words in their voices: *HowyougonnaeatthemImgonnaeatthemHowyougonnaeatthem ImgonnaeatthemHowyougonnaeatthemImgonnaeatthem HowyougonnaeatthemImgonnaeatthemHowyougonnaeatthem Imgonnaeatthem . . .*

'What do we do?' asked Junk, so quietly he wasn't sure if the words had been audible, but Garvan looked at him so he must have made some sort of sound. Garvan moved his eyes, leading Junk's attention through the birdmen, through the trees, to his cabin fifty metres away. Junk understood. They needed to get there. The cabin was their only chance of survival. Junk nodded. 'OK,' he said. 'On three?' Garvan didn't respond, but Junk chose to believe he understood. 'One . . .'

The birdmen were edging closer.

'Two . . .'

Their beaks were opening, ready to feast.

'Thr—' Before Junk could finish the word, Garvan leaped forward and let out an almighty bellow. It was the roar of a lion, the trumpet of an elephant and the fury of a silverback all rolled into one deafening outburst. It made the birdmen hesitate for a moment. A moment was enough. Pushing Junk into a run, Garvan charged at the predators. He was brutal. He grabbed at wings, twisted and snapped bone and cartilage. Always moving, flowing, dipping to scoop a rock from the ground, up again, turning, smashing the rock on the side of one birdman's head, his arm carrying through, taking out another.

In the first few moments of the battle Garvan had put down five before Junk even knew what was happening. Then movement out of the corner of his eye made Junk turn. Another of the birdmen was coming directly for him. Junk let himself drop like a dead weight half a second before a mass of feathers and claws shrieked through the air above him. He scrambled to his feet and started running. He had never run so fast in his entire life. The birdman skidded across the dusty ground, twisted, turned and got back to his feet. He took off after Junk. He ran like a man, not like a bird. His legs were long, his strides massive. He gained ground quickly.

Junk reached the cabin and threw himself through the open door. He turned in time to see the birdman coming for him. He kicked out at the door and it slammed shut in the advancing predator's path and Junk heard a crunching thud as the birdman smashed into the heavy wooden door. The impact made the whole cabin shudder.

Junk lay still, listening, feeling every part of his body complaining. Every pain receptor in him was jostling to be at the front of the queue to lodge a strongly worded complaint about their recent treatment.

Then he heard the birdman on the other side of the door groaning. He could hear the sound of his talons scraping on the wooden porch as he pulled himself upright. Again Junk's imagination made sense of the didgeridoo-like cadence of its voice: *Iwanna getinthereIwannariphimapartIwannagetinthereIwannariphim apartIwannagetinthereIwannariphimapartIwannagetinthere Iwannariphimapart.*

Suddenly there was a second voice and then a third all saying the same thing. Junk pulled a chair over to the translucent window and looked out. More birdmen were arriving. The chorus of voices swelled. Four, five, six, seven, eight . . .

They were all around the cabin. Their chanting increased. Then they started kicking at the doors and walls. The suddenness and the ferocity of their attack startled Junk and he leaped back. He hit the table, upsetting an earthenware jug. It smashed on the floor and silver lines of water spidered outwards.

As sturdy as the cabin was, it wouldn't take them long to break in. Junk sank to the floor, squirming in under the table, and tried not to cry. His mind was full of images of what would happen to him when they got in. There was no way out. He was trapped. He would surely die. He screwed his eyes tightly shut and clamped his hands over his ears, trying to block out his senses. But it was no good. He could hear their incessant droning voices: *IwannagetthereIwannariphimapartIwannagetinthere IwannariphimapartIwannagetinthereIwannariphimapart IwannariphimapartIwannariphimapartIwannariphimapart.*

He opened his eyes and saw the water from the broken jug. It had flowed freely across the smooth floor under the table to a point. To a line, near invisible unless one was looking for it, where it collected and then vanished. A door. A trapdoor.

There was a sharp crack as the first window broke. Junk peered up from under the table to see the head of one of the birdmen pushing through the gap. He let out a shrill screech of triumph that reverberated around the cabin, stinging Junk's hearing. A flood of adrenalin shot Junk up on to his knees and he started feeling around the perimeter of the trapdoor. There were no visible hinges and no handle. From all around him now he could hear more windows breaking, and the screeching and clawing of talons on wood increased. Junk let out a pathetic little whimper.

Then he found it: a small concealed flap. As with the puzzles, the craftsmanship was so masterful that it was almost impossible to detect. The flap slid smoothly to the side to reveal a handle. With no time to lose, Junk wrapped both hands around the handle and pulled. The trapdoor lifted up quietly and efficiently. He found himself looking down a set of steps cut into the rock, leading into darkness. More birdmen were invading the room all around him. He saw their scrawny, plucked legs surrounding him. Junk slithered through the hole in the floor, on to the steps, and pulled the trapdoor closed after him.

Some of the birdmen looked under the table but were a second too late. They were confused. They didn't understand why no one was there. Then they quickly forgot why they were there and started fighting among themselves.

Junk moved cautiously down the steps, keeping one hand on the wall to his right at all times. The sounds of battle from above quickly dwindled, dampened by the thick stone walls. There was no light. In total darkness Junk continued blindly, feeling each successive step with his foot before putting his weight on it. After about a minute, though it felt longer in the dark, Junk realized light was coming up from below. Ten seconds later and the blackness all around him started to take on form. He could make out the steps and only now realized that they were curving slightly. The treads were becoming deeper towards the bottom. Another dozen steps and Junk saw an archway carved into the rock. Bright sunlight was spilling out.

He reached the bottom and stepped through the doorway. He found himself in an expansive cave at sea level. There was a fishing boat moored against a wooden jetty, bobbing gently up and down on the water that slupped in and out of the cave mouth. Junk saw the open sea and sky beyond. The walls of the cave were covered with fishing tackle, nets, sails, oars and other such paraphernalia. At last Junk had found a way off this island.

The boat cut through the water. It was big for Junk to man alone, but he was familiar enough around boats to pilot something twice the size. Though to use the oars he had to spread his arms as wide as possible. His muscles screamed. As he rowed, sweat was pouring down his face as much from the pain as from the exertion.

He had only travelled for about a minute out and away from the island when he looked back and spotted Garvan at the top of the cliffs directly above the cave mouth. A dozen birdmen were tightening their circle around him. Garvan was armed only with his bow, though the arrows were long spent so he was using it like a staff, swinging it back and forth in an attempt to keep his attackers at bay. To Junk it seemed that Garvan was on his last reserve of energy. He wouldn't be able to keep his defences up for much longer. The birdmen were holding off, waiting for their prey to give in and collapse rather than risk taking a blow.

Junk stared, confused by his feelings. Garvan had been his jailer for weeks. Why should he care what happened to him? But then he'd be dead now if it hadn't been for Garvan rescuing him from that first birdman assault. He knew he should put his head down and just keep rowing but that also meant that he was taking Garvan's only means of escape from the island. Which of course he wouldn't need when he was ripped to shreds. That thought settled it. He couldn't do it. He pulled back on the starboard oar and started to turn the nose of the boat back to the island. Chances were that Garvan would be gone by the time he got there, and even if he got there, what the hell was he supposed to do? But he knew he had to try.

By the time he reached the cliffs, his head was throbbing from overexertion. He kicked out at the anchor and it rattled over the side. The boat floated to the edge of the rocks. He took a moment to catch his breath and then, with difficulty, drew the oars in. He stood. The boat was big enough that his movements had little impact on its stability. Only the gently lapping waves jostled it. He put one foot on the side of the boat and jumped off on to the rocks. He hurried to the cliff-face and launched himself up on to a small ledge. The cliff was ragged, covered with nodules and outcroppings. He was spoiled for hand- and footholds and scampered up to the top quickly.

Junk pulled himself over the lip of the cliff silently and slid into the undergrowth. Barbed bushes scratched at him and he gritted his teeth, desperate not to make a sound.

He peered out of the bushes to see one of the birdmen pecking at Garvan. The attack drew blood. Garvan roared in pain and swung the bow. It hit the birdman hard, sending him staggering back, but in the process the bow snapped in two. His weapon was gone. The birdmen sensed that the end was near. Dinnertime was upon them. They jostled one another for prime position, each wanting to lead the feeding frenzy that seemed inevitable.

Junk stayed low and circled around so that he was inland of Garvan and the birdmen. He waited for the right moment. He didn't have to wait long. Garvan, breathing hard, looked at the broken bow in his hands. He knew it was over. He cast the two halves of the bow to the ground and stood, arms spread, eyes closed, resigned to his imminent death. Junk shot out of his hiding place and ran as fast as he could. He bellowed at the top of his lungs to drown out any second thoughts as he flung himself at Garvan's considerable midriff. Garvan's eyes snapped open and he had but a split second to register Junk's approach. Junk collided with him and the momentum took both of them over the edge of the cliff. The squabbling birdmen had taken their collective eye off their prize and it had suddenly vanished. They glanced around, confused.

Garvan and Junk fell, missing the rocks by the slimmest of margins, and plunged into the foaming sea, where they were sucked down in a maelstrom of frenzied bubbles. The rock shelf sliced and hacked at their skin, their blood mixing with the water and swirling around them in a cloak of red mist. After a few moments, gravity took a hold and they started to rise.

Exploding to the surface, Junk choked out the salty water, coughing and spluttering. He twisted about to get his bearings, looking for Garvan, but there was no sign of him. Junk started to gulp in air, ready to submerge again to go and find him, when suddenly Garvan rose up like a surfacing submarine. He came down with a thunderous splash and then floated, not moving, out cold.

Junk grabbed hold of Garvan's gargantuan arm and looked towards the boat, a few metres away. He was going to have to get him there, but moving him was like trying to manoeuvre a shed. Garvan's dead weight and waterlogged clothes kept dragging him under. Junk reached the boat and scrambled in. He turned instantly for Garvan, but he was already sinking. He latched on to him.

'Help me, Frank,' he shouted through gritted teeth as he pulled at Garvan. 'Wake up, you stupid great lump, and help me!' But Garvan continued to slip away. Junk headbutted the side of Garvan's head in an attempt to rouse him. Hitting Garvan's head was similar to beating one's head against a lump of granite. A welt opened up on Junk's forehead and blood flowed down his face. A surge of strength rippled through him and Junk roared as he put everything he had left into pulling Garvan into the boat. Just at that moment, a wave tucked under the stern and tossed the boat up. It came down hard and the momentum caused Garvan's dead weight to move with it and like a calf being spat out of the birth canal Garvan and Junk slithered fully into the boat. Junk hauled the anchor in and pushed away from the rocks.

After all the exertion, Junk was spent. Unconsciousness overcame him and he collapsed. The boat drifted.

8

When Junk woke next, he was disorientated. It was still bright. His mind and body felt as if he had been asleep for hours, but the sun was pretty much in the same position in the sky so clearly not much time had passed. He rubbed a hand over his face and felt the caked-on blood from the cut on his forehead. He looked at his hands and his arms. All his wounds were at least a day old, maybe two. He realized he must have been unconscious for at least twenty-four hours. He pushed himself up and saw that he was still lying on top of Garvan. The big man's chest was rising and falling gently as he breathed. He was alive.

Junk slid off him. Every inch of his body ached. His mouth was dry and felt gritty. He looked around and discovered that they had run aground on a wide, sandy beach that stretched both ways as far as he could see. Straight ahead was the open sea. No landmarks. No islands. Nothing but water. He turned and saw that behind them, the beach reached inland for about another hundred metres or so and then became forest. Dense and not particularly inviting.

The sun beat down on them. They were completely

exposed. They needed shelter, Junk knew that, but his options were limited. He leaned over and shook Garvan vigorously.

'Frank! Wake up. Frank. Frank. Frank.' He kept shaking him for the best part of a minute, but Garvan didn't react at all. Not so much as a grunt or a murmur. Junk knew he wouldn't be able to move Garvan any distance, so his only option was to build them a shelter where they were.

He searched the boat and found several concealed compartments secreted in the hull. He found five animal-hide water butts, which he filled from a nearby spring, and an expansive sail with which he was able to rig a sun canopy using half a dozen of the longest branches he could scavenge from the edge of the forest. The sail was so big that it could enclose them if the wind got up or be hiked up like the sides of a bell tent if they wanted a breeze.

Once the shelter was erected, Junk's thoughts turned to food. He found one of Garvan's fishing nets in another of the compartments. He could see that there was a shelf that stretched out a good two hundred metres from the beach before dropping off dramatically. Junk waded out as far as he could before trying to cast the net. However, it was too big or he was too small to launch it properly and it just plopped into the sea three metres in front of him and sank.

So Junk gathered the net up and dived into the sea. He swam down for several metres and then let the net unfurl naturally. The weights around the edge dragged it down and Junk swam back to the surface with the net leash around his wrist. He started to haul it in, wrapping the trailing rope around his arm, from his elbow to his thumb. When he retrieved the net it was teeming with fish, nothing too big but lots of smaller fish about the size of sardines.

He built a fire close to the boat and cooked the fish on sticks, which he sharpened with a hefty knife he had also found in the boat.

As night scuttled in, he looked up at the sky and frowned. The moon looked like the moon, but he figured his was the only one he had ever seen and maybe moons all look the same. What was different were the stars. There wasn't a single constellation he recognized and there were very few places on Earth where he hadn't at some point in the last three plus years sat and looked up at the night sky. Wherever he was, it wasn't Earth.

Junk slept in the boat, which moved with the current and the tide, but he had had the forethought to anchor it securely so all it did was bob about a bit and was pretty much in the same spot the next morning.

He cooked more fish for breakfast and sat and looked at Garvan as he ate.

'Look, Frank, we need to talk,' he said to the unconscious giant. 'I need to go. I don't know how long I was tied up in your place. Seemed a long time, I can tell ya. You know I'm looking for someone. I've told you. Person who killed my little sister. I haven't got the first clue where to find him, other than he's not on this beach or your island. I can't stay here with you. You understand, right? I need to find out where I am and where he might be, and to do that I need someone who speaks. You weren't the chattiest person I ever met before, but now you're taking being the strong, silent type to a whole new level. I don't know how long you're going to be like this. You do understand, right? I mean it could be another day, another week, another month. I can't just wait around for another month. Ambeline's killer might be on the other side of the world by now. Whatever world this is.'

Junk put down the fish he was picking at as a shudder of sadness pushed through him. A palpable throb of loneliness. It was homesickness. He had felt the same thing many times over the last three years. He was now further from home than ever, but at the same time a little closer. Closer than he'd ever been to Ambeline's killer, which meant closer to being able to prove to his mother what really happened. He thought about his parents then. Something he tried not to do. He tried not to imagine what they were doing at that very moment. He wasn't sure of the time wherever he was now, and he didn't know the time difference between here and Murroughtoohy so had no idea what time it was back home. It might be morning; it might be last thing at night. That's even if they were still at home. It had been more than three years. One thousand, one hundred and nineteen days, plus however long he had been here. For all he knew, they might have moved. Too many ghosts in the house to stay. He pushed those thoughts away. Nothing he could do about that. He concentrated on the pulsating surge of homesickness and forced it to retreat. He locked it in the deep, dark coal cellar of his mind and looked back at Garvan.

'I have to go. You understand. I can't move you. You're too big. I could maybe make some sort of stretcher. Plenty of wood. Wheels would be harder. But I've got no tools apart from your big ol' knife. And even if I could, I'd never be able to move it. Not unless it was downhill all the way. No, it's best if you stay in the boat. I think you just need rest. I've dressed all your wounds. Nothing's infected. Frankly, I don't know why you're still out. Can't see any reason why you should be, but I'm no expert. Only know what I've picked up along the way. I know how to cure dysentery, but I'd need a kapok tree, and luckily for us you don't have that. That'd be awful messy.' Junk actually shuddered at the thought.

'So we're agreed then. I need to go. I can't stay and I can't take you with me. So the only option is for me to go and leave you here.' He looked at Garvan as if expecting a reply. None came, but Junk nodded in agreement anyway. 'So that's settled then. Good.' Junk looked at his fish again but it had gone cold by now and its opaque little eye was staring up at him accusingly. He tossed it aside.

Junk spent the rest of the day preparing for his onward journey. He caught more fish, fashioned a smokehouse out of several large flat stones he found a little further along the shoreline and hung the majority of his catch up to smoke. It was a technique he had learned in Russia a little over a year before. The process would keep the catch edible for longer. He had no way of knowing what was to come, so couldn't rely on finding more fresh food.

He debated with himself whether or not to take the knife with him. Garvan's knife. It felt wrong to steal a man's only knife. And it would very much be stealing. It wasn't borrowing. He didn't think he'd ever see Garvan again after he left, so he didn't think he would have the opportunity to return it. However, he decided that if Garvan remained comatose he wouldn't have need of the knife, and if he gained consciousness, he was bigger, stronger and better able to defend himself than Junk was, so the only sensible option was for him to take the knife. He knew it was the wrong decision, so he stopped thinking about it.

He topped up the water butts and decided, because he was still feeling guilty about the knife, to leave three for Garvan and take two himself.

He went to sleep as soon as the sky started to darken, planning on setting off at first light.

Junk found himself sitting at an unfamiliar table in an unfamiliar room surrounded by unfamiliar figures bathed in shadow. The room was vast. Cavernous even. So large that the walls and ceiling disappeared into blackness. It reminded him of somewhere else, but he couldn't remember where exactly.

The table stretched away from him. He was seated at the head. There were people sitting on either side of the length of the table but they had no detail to them. They were just eyes glinting in the dark. They were all talking at once, speaking over one another, but Junk couldn't make out any of the words.

He looked down and in front of him was a box. One of Garvan's puzzle boxes. He picked it up and knew instinctively what to do, how to manipulate it to make it open. As his fingers twisted, pushed and pulled at the panels, he became aware that the garbled conversations of his companions were dying away. All eyes turned to look at him. Junk stopped and looked around, not comfortable with the scrutiny. Then his gaze settled on a single yellow eye at the opposite end of the table. The one eye was looking back at him, glaring. It was a malevolent eye – if such a thing was possible. He caught his breath.

Junk became aware that his fingers had started to manipulate the box again, seemingly on their own, without his brain being involved. He heard a click and looked down as the box split open on his lap. Inside were two small green stones. Junk lifted them out and set the box aside. He knew what to do with them even though he didn't know how he knew. He held the two stones out in front of him, just above the table, and cracked them together. A small green flame shot out, igniting an invisible wick. The green flame spread down the centre of the table, illuminating the people on either side as it progressed. Except they weren't people, they were animals. They sat like people, wore clothes like people, but their bodies were scaled or furred.

To Junk's immediate left was a goat, wearing a white coat and a pair of pince-nez. Next to him a tiger, opposite a snake smoking a pipe. Next to the snake was a porcupine pulling a sour face.

'Ugh, what's in this pâté?' asked the porcupine. Now Junk could understand what was being said around him.

The green flame continued down the table, illuminating more and more animals: a walrus polishing his tusks, a crow playing a ukulele, a rhinoceros doing sleight-of-hand card tricks, a capybara with a yo-yo, a bear making the sign of the cross over and over, muttering a little rhyme under his breath as he did so, a flamingo applying lipstick and a cow nodding sagely.

The flame went on until it reached the far end of the table, where it fizzed and sparkled and lit up the occupant of the seat directly opposite Junk. It was a shark. A great white, covered in scars, the most prominent of which was in the shape of a cross over its left eye. The eye was milky and dead just like the eye of the creature who took Ambeline. Junk stood up violently, knocking his chair back as he did so. As the chair hit the floor, all conversation in the room stopped again and everyone looked from Junk to the shark and back again.

'Sit down, boy,' said the shark. His voice was deep and slow. He spoke from the back of his throat.

'I'm here to kill you!' shouted Junk. The shark laughed, his fleshy throat pulsing. The laughter enraged

Junk. His hands curled into fists, his fingernails digging into his palms. His face was puce with burgeoning rage.

Then, in the blink of an eye, the shark stopped laughing. 'Impertinent worm.' And with that, the creature launched himself out of his seat and flew the length of the table at lightning speed, coming straight for Junk, his mouth open, multiple rows of teeth glinting. Junk couldn't move. No time to react. And then, just as the shark reached him, just as the shark's jaws were about to snap down on him, a hand came out of nowhere. A fist moving like a cannonball. It hit the shark on the top of its nose, smashing him down on to the table, where all life left the one good eye.

Junk breathed again and looked up to see Garvan standing over him. Garvan unclenched his fist and shook out his fingers. Then he grabbed the dead shark, hoisted him over his shoulder and walked away. The shadows at the edge of the room swallowed them both.

Junk woke with a start. He was lying in the boat and Garvan was next to him. Still unconscious. Junk sat up, leaning back against the side of the boat, and thought about the dream.

9

By the time the sun started to rise the next morning, Junk
had decided what the dream meant and what to do. So
instead of abandoning Garvan, he took down the canvas
he had used as a shelter and rigged it to the boat's mast,
returning it to its intended purpose. He untethered the
boat and set sail. He and Garvan would stay together a
little longer.

They headed south, keeping the coastline in view off the
starboard side. The wind was gentle so it was slow going.
For hours Junk saw nothing but open water and forested
land. Garvan's boat sliced through the calm seas easily
and there wasn't much Junk had to do. As the hot sun
bore down on him, Junk's eyes grew heavy and he started
to slip into sleep, which was why he didn't notice the
approaching ship until it was almost too late.

It was a job to not notice it. The ship was huge. Vast.
So vast in fact that it was hard to comprehend. It was eight
hundred metres in length, three hundred metres wide
and towered a hundred metres out of the water, with

fourteen masts adding further to its height. It seemed to be made of wood so had the look of a galleon or a barque but on a scale that would dwarf a supertanker.

The reason Junk didn't see it was because the coastline cut away sharply. Had he been awake he would have been getting ready to turn to starboard to continue following the land and would have turned unwittingly straight into the path of the behemoth. Ironically, falling asleep was what saved his and Garvan's lives. He ploughed on straight and in doing so cut across the bow of the big ship. As he drew closer, someone on board miraculously noticed Garvan's little boat and sounded a warning. The cacophonous blast yanked Junk from his dreams. He cried out as he leaped to his feet and looked around just in time to see the skyscraper-like bow bearing down on them. He screamed in horror and panic. There was nothing he could do. He grabbed hold of the rudder and held it firm and true and just managed to cut across the front of the giant ship with the narrowest of margins to spare.

The wash from the big ship tossed the little boat about as if it was a leaf in a washing machine. Fortunately Junk had lashed Garvan to the deck in case they experienced any storms. Junk however was flipped overboard and only just managed to grab the little boat's perimeter rail. He held on with one hand and refused to relinquish his grip no matter how much the boat was tossed to and fro. After a minute the massive ship passed by and the sea returned to its former calm. Junk hauled himself up and into the boat. He lay on the deck panting until he regained his breath. He looked up to see the stern of the huge ship moving away. It was like watching an office block sailing out to sea.

Junk turned and looked the other way, in the direction the ship had come from. He was startled to see a town nestled in an expansive cove. Stone buildings littered the shoreline and rose up behind on steep hills. He was reminded of the Greek island of Santorini. Though whereas the buildings there were predominantly white, here they were many different colours. Here also the buildings were bifurcated by an enormous railway line that ran, rather incongruously, straight into the sea and disappeared beneath the waterline.

The town was buzzing with activity. There were three dozen boats of various sizes moored in the cove, much closer to shore. Nothing was on a scale with the supership that had narrowly missed flattening them. They were mostly fishing boats, roughly the same size as Garvan's. From where he was, a clear mile out to sea, Junk could see what looked like a bustling market on the quayside. There were people of all shapes and sizes milling to and fro. Not people, Junk reminded himself. Aliens.

Junk had no way of knowing whether or not the inhabitants of the town were friendly. He decided caution was the best approach. He sailed on past the cove and around the next headland he found another smaller, deserted cove and anchored the boat there. He unrigged the sail and used it again to shade Garvan from the harsh sun. Then he secreted Garvan's knife under his jacket, which wasn't easy, seeing it was the size of a frying pan, and set off.

He climbed up the hill. When he reached the summit, he looked down and discovered that the part of the town visible from the water was small compared to the rest. It was sprawling, reaching back for a couple of miles before the buildings started to thin out. He could see the huge railway line stretching off into the distance. Just below where he stood, the tracks split into two at the largest structure in the town, which appeared to be a station.

Junk made his way down the hillside on to a dirt road, which he followed into the town. Single-storey stone houses gave way to municipal buildings and shops. Junk passed one building that made him think of a sheriff's jail in a western. Three big glowering men were loitering outside, all wearing the same uniform of red-stained hide long coats. The men were big, though not as big as Garvan. Seven or eight feet tall, broad-shouldered, with big hands, big feet, big features. They looked like brothers. All had dark brown skin and white-blond hair cut short at the front but tied back into a long, thin ponytail behind. They had heavy brows and thick blond moustaches that were in need of trimming. They sat or leaned outside their building, eyeing the passers-by with undisguised suspicion. Hanging by their sides were foot-long leather saps, and their expressions were begging for a reason to wield them. Junk kept his head down and hurried on.

As he went he looked at all the different aliens and

marvelled at their uniqueness. Not just from him but from one another. People here were all sizes, shapes and colours. Then it occurred to him that they weren't the aliens; he was. He was on their planet, not the other way around.

He passed shops selling fruit, bread (or at least the bread-like substance that Garvan had given him), fish and meat. The smells of cooking flowed over and around him, caressing his senses and making him realize how ravenously hungry he was. He hadn't eaten in several hours. He felt his pockets for money and realized that he had neither money nor pockets.

The winding streets were narrow. He followed the sound of the sea to the quayside that he had observed from the boat. As he had thought, there was a market set up here. Dozens of stalls were selling food (more divine smells teased him), clothes, tools, books, artwork, all sorts of things. As Junk listened to the myriad voices around him, the first he had heard since his arrival (the didgeridoo calls of the birdmen didn't count), he realized that he couldn't understand one word of what was being said. The local language was spoken quickly and rhythmically. There was almost a musical quality to it, similar to Italian, though the words were most definitely not Italian or French or Spanish or English or Russian or Chinese or any other of the hundred languages that Junk could speak to some degree or had heard on his globe-trotting travels. The signs on the stalls, the street names and the titles of the books for sale were indecipherable to him.

There seemed to be distinct characters, but it was like the first time he had ever visited Japan: he couldn't work out what anything meant.

He spotted another of the dark-skinned, blond policemen (if that's what they were). He wore the same uniform as the others Junk had seen and had the same distinctive hairstyle. He walked casually between the stalls, as if on his beat. He had an air of chilly superiority about him, glancing at the people he passed with a curled lip of contempt, and everyone knew to get out of his path rather than the other way round. Junk gave him a wide berth for no other reason than that Junk didn't belong here.

At that moment, he had the strangest feeling that he was being watched. He glanced around but didn't see anyone paying him any undue attention. He looked up and caught sight of a silhouetted figure standing on the roof of one of the buildings overlooking the marketplace. The figure was tall and lithe and after a second disappeared from view.

The person who had been standing on the rooftop was a young woman by the name of Lasel Mowtay and she had indeed been watching Junk. Her green eyes were large and oval and there was a subtle point to the top of her ears. Her legs were impossibly long. Slender but muscular, like a dancer's. She had long copper-coloured hair, thrown behind her in a carefree ponytail that reached down almost to the small of her back. She looked about sixteen years old but was an old soul in a young body. To Lasel, everything was possible. Occasionally a solution to a problem wasn't glaringly obvious, but it was always there somewhere. The trick was to find it.

She skipped off from the parapet at the front of the building and slid down the sloping roof behind. Her movements were wonderfully balletic. She let herself drop down into an alleyway. She slowed her descent by pushing herself from one wall to the one opposite and back again. Her movements seemed to defy gravity though in reality they merely made the most out of gravity. She landed silently on the ground and moved towards the quayside.

Lasel fell into step a short distance behind Junk and started to shadow him. She drew closer without alerting him to her presence. As they passed one of the bookstalls, her hand shot out in a blur of motion, whipped a book away and secreted it beneath her leather waistcoat. She advanced on Junk with the intention of slipping the book into his pocket. Only as she got closer did she realize that he didn't have any pockets.

'Cootun,' she muttered with a frown, and continued to follow him. Junk turned left, saw the policeman ahead and turned back. Lasel's reaction was casual. She didn't make eye contact with Junk, didn't hesitate, didn't falter. She moved past him, then turned blithely and fell into step behind him again as Junk made his way back towards the bookstall. As he passed the stall, Lasel moved quickly forward and in one fluid motion slipped the book into his hand and moved away before Junk was even aware that he was holding it.

'Dattakar!' came a shout from Lasel. Everyone including Junk turned. The bookseller spotted the book in Junk's hand at about the same time as Junk did. As far as he was concerned, it had magically appeared there.

'Dattakar! DATTAKAR!' shouted the bookseller, and started coming around his table towards Junk, who was shaking his head, at a loss to explain why or how he was holding the book. 'JUNTA!' shouted the bookseller.

Junk saw the policeman turn and start running towards him. 'Junta' must mean 'police', thought Junk. Then he thought, Run. So he ran.

Junk avoided the bookseller as he lunged for him by slipping under his grasping hands. The bookseller was a small man, who reminded Junk of a jockey. There was an old manor house back in Murroughtoohy, and the lord of the manor, a man called Eales, trained racehorses. Junk would see the diminutive jockeys in town from time to time and that's who he thought of now as the bookseller pursued him.

'TUNK ET! TUNK ET!' shouted the big policeman as he pounded towards Junk. All eyes in the market were on Junk and no one was paying Lasel the slightest bit of notice, which was just what she planned. She moved in behind the bookseller's counter, produced a small crooked piece of metal and deftly picked the lock on his cash till. She lifted the tray, revealing a stash of colourful paper money. She smiled and pocketed it all. She was in and out in less than twenty seconds.

Other people in the marketplace tried to grab Junk as he passed them. He was forced to twist and turn and weave to avoid capture. He turned a corner and saw the bookseller coming towards him. The policeman was gaining behind. Realizing he was still holding the book, Junk tossed it in the air as he passed the bookseller. The little man instinctively made to catch it and Junk slid past.

He emerged from the market stalls and ran down the first street he came to. The policeman was still in pursuit. He reached into his coat, withdrew a small horn made of shell and blew hard as he ran. It made no sound.

However, some distance away, at the police station, his three colleagues all reacted. They were attuned to the shell horn's frequency, like dogs to a dog whistle. Each drew his billy club and started running.

The narrow streets were a maze and Junk quickly lost all sense of direction. All he heard was the sound of feet thundering towards him. Panicking, he turned down one street and saw one of the policeman charging straight at him. He turned back the way he had come and zigzagged down a side street. Two quick turns brought him to a small open square with a fountain in the middle. The buildings here were higher. Three or four storeys. There were a dozen alleyways and openings leading off the square. He didn't pause. He chose one at random and continued running.

On the rooftops above, Lasel sat and counted her

plunder. She looked down to see Junk run out of the square. A moment later two of the pursuing policemen entered, hesitated, chose two random exits (both different to Junk) and carried on. Then a third policeman came and went. He chose the route that Junk had taken. Lasel stopped counting and wrestled briefly with her conscience. She sighed and pocketed the money. Then she stood and leaped gracefully into the air and off the roof.

Junk stopped at an intersection to catch his breath. He heard the policemen's shouts echoing all around him. He didn't know which way to go. It sounded as if they were getting closer. Just then he heard a soft, short whistle and looked up to see Lasel perched like a cat on a windowsill.

'Puttum,' she said, gesturing with a nod of her head.

'I don't understand,' said Junk, with a panicked strain to his voice.

From her slightly elevated position Lasel could see one of the policemen approaching. Another few seconds and he would have Junk. She reached down her hand. 'Puttum! Puttum!' she said again, more forcefully. The outstretched hand spoke for itself. He grabbed it and she pulled him up, yanking him back into the recess of the window just as the policeman lumbered past below, panting audibly. They waited until he had passed and then Lasel pointed a thumb upwards. 'Tankata solip.'

Junk shook his head. 'I don't speak your language. I don't understand.'

'Criptik tapar,' said Lasel. 'Mullatapar.' Which ironically means, 'I don't speak your language. I don't understand.' 'Tankata,' she said again and pointed. Then she started to climb up the side of the building. Junk was pretty sure she wanted him to follow her. So he did.

At the top of the building was an ornate dome. By the time Junk reached the top Lasel was sitting there eating a red fruit. He sat next to her and caught his breath.

'Thanks for your help,' he said. 'My name's Junk.' He patted his chest. 'Junk. Junk. Me Junk.' Lasel ate her fruit, frowning a little as she scrutinized him. Then she retrieved a second fruit from one of her many pockets and tossed it to Junk. He caught it and ate it quickly. 'Wow, this is nice,' he said, juice running down his chin. 'Juicy.'

He tried again. He pointed to himself and said, 'Junk.' Then he pointed to Lasel. He did this several times until she smiled, seeming to understand what he meant. She pointed to him. 'Junk,' she said.

Junk grinned and nodded. 'Yeah. Junk.'

Then Lasel pointed to herself and said, 'Lasel.' She pronounced it 'Lay-sell'.

'Lasel,' said Junk, pointing. Lasel smiled and continued eating her fruit.

Then Junk moved his arm in a wide, sweeping motion taking in the town around them. 'And where's this? Where are we?' He shrugged.

It took Lasel several moments to process what Junk might be saying. Then she gestured with both hands, much as he had done and said, 'Corraway.' She rolled the r's lyrically.

'Corraway,' repeated Junk. He thought for a moment and then raised his hands to the blue sky in another grand, sweeping gesture. 'And what planet is this?'

Lasel looked at the sky and thought hard about what Junk might be asking. She shook her head. She didn't understand.

10

When night fell, Junk and Lasel climbed down from the rooftop cupola. They walked through the town cloaked in the anonymity of darkness. Junk noticed they had electricity or something similar here. Some streets were lit by electric lights. They stuck to the ones that were not. They made their way out of town, passing close to the police station. Close enough to see inside. The four policemen from earlier were sitting at a large table eating and drinking. Their long leather coats hung from hooks on the wall. They all wore sleeveless black shirts and black leather trousers.

Once out of town, Lasel and Junk took to the hills and he led her to where he had left Garvan's boat anchored in the next cove. Junk was relieved to see that Garvan was still there, just as he had left him. The first thing he did was check to see if he was still alive. He was. Junk looked to Lasel. He pointed at Garvan.

'This is Frank. My . . . friend.' He flapped his arms and mimicked the didgeridoo call of the birdmen, then mimed them attacking Garvan. When he reached the end of his visual explanation, he had no idea if Lasel had understood him. She stood frowning, trying to decipher everything he had done. Then she crouched next to Garvan and examined him. She wasn't gentle, and Junk squirmed as she pinched and pulled at his eyelids, revealing his dilated pupils. She pushed and moved his bulky body as much as she could and started nodding.

'Ta pody ti veta chet,' she said. Junk looked blankly at her and shrugged. Of course he didn't understand. 'Ta pody ti cluka. Kimmer.' She pointed to the ground beneath her feet and said it again: 'Kimmer.' Then she turned and walked away.

Junk watched her go, playing her alien words over and over in his head, hoping a translation would reveal itself. It didn't.

Lasel was gone for the best part of two hours and Junk had almost given up on her when she returned. She brought with her a bag of provisions from which she extracted a small blue bottle. She gestured to Junk and he followed her to Garvan's side.

'Tumpah plugh –' and she mimed opening her mouth but nodded her head to Garvan. Junk understood. He knelt and pulled Garvan's jaws apart. They were rigid and it took some effort to prise them open. They parted with an aggressive exhalation of foul-smelling breath and Junk gagged. Lasel knelt on the other side of Garvan, uncorked the bottle and tipped it up over his mouth. Ever so carefully she let one . . . two . . . three . . . drops fall into his mouth, making sure they went straight in and didn't touch his lips. She took the bottle away, re-corked it and pushed Garvan's mouth closed. They waited a moment and then . . . nothing happened. So they waited some more and still nothing happened. Junk looked at her and shrugged.

'Is that it?' Lasel might not have understood his words, but she did understand the sentiment. She put up a hand, preaching patience, and Junk waited some more. His mind began to wander and so Garvan's return to life took him by surprise. The fact that his resuscitation was so brutal didn't help either. Garvan sat up sharply, wailing. His sudden movement made the boat rock so forcefully that it almost capsized. He lurched to the side rail and vomited violently. Junk and Lasel held on to the bucking boat while Garvan vomited again. And again. And again. Junk wasn't sure he was ever going to stop, but finally he did. He wiped his mouth and sat back to catch his breath. After a few moments the boat settled down too. Junk smiled at Garvan.

'Welcome back, Frank. Had me worried there.' Garvan looked at Junk with bloodshot eyes and belched loudly. 'Nice,' said Junk. He pointed to Lasel. 'This is Lasel. She helped you. Lasel, this is Frank. He doesn't talk.'

'Occootoo, Lasel,' said Garvan. Junk was stunned. These were the very first words he had heard the big man say. Garvan's voice was deep, echoing up from his belly, and the ends of his words were crisp and clipped.

'OK,' said Junk. 'Evidently you do speak. Just not to me.'

'Occootoo, Frank,' said Lasel.

'Nenga Frank. Garvan. Garvan Fiske,' said Garvan, putting a hand on his big chest. He too rolled his r's.

'Utta Junk cascaba Frank?' asked Lasel. Garvan shrugged.

'Well, ain't you chatty all of a sudden? I'm feeling a little left out here,' said Junk.

'Sorry, Junk,' said Garvan, in English with a hint of an Irish accent. 'I was telling Lasel that my name's not Frank, it's Garvan. Garvan Fiske. She asked why you call me Frank and I wasn't sure.'

Junk stared at Garvan for the best part of twenty seconds as his mind whirled, trying to make sense of the words he had just heard.

'Y-you speak English?' said Junk.

'Is that what your language is?' asked Garvan.

'Yes. What? How do you not know? You're speaking it.'

'It's my first time,' said Garvan.

'Your first time speaking English?' said Junk, the incredulity clear in his tone. 'I don't understand.'

'You talked a lot, and I listened.'

Junk thought about that. Played the words over and over in his head to make sure he wasn't misinterpreting what Garvan was trying to say. 'Are you saying you taught yourself to speak English just by listening to me talk?' asked Junk.

Garvan nodded. 'Well, you did talk a lot.'

'How come you never said anything back?' asked Junk, starting to get a little angry now. He felt that maybe he had been the butt of a joke.

'I like to listen,' said Garvan, with an apologetic shrug.

'You like to listen?' Junk was properly annoyed now. There was so much he wanted to say and everything vied to come out at the same time until he decided he needed to be somewhere else. He shook his head, jumped out of the boat and stomped off up the beach.

Garvan and Lasel watched him go.

'Dusca?' asked Garvan.

Lasel pointed over the hill and said, 'Corraway.'

Now Garvan knew. Junk was the one he had been waiting for. Garvan had learned to speak his language, Junk had solved the puzzle boxes and he had saved Garvan's life, just as had been predicted. Now their journeys were linked. Because of Junk, now Garvan wouldn't have to kill his own father. It was quite a relief. However, there was much that would happen before they returned to Garvan's home. His real home and his family.

Junk cooled off some and returned to the boat. Lasel and Garvan had made a fire on the beach and were cooking what looked like two small pigs on a spit.

'Sorry about that,' said Junk as he sat down by them.

Garvan shook his head. 'No. It is me who should to apologize.' Now and then his English faltered.

'Well, you did keep me prisoner for . . . How long was I there?' asked Junk.

Garvan shrugged. 'Twenty-four . . . twenty-five hyka. Umm . . .' He struggled to find the word. 'Days? You say days?'

'You learned to speak English this well in twenty-five days? What are you? Like a mental genius or something?'

Garvan frowned. His English wasn't complete.

'Well, you'll have to teach me your language,' said Junk.

'Which one?' asked Garvan.

'How many do you speak?'

'Eighteen . . . or so.'

Junk blinked at him. 'That's a lot.' He looked to Lasel. 'How many do you speak?'

English not being one of hers, Lasel looked to Garvan for a translation: 'Krimpta criptik te?'

'Oh.' Lasel had to think. 'Fal. Fal-gi.'

'Ten or eleven. It is normal. There are many languages spoken in the world.'

'I guess,' said Junk, thinking about it. 'In mine too. I mean, I speak a fair few cos I've been moving around like. Not much use to me here though. Which brings me to . . . Where is here? Where am I?'

'The town over the hill is—' Garvan started but Junk interrupted.

'Called Corraway. I know. That much Lasel and I

got.' He smiled at Lasel. She smiled back but wasn't sure what they were talking about.

'You are on the southern coast of Jansia.' Garvan picked up a spare spit and started drawing a crude map of his world in the sand. Jansia was part of a continent that vaguely resembled Europe, though, in comparison to a similar-sized map of Earth, the land mass was far smaller and there was a lot more water. This was true of the rest of this world. 'This area is Bartaya,' he said, motioning to the continent of which Jansia was a part. To the east of Bartaya were two massive areas of land separated in the middle by a strip of ocean. 'Tayana,' he pointed to what was vaguely northern Asia. 'Payana.' He pointed to what would be southern Asia, then drew four separate land masses where Africa would have been. He tapped the northernmost one: 'Glarn Sita.' He indicated the eastern one: 'Unta Sita. To the south was 'Cul Sita' and the last area he called 'Daté Sita'. He drew land at both poles: 'Jjen' – the northern one. 'Pjen' was in the south. To the east of Tayana and Payana, he drew something shaped like a sickle. 'Mallia,' he said. The two l's made an *ee* sound. Mallia was roughly in the same position as the Americas would be back home, but there was a lot more sea around a lot less land.

'So you remember I was talking and you were listening, back in your cabin . . . you remember I mentioned the League of Sharks?' said Junk.

'I was listening,' agreed Garvan. 'Learning.'

'Right. Clearly. So any idea where I start looking for them?'

'Dint criptik oot?' Now Lasel was feeling left out.

Garvan turned to Junk, pointing at Lasel. 'I say to her your story? Explain?'

'Sure.' Junk shrugged and then listened, picking out the odd word here and there, as Garvan recounted to Lasel the story of the man who took Ambeline, of Junk's search around the world, of his discovery of La Liga de los Tiburones and then the green door that took him to the Room of Doors – Bosck dei Varm in their language. At that point, Junk noticed Lasel's brow furrow where before she had just been listening intently. He didn't say anything straight away and let Garvan go on to explain how Junk had a choice of two doors, went through one that brought him here, how he caught Junk in his net, kept him prisoner until he was sure he was harmless. He described the birdmen attack and that was the last thing he remembered until waking up here.

'Dinta took,' said Lasel once Garvan had finished.

'She said, "What a story,"' said Garvan to Junk. 'To answer your question, I've never heard of this League of Sharks. I don't know where for you to start to look.' He turned to Lasel and asked her, but she just shook her head. She hadn't heard of them either.

'But have you heard of the Room of Doors?' asked Junk. Garvan translated. 'You frowned when Frank . . . I mean Garvan . . . mentioned it.' Again Garvan translated for Lasel. She thought for a moment before answering. She spoke in her native Jansian and Garvan translated her reply for Junk.

'There is a man in Arrapia.' Garvan added an explanation: 'Arrapia is a city to the north.' Lasel continued and Garvan translated. 'He is called Otravinicus. He is a scientist. A doctor. Doctor Otravinicus. He wrote a book about a mythical place called the Room of Doors.' Junk was drawn deeper into her story with every word. He sat up a little straighter as he listened. 'The Church wasn't happy with the book. The Room of Doors is supposed to be a very sacred and holy place. There was much argumenting.'

'Arguing,' corrected Junk.

Garvan nodded and continued. 'Much anger. It was very famous. The Church put him on trial. I'm surprised you don't know about this.' It took Garvan a moment to realize Lasel meant that last comment for him. 'Nenga. Garvan shook his head. 'Penca tamatay inta vol. Tapar its oot a barrat.' He looked at Junk. 'I was explaining that I usually just stay on my island. I don't hear things about the outside world.'

'Fair enough,' said Junk with a shrug.

He looked at Lasel and she resumed her story. Garvan continued his translation: 'The Church wanted him to be punished because of what he had written, but he didn't say in the book where the Room of Doors is. Maybe he doesn't know. Anyway, maybe he could help you.' She shrugged. That was all she had.

Junk considered what he had heard. He nodded and then looked at Garvan. 'How do I get to Arrapia?'

'It's a long way. You'd have to take a land-ship.'

'Land-ship?' asked Junk.

'Great boats that travel on rails over land, go straight into the water.'

Junk nodded, remembering. 'I saw one earlier. We almost got crushed by it.'

'That wouldn't have been good,' said Garvan. 'There's a station on the outskirts of Corraway.' He looked at Lasel and asked her a question, which she answered. 'Lasel says there will be a land-ship we can get tomorrow that will take us to Arrapia.'

'We?' asked Junk.

Garvan nodded. 'You saved me. You didn't have to do that. You looked after me. You didn't have to do that either. You could have just left me. I did tie you up after all. I think we are friends. Yes?'

Junk shrugged. 'Yeah, I guess.'

'I will help you in your quest,' announced Garvan.

Junk smiled. 'Thank you.' Then a thought occurred to him. 'Wait. Does it cost money to ride on one of these land-ships?'

'Yes,' said Garvan. 'Of course.'

'We don't have any money,' said Junk.

'Oh,' said Garvan.

'Hupta?' asked Lasel. *Problem?*

'Nenga salli,' said Garvan, holding both hands open.

Lasel smiled. 'Nenga hupta.'

11

The next morning Garvan, Lasel and Junk stood on the brow of the hill looking down on Corraway. It was the exact spot where Junk had stood the previous day. They saw the huge land-ship station. There was a ship there waiting, though it was facing south. A second, identical ship was coming in from the sea. The ship at the station had all its sails furled.

The arriving vessel was alive with activity as the captain piloted it towards the land and the crew readied it for the transfer from water to rails. Two small tugboats had come out to greet the land-ship and attached themselves via guidelines to the bow. They were now helping to line the land-ship up correctly. There was little room for error. However, this was clearly something that happened on a regular basis and it went off without a hitch.

A row of wheels ran the length of the underside of the land-ship. Between the captain and the tugs, the ship and the rails were lined up and embedded magnets did the rest. The wheels locked into place with a resounding clank. A pulley system clamped the wheels on to the rail and the land-ship heaved out of the water without so much as a stutter. The crew tied up the sails as it made its way through the middle of Corraway, towering over the low buildings, and came to a stop at the station.

As it did the second land-ship was cleared for departure and it rumbled towards the sea. Gravity took hold as it slipped down the rails running through the town. As it went its sails unfurled and an enormous curtain of water curled into the air as the land-ship hit the sea and it detached from the rails. It headed steadily out to sea.

'Chiva,' said Lasel and she started down the hill towards the town.

'Let's go,' translated Garvan, and set off after her. Junk followed.

They made their way into town and headed to the station. The huge concourse was teeming with life. Fifty stalls dotted the immense forecourt, selling food and souvenirs and everything else a departing or arriving traveller might need.

On the eastern side of the building there were eight gangplanks leading into the body of the land-ship, half for those alighting, half for those embarking; all were choked with passengers. Station officials wore a distinctive orange-and-grey livery that made Junk think of the Swiss Guards of Vatican City, whom he had seen in Rome a year or so earlier. They might not have been as colourfully attired as the red, blue and gold Swiss Guards, but they certainly stood out.

Lasel put a hand on Junk's arm and drew his attention to an octagonal structure in the centre of the concourse. 'Tarra dei omm,' she said.

'Ticket office,' said Garvan.

Junk and Garvan followed Lasel a little closer to the octagonal structure. They circled around to the far side where they saw a door ajar. They could see the backs of six cashiers who were facing the windows on the opposite side. Lasel explained the plan and Garvan translated.

'Inside, to the . . .' He faltered, not knowing the correct word, and held up his left hand. 'This side.'

'Left,' said Junk.

'Yes,' continued Garvan. 'Inside, to the left is a drawer. The top one of three. It is unlocked and inside they keep blank tickets. Spares, if you like. All you have to do is get in and out quickly and don't be seen.'

'Me?' said Junk, it not having occurred to him that he would have to steal.

'I'm too big,' said Garvan. 'I think they might spot me.' He was of course right. Junk looked to Lasel. After all, she was the one who knew what to do. She understood from the look on his face what he was thinking. She frowned and shook her head.

'Chuva tapar ante,' she said.

'I'm not going anywhere,' said Garvan, translating.

'I guess not,' said Junk, resigning himself to what he was about to do. 'How about you two go around the front and cause a distraction or something? Try to get everyone in the ticket office looking out the front and not behind them. Yeah?'

'Seems sensible,' said Garvan, and he translated for Lasel. She nodded in agreement. The two of them walked away from Junk, who looked down and saw that his hands were shaking. He closed his eyes and took a deep breath, steeling his nerve.

'OK,' he said quietly to himself, his eyes still closed. 'One. Two. Three. Go.' With that, he opened his eyes ready to make a dash towards the ticket office but found himself looking straight at the hulking policeman who had chased him through the market the day before. Junk could see the look of recognition on the man's face.

'Tunk!' he shouted, pointing at Junk, who turned and ran. The policeman blew his silent horn as he sped off in pursuit.

At the front of the ticket office, Garvan and Lasel looked to see what the commotion was all about and saw Junk sprinting away with the red-coated policeman charging after him. Lasel looked to the land-ship. The number of passengers on the gangplanks had lessened considerably. Boarding was almost done.

'The ship's going to leave very soon,' said Lasel to Garvan in Jansian. 'Find a way to hold it up. I'll get Junk.' She was gone, racing out of the station, before Garvan had a chance to argue. He turned to the ship. How on earth was he going to delay it?

*

Junk came hurtling out of the station and took off across the road into the labyrinth of narrow streets where he had lost the policemen the day before. Maybe he could do the same thing again, he thought. He weaved left and right, conscious of the fact that he really didn't know where he was going. That fact became horrifyingly evident when he turned into a dead end. He stuttered to a halt and did a quick one-eighty, but suddenly his exit was blocked by the policeman. The man was panting hard, sweat coursing down his brow. His lip curled up into an irritated snarl.

'Criptiktar tunk, ba tunty dattakar,' he panted. Of course Junk had no idea what he was saying.

The sun was high in the sky and both the policeman and Junk were distracted by a shadow that flitted over the ground between them, but when they looked up neither of them could see what had caused it.

It was Lasel. She was on the rooftops above. She looked around for anything useful and found a length of strong rope attached to what looked like a long-abandoned birdhouse. She pulled it free and stopped for a moment to consider what to do with it. An idea blossomed and she smiled as she started to tie a loop at each end.

In the alleyway below, the policeman had Junk up against the wall. He was holding him in place with one large hand clamped on to the back of Junk's head, pushing his face into the rough stonework as he patted him down.

'Dint cascaba?'

'I don't understand,' said Junk, scared. The policeman unsheathed his long leather sap and tapped it against Junk's cheek with menacing glee.

'Dusca ba galm?'

'I don't know what you're saying,' pleaded Junk. He was almost in tears. The policeman liked that. He put his mouth close to Junk's ear and was just about to say something else no doubt scary and menacing and not at all pleasant when he heard the sound of someone landing on the ground behind him. He spun round to see that Lasel had jumped down from the roof. She was crouching. As the policeman turned she sprang up and grabbed Junk by the hand.

'CHIVA!' she shouted. Junk searched his memory. She had said that earlier. What did it mean? But she didn't give him time to remember. She dragged him away from the policeman, who was momentarily startled by her sudden appearance.

'TUNK!' shouted the policeman and set off after them, taking out his shell horn. He didn't manage to take more than a step before he was pulled up short by the length of rope that he discovered Lasel had looped around his ponytail. The other end was tied to the rooftop and he was held securely in place. He jerked to a stop and the horn flew from his grasp. He struggled to pull the rope free but it was too tough to break, and pulling it only made the loops on either end tighten all the more. He was powerless. Lasel and Junk stopped at the entrance to the cul-de-sac and saw he was impotent. They laughed as they watched his comically manic attempts to free himself.

'See ya later. Sorry about that,' shouted Junk as he and Lasel ran away.

Lasel led the way as they raced back through the narrow streets towards the station. She was about to explain to Junk that the land-ship was on the verge of leaving and if Garvan hadn't found a way to delay it they would be too late, but she knew he wouldn't understand a word of it so she put all her efforts into running as fast as she could, Junk on her heels.

As they came out of a side street and saw the station opposite, Lasel breathed a sigh of relief to see that the land-ship was still in situ. Garvan had done it.

They ran into the station and found Garvan sitting on an upturned bin. There was much activity going on among the orange-and-grey-suited station personnel. They were racing back and forth all over the concourse.

'You did it,' said Lasel. 'You stopped the ship leaving.'

'And you got Junk back.' Garvan smiled at Junk, who of course didn't know what either was saying.

'How did you do it?' asked Lasel.

'They couldn't very well leave without the captain.'

Lasel frowned. 'The captain?'

Garvan merely looked down at the bin he was sitting on. 'Please let me out,' said a small, muffled voice from within. Garvan thumped on the bin. Lasel said something else that Junk didn't understand and then hurried away. 'She's gone to get the tickets this time,' said Garvan in English to Junk.

Junk nodded towards the bin. 'Is there someone in there?'

'Yes,' said Garvan matter-of-factly.

'How come he's not shouting?'

'I told him not to.'

The two of them waited in silence. They didn't have to wait long. Lasel returned quickly and gestured for them to follow her to one of the gangplanks.

Garvan slid off the bin and crouched down next to it. He tapped on the side and said something Junk didn't catch.

'Maro,' came the muted reply from within.

Garvan caught up with Lasel and Junk as the three of them reached the gangplank. One of the station staff looked up as they approached. Lasel held out three tickets. Junk spotted this.

'You're coming too?' he asked, and prodded Garvan to translate, which he did.

'Maro,' said Lasel. 'Nenga rooth tuug.'

Garvan translated back again: 'Yes. No choice now.'

Junk thought about that. 'I suppose not. Sorry.'

The ticket attendant smiled broadly at them and handed back the tickets.

'Zebla jard,' he said, and ushered them up the gangplank.

*

A short time later and Junk, Garvan and Lasel were settled into a luxurious state cabin with fruit, food and drink laid out in abundance. There were expansive, well-stuffed daybeds and panoramic windows. Junk grabbed a piece of fruit that resembled an apple and bit into it. It was delicious.

'I can't believe this is what you got. Is the whole ship like this?' asked Junk.

'No, this is first class,' said Garvan. Lasel said something and Garvan translated with a shrug. 'She said if we were going to steal tickets anyway, she figured we might as well steal the best.'

'Well, it makes sense,' said Junk. Just then there was a mounting rumble and the land-ship started moving with a judder. Junk looked out of the window and saw them leaving Corraway behind as their speed increased.

Lasel opened a door off the main room, revealing a palatial bathroom. She grinned broadly and went inside, locking the door behind her.

'Bagsy next,' said Junk to Garvan.

'Bagsy?' said Garvan. Not a word he had learned yet.

The journey to Arrapia would take several hours with half a dozen stops along the way, but Junk was grateful for the time to relax. He spent the best part of an hour soaking in the bathtub, which was big enough for Garvan to be able to stretch out in, so for Junk it was like lying in a swimming pool.

There was an onboard laundry service so they all sent their clothes to be cleaned and sat around the suite in robes, filling their bellies.

When it was Garvan's turn to bathe, Lasel and Junk spent the time teaching one another words from their respective languages. Junk had a good ear and quickly started to grasp the syntax and structure of Jansian. He had once learned Portuguese in a weekend, at least well enough to avoid getting into a fight with an eighty-year-old man who wore a penguin costume and swore blind he was Elvis Presley.

By the time they reached the outskirts of Arrapia, they were all clean, fed and rested. Junk felt ready for whatever was going to happen next. However, as he turned to look out of the window of their cabin, he saw the last thing in the world he expected: the Eiffel Tower.

He stood and stared, blinking, trying to force his brain to process what he was seeing. The tower wasn't standing erect. It was lying on its side as if its legs had buckled beneath it and it had toppled over. Vegetation had grown up and through it, but it was unmistakably the Eiffel Tower. Arrapia, he realized at that moment, was Paris. He wasn't on an alien world. He was on his world. He was on Earth. Except Earth was an alien world to him.

12

'How can this be . . . Paris?'

Junk, Lasel and Garvan were standing in the shadow of the fallen Eiffel Tower. Junk was shaking his head in disbelief.

'I don't understand,' said Garvan. 'You have one of these in your world?'

'No,' said Junk, turning. 'I have *this* in my world. This city is Paris. It's called Paris.' He was sure of it. He had been to Paris, his Paris, several times over the last three years. Even though the buildings were different, he recognized the layout. The river ran next to them. It was unmistakably the Seine. Though the Pont d'Iéna was missing, as was the Champ de Mars behind them and the Jardins du Trocadéro on the opposite bank. Even though Arrapia was a city compared to Corraway, it wasn't as built up as the Paris Junk knew.

'How?' he said again.

'I don't know,' said Garvan.

'What do you call this?' He waved his arms around, gesturing to everything. 'What do you call this planet?'

'Jorda,' replied Garvan, rolling the r.

'And what does Jorda mean? The word. Translate it for me.'

'It means "ground",' said Garvan. 'Ground . . . Or earth.'

They stood in silence until Lasel spoke:

'Dr Otravinicus will know,' she said in English. She too picked up languages quickly. Though she struggled to say any more and reverted to Jansian, which Garvan had to translate.

'We need to work out how to find him,' Garvan repeated in English. That made sense to Junk. He nodded in agreement.

They found a hotel for the night. Lasel paid with the money she had stolen the day before from the bookseller in Corraway. She didn't bother explaining to Junk and Garvan how she had got the money. The place was cheap and clean and she paid for two rooms. She took one for herself, and Garvan and Junk shared the other. The place catered for people of all shapes and sizes and the beds were easily big enough to accommodate Garvan's bulk. However, it turned out that he snored like a bulldozer, and in the end Junk took the blanket and spent the night on the balcony outside, huddled into a rickety wooden lounger.

He looked out across the city. The buildings were made of black brick and were much larger and grander than those in Corraway. The scale of the city made him feel small and insignificant. He felt confused, which made him feel alone. He didn't have his parents to rely on. He was still only fifteen. Even he forgot that from time to time. Because he looked older, people treated him as older, but he was still a kid. The feeling of solitude overwhelmed him and he started to cry. He fought to hold back the tears but it was a losing battle. He hugged his knees and pushed his face into the blanket to muffle his sobs.

Lasel was sitting in darkness on the balcony of her room, one along from Junk's on the floor above. She had heard Junk come out and had watched him silently. His sadness took her by surprise and she wasn't sure what to do. Should she say something? What could she say that he would understand? Should she ignore him? Leave him to what was clearly a private moment?

Lasel had been on her own for most of her life. Her mother had left when she was a baby. She had no memory of her. Her father was an angry man. She assumed he was bitter because her mother had left, but maybe her mother had left because of his bitterness. As far as Lasel was concerned, he did the very best he could for her but unfortunately his best was rather pathetic. She was quick-witted, fast to learn new things and she too abandoned him, when she was just seven years old. She assumed this would have made him even more angry and bitter, but she had never gone back to find out. Her old home was not far from Arrapia. Just slightly north-west of the city in a small town called Dissel. Maybe she should go back and find out what had become of him.

She pushed such thoughts away. They weren't healthy, she told herself. That was the past. Almost ten years ago. Chances were her father was dead by now, and as she had no intention of returning home, what was the point of even remembering it?

She turned her attention back to Junk to distract herself from the memories of her childhood. He was still crying. Still trying to smother the great sobs of emotion that were pulsing through him and gave no sign of stopping. She made a decision and stood up. She swung her legs over the side of the balcony and dropped, catching hold of a baluster as she went to control her descent. She lowered herself on to the balcony below and stepped across the gap between that one and Junk's.

Junk felt a hand on him and for a moment thought it was his mother, coming to comfort him as she would when he was little. Back when life was perfect. The moment quickly passed and he was sorry to see it go. He looked up to see Lasel. She didn't say anything and neither did Junk. He wiped his sleeve across his face. Strangely, there was no feeling of embarrassment.

Lasel picked up one corner of his blanket and slipped underneath. She curled her arms around Junk and stroked his hair. He was tense to begin with but that quickly dissipated. He relaxed into her embrace and felt safe. He didn't question it, even to himself. There was nothing he wanted more in the world right now than the comfort of his new friend. They both closed their eyes and slept.

The next morning Junk, Lasel and Garvan walked through the broad streets of Arrapia, wondering how they were going to find Dr Otravinicus. They passed a bookshop and an idea occurred to Lasel. She dashed inside and returned clutching a copy of the controversial book written by Dr Sznarzel Otravinicus. There was a photograph of the man himself on the back cover. He was small and erudite-looking with a long, thin face and a pair of pince-nez perched on the end of his nose. Something about the picture sparked a memory in Junk but he couldn't recall what it was exactly.

'How does this help?' he asked, and Garvan relayed the question to Lasel. She tapped the picture.

'Harru,' she said, pointing. *Look.* The photograph had been taken on a rooftop in Arrapia. Dr Otravinicus was learning against a low wall, trying to smile but not entirely succeeding. In the background was a large, ornate building that looked, to Junk, a little like a church. It had a tower with a spire at one end. It was one of the tallest buildings in Arrapia. Lasel turned and pointed. Garvan and Junk followed her finger and saw the tip of the very same spire rising up behind some buildings at the end of the street.

*

They stood outside the property with the spire and then turned their backs to it. In front of them were dozens of buildings.

'There's nothing to say that's necessarily his house in the photo. Could've been taken anywhere,' said Junk.

'Have you idea different?' asked Lasel in fractured English.

'Nenga,' replied Junk. They shared a smile. Lasel had been gone by the time Junk woke that morning so he had no idea how long she had spent with him, but something between them had changed. There was a link. A connection. An attraction. Junk didn't know what it was, but he got a buzz whenever she was near him. He felt stronger just being with her. 'Palar harru?' He pointed to the book, hoping he had said, *Can I look?* He must have been close enough because Lasel held it out to him. He studied the photograph and the buildings in front of him. 'It's down that street,' he said, his Jansian failing him, so Garvan translated. 'On that side of the road.' He waved his hand to the left side.

'Harru . . . harru,' said Lasel, taking the book from him. She pointed to a flagpole, the tip of which was visible in the photograph just behind Dr Otravinicus, at a jaunty forty-five-degree angle. They looked along the street and only one building on the left-hand side had a flagpole out front at the same angle. It meant that the photo had been taken on the rooftop of the next building along.

*

135

They approached the building. It was a seven-storey apartment block made from the same black brick as the rest of Arrapia. There was a large, ornate canopied entrance. So large in fact that Garvan would not have to bend down to enter.

'What do we say to him?' asked Junk.

'We'll think of something,' said Garvan.

Junk nodded and stepped towards the door. It opened outwards before he reached it and a huge, silver-skinned man stepped out wearing a military-style greatcoat. Junk gasped and stuttered to a stop. Garvan walked into the back of him and knocked him off his feet. Junk fell to the ground and looked up. It was another Sharlem, like the man who had killed Ambeline. But not the same man.

'Palar vestum?' he said. A phrase Junk recognized. *Can I help?* He realized that the man wasn't wearing a greatcoat; he was wearing a uniform. He was a doorman. Garvan grabbed Junk by the back of his jacket and hoicked him to his feet.

'Carrollotu criptik sonta Vontra Otravinicus,' said Garvan. *We would like to speak to Dr Otravinicus.*

'Lanatar brask?' asked the doorman with a plastic smile. *Do you have an appointment?*

'Nenga.' *No.*

The plastic smile became a plastic frown. 'Vontra Otravinicus nenga harru ambe sonti brask.' *Dr Otravinicus never sees anyone without an appointment.*

'Papakar song brask?' *How do I make an appointment?*

'Sonta Vontra Otravinicus.' *With Dr Otravinicus.*

Now Garvan was getting a little confused. 'Papakar song brask sonta Vontra Otravinicus sonti criptik sonta Vontra Otravinicus?' *How do I make an appointment with Dr Otravinicus without speaking with Dr Otravinicus?*

'Vontra Otravinicus nenga car harru ambe.' *Dr Otravinicus doesn't like to see anyone.*

'Palar gusk lugh?' *Can I leave a note?*

'Nenga.' *No.* Garvan threw up his hands in frustration. Lasel put her hand on his arm and shook her head.

'Chiva,' she said. *Let's go.*

'Tub . . .' said Garvan, gearing up for an argument but Lasel shook her head more firmly.

'Chiva.' They walked away and the doorman made a point of standing and watching until they were out of sight.

They found a cafe and discussed their next move. Lasel pointed out that on the plus side they were right about Dr Otravinicus living there. Now all they had to do was work out how to get to him.

Junk was a bit shaken by seeing the doorman. All he could think about was whether or not he had a tattoo of a shark's fin and five stars on his left bicep. Was he a member of the League of Sharks? Could he lead him to Ambeline's killer?

'Junk!' It was Garvan. Junk hadn't heard him calling his name repeatedly, trying to get his attention.

137

'What?' said Junk. 'What is it?'

'You weren't listening,' said Garvan.

'Sorry.'

'Lasel was saying we could keep watch on Otravinicus's building and hope he comes out, but for all we know he's a recluse. After all the trouble he got into with the Church people, he might never come out.'

'Maybe. Yeah,' said Junk. 'So what do you think we should do?'

'We get that doorman out of the way and you sneak in,' said Garvan.

Junk shrugged. 'OK.'

The doorman had a small office adjacent to the lobby. It was big enough for a small desk and a chair and he kept his lunch in a bag on the desk. He rarely spent any time in the office as it was cramped and claustrophobic. The man who had had the job before him had been half his size. It had been fine for him. The doorman had popped into the office to get a brush to sweep up some leaves that were collecting outside when he heard the front door open. He hurried out of his office to see who was there.

He was surprised to find the lobby empty. There was a chest-high counter directly outside the door to his office. This was where he usually sat. From where he was standing he couldn't see Lasel crouched down in front of it.

'Occootoo?' he called, and listened. He heard nothing.

He shrugged and went back into the office. Lasel kept low and scampered for the stairs. The doorman was only gone for a moment. He returned in time to see her running up the staircase. 'AI!' he shouted and, dropping the broom, set off after her.

The moment he was gone, Junk hurried in and hid behind the counter. He heard Lasel and the doorman coming back down. They were arguing, or rather Lasel was arguing; the doorman hardly said anything. Junk peeked out and watched as he frogmarched her outside.

As soon as the door closed behind them, Junk raced for the stairs. They were broad with deep treads. He took them two at a time, but the muscles in his legs quickly started to burn and he had to slow down.

He stopped and looked down the stairwell to see if the doorman was coming after him. He couldn't hear anything so thought he was probably safe.

Eventually he reached the top floor. There was only one apartment. There was no name or bell next to the door so Junk decided to just knock, but as he raised his hand, he stopped. He had realized they had made a mistake. He should have been the one to distract the doorman and Lasel should have come up here. He couldn't speak Jansian and he was pretty sure the doctor wouldn't speak English. How was he going to explain himself? The Room of Doors. That was all he had to say. He had heard Garvan say it when he was telling Lasel Junk's story. What was it? Tarra dei omm? No, no, that meant ticket office. It was dei-something though. Dei Varm. That was it. Bosck dei Varm. Room of Doors. He said it to himself under his breath a couple of times to make sure it sounded right, and then he knocked and waited. And waited some more. He knocked again. He waited some more. He knocked again. After all that, Dr Otravinicus wasn't in.

There was a window at the end of the hallway. He opened it and looked out. It was a precipitous drop but there was a ledge that went all the way to an open terrace that was outside Otravinicus's apartment. He couldn't leave without trying absolutely everything. Maybe Otravinicus was in but ignoring the knocking on the door, or maybe he could get into his place and find a clue to his whereabouts. He took a deep breath and stepped out.

He had to close the window behind to clear his path. The wind whistled like a yawn up here, buffeting him against the side of the building. There was nothing to hold on to. The wall was smooth. He faced it, spread his arms out and moved slowly one step at a time. The ledge was narrow, only enough room on it for his toes. He kept moving until he reached the terrace and was able to grab on to the balustrade. He slithered over the top and hugged the wide expanse of stone floor.

Once his heart had stopped pounding quite so aggressively he got to his feet. He looked around and recognized the view from the photograph on the back of Otravinicus's book. This was the exact spot where it had been taken.

He turned to the large windows and pressed his face

up against them to peer inside. Dr Otravinicus's apartment was a tip. At first, Junk wondered if he had been robbed, but as he looked closer he realized it was accumulated mess. Clothes and magazines discarded here and there. Forgotten plates of food festering. He hoped Otravinicus wasn't dead in there somewhere. He tried the handle and found that the door was unlocked. He hesitated, but only for a moment, before opening it and stepping inside.

The apartment smelled stale, well lived in. Something was rotting here, but it wasn't a body.

'Occootoo,' Junk called out. He searched his memory for the right words and remembered them. 'Vontra Otravinicus?' No answer.

There was a large main room that was a kitchen at one end and a living room at the other. Three doors led off it. The first was a windowless bathroom. Empty. The second an office. Also empty. And the third was a bedroom. Empty. *Now what?*

Junk started to look around for a clue as to where the doctor might be, but it was pointless. He couldn't read a word of Jansian, so even if the man's location was writ large somewhere right in front of him, he would never know. He could either wait in the hope that the doctor would soon return or go back and rejoin Garvan and Lasel in the cafe to come up with a plan B. He decided on the latter and left through the front door, which he discovered had been unlocked all along.

*

'Well, we could try again, I suppose,' said Garvan. 'If Lasel or I go this time, we'll be able to read through his papers at least. Did you leave the door unlocked?'

'Yes,' said Junk. 'Of course.'

Just then a shadow fell across the table. All three looked up to see a diminutive, bespectacled man with a long, thin face. He sat down without being asked. It was Dr Otravinicus himself.

'I've been sitting three tables away all morning, listening to you a-plotting and a-planning,' he said, oddly enough in English with a distinctive southern American accent. 'It sounds like you have been trying very hard to find me. I must say I am intrigued to discover why.'

13

Otravinicus listened as Junk and Garvan took it in turns to recount their story – from the man who killed Ambeline to the reason why they were in Arrapia looking for Otravinicus. When they had finished, he was quiet and contemplative. He nodded and Junk thought he was considering whether their story was true.

'I believe the story,' he said eventually, as if he could read Junk's mind. 'It's fascinating. Just fascinating. But if I am correct, you –' he was addressing Junk – 'could not find the Room of Doors again.'

'I possibly could,' said Junk. 'It would depend.'

'On?' asked Otravinicus.

'On Garvan. If he knew the exact spot where he caught me in his net.'

'Well, Mr Fiske,' said Otravinicus, turning to Garvan, 'do you?'

'Yes. I always go to the same spot,' he said.

'So the only problem . . .' continued Junk, '. . . is that I don't know how deep I was when I came through, but I assume there's a bottom to the sea there.

I went straight up. So if I was to go straight down again . . .'

'In theory we could find an entrance to the Room of Doors. I would be very interested in that, Mr Doyle.'

'Well,' said Junk, 'if you can help me, I can help you.'

Dr Otravinicus didn't say anything in reply. He just sat staring at Junk and nodding his head. Then he jumped to his feet and threw some money on the table.

'Come on,' he said. 'Let's go back to my home. I have a lot to explain to you.'

When they returned to Dr Otravinicus's building, the doorman glared as he saw them. Not them again! He had already had to throw them out. First the girl, and then the boy when he found him coming casually down the stairs as if he belonged there. It took him a moment to realize they were with one of the tenants. This stopped him. He spoke to Otravinicus and explained the trouble these three had caused. He wanted to call the police on them but the doctor waved him away and announced that they were his guests. The doorman did not look happy as they mounted the stairs. Junk wanted to ask Otravinicus about the League of Sharks and the doorman's possible connection to them, but he felt it wasn't the best time. It would have to wait.

When they reached the apartment the doctor threw off his coat. It fell on top of some other clothes in a pile by the front door.

'Come in,' he said. 'Throw your coats anywhere.

Can I get you anything? I don't really have anything.' All three said no. The doctor opened up the door to the terrace, picked up some newspapers and magazines from one of the large sofas and tossed them into a convenient but already cluttered corner. He threw himself back. 'Sit anywhere. Just push things out of your way. I'll tidy up later.' No one believed that. The three of them found places to sit. 'Junk – interesting name, by the way. Maybe you and I are kindred spirits. Go to that bookshelf. There's a book of maps at the bottom. Fetch it here, will you?'

Junk did as requested and found an atlas. He took it over to Otravinicus, who laid it on the coffee table in front of him and opened it up to a double-page map of the world of Jorda. Junk saw immediately how impressively accurate Garvan's sketch in the sand had been.

'Where to start? Where to start?' said Otravinicus. 'The beginning is always a good place, but in this instance it's hard to say where exactly the beginning resides. This is a map of the world as it is today. You have of course realized by now that you're on Earth, that Arrapia was called Paris in your day.'

'My day?' asked Junk, frowning.

'Your day, hard as this may be to comprehend, was some three million years ago.' He let the words hang in the air. The very idea made Junk's brain throb. He massaged his temples and shook his head, as if he could make all the hundreds of thoughts currently raging through his mind sort themselves out with a little jiggle.

It didn't work exactly, though one thought did rise to the top.

'But the Eiffel Tower . . . ?' he said, the question finding its own form as the words came out of his mouth. 'Metal wouldn't last that long, would it?' He wasn't one hundred per cent sure. 'I mean iron would rust away to nothing over such a long time. Wouldn't it?'

'You're not wrong,' said Otravinicus, 'except it's not iron. It's not actually the same Eiffel Tower at all. It was replaced at some point in its lifetime, when exactly is unknown, with a synthetic metal called falakite.'

'Never heard of it,' said Junk.

'No, you wouldn't have,' said Otravinicus. 'It would have been a good while after your time. Falakite is virtually indestructible, as far as anything can be. It weakens, hence it being on its side now, but it'll be there for another three million years and maybe three million years after that. No one knows exactly. There are bits and pieces of falakite all over the planet.'

Otravinicus turned his attention back to the map in front of him. 'This is what your world looks like today.' He wafted a hand across the book.

'Ireland's gone,' is all Junk could think to say.

'Land masses change over such a period of time. Usually with some help. Countries come and go.'

'What does that mean?' asked Junk. 'Help? What help?'

'Technology and industry from your time and for several centuries after, possibly even for millennia,

146

ravaged the planet. Absolutely devastated it. You were a short-sighted bunch. Your cities grew bigger and bigger. You cut down forests. Decimated the ice caps. Sea levels rose. The Final War split continents. I mean that literally. I'm massively oversimplifying thousands of years of misuse and stupidity of course. The thing is, geologically speaking, ape-descended man was a blip. A footnote. We try not to make the same mistakes but end up making brand-new ones.'

'What do you mean, "blip"?' asked Junk.

'There are no ape-descendants on the planet any more. Humans who evolved from apes died out completely about two thousand years after your time. So that would be what? About the mid-forty-first century? Am I correct? I studied your calendar system, but it's been a while.'

Junk just nodded. This was a lot to take in. 'So we destroyed ourselves?'

'Don't feel bad about it. You would have been long dead by then, and your children's children's children's children would all be dead too. No one's quite sure now, but they think there were about eighteen billion people on the planet by the end. Earth just wasn't able to sustain that kind of population. You tried to cheat nature. You tried to play God in so many ways: genetically modified foods and genetically modified people and genetically modified animals. In the end it was a disease, we think, of your own making that wiped you out. Your legacy changed the face of the world to what you see now.

'Ironically though, many people, myself included, believe that it was your playing God that's responsible for us –' he gestured to himself, Lasel and Garvan – 'being here today.'

'I don't understand,' said Junk. 'What does that mean?'

'Well, history is . . .' he searched for the word, '. . . patchy at best' was all he could come up with. 'You see, a few hundred years ago the Church had a cull of sorts. A cull on the past. The Church doesn't believe we are the result of scientific endeavour of course. The Church never does.'

'Same in my time,' said Junk.

The doctor continued. 'They tried, and for the most part succeeded in, eradicating history. There are huge gaping holes in our knowledge, but as far as we can tell, you – by which I mean ape-descendants – were tinkering with the DNA of our ancestors. You know DNA, right? That wasn't after your time?'

'No, I know all about it. Did a project on it at school. Deoxyribonucleic acid – DNA.' Junk repeated it for no other reason than that was pretty much all he remembered on the subject.

Otravinicus went on. 'Well, at the same time you were destroying yourselves by perverting your own DNA you were pushing forward the building blocks of our evolution by perverting our DNA. In much the same way that your distant ancestors were apes, I can trace my genetic code to the genus *Capra*.'

Junk looked blank.

'Goats,' said Otravinicus to clarify.

'Goats?' said Junk, wondering if this was a joke. Though when he stopped and looked at Otravinicus, he could see something a little goat-like about him. Otravinicus was a small, slight man with a puny, insubstantial body. His neck didn't look robust enough to be able to hold up his oversized head, which was looking more and more bulbous to Junk now he scrutinized it, but it did, so appearances must be deceptive. His limbs were long but anorexically thin. When the man sat, it was clear through the material of his trousers that his thigh was only a little wider than Junk's (admittedly muscular) forearm.

'Mr Fiske here clearly shares his ancestry with the noble elephant.' No argument there from Junk. That made perfect sense. Otravinicus continued. 'From his size, I would say genus *Loxodonta*. For Ms Mowtay, I would hazard a guess at *Cervine*.'

'What's that?' asked Junk.

'Deer and the like,' replied the doctor. He looked to Lasel for confirmation and she nodded. That made sense too. The big round eyes and impossibly long legs. Maybe her agile movement as well, but then Junk thought about it and he assumed his ape ancestors were a lot more agile than he would ever be, so Lasel's grace was less a product of her evolution than a result of her environment.

Junk looked at Lasel. 'You're a deer?'

'You're a monkey,' she pointed out with a smirk. Junk smiled back.

'We're no more goat and deer and elephant than you are an orang-utan,' said Otravinicus. 'Your descendants gave our ancestors a prod in the right direction. Everything else was evolution.'

'You know how crazy this sounds, right?' said Junk. 'Back in my time, there were still people who didn't accept that we evolved from apes. Who knows what they'd make of the idea of all animals evolving.'

'Not all,' said Otravinicus. 'Many but not all. Look around you. Not just at us but at everyone you've seen since you arrived here.'

'Made more sense when I thought I was on an alien planet.'

'I suppose you are in a way. Three million years is a very long time.'

'You're telling me,' said Junk. He tried to process all this information. It made his head spin so he changed the subject. 'Why do you have an American accent?'

'I suppose for the same recent that Mr Fiske here sounds a lot like you,' said Otravinicus. 'I learned to speak your language from an American.'

It took a few moments for the implications of that to register with Junk. 'You mean someone from my time?' he asked.

'Correct.'

'Then I'm not the first to find the Room of Doors,' he said.

'No, you're not.'

'Who is he? Is he still here? Are there other people here?' asked Junk.

'That I cannot answer. He and I had an agreement but unfortunately he chose not to honour the deal.' From the way he spat the last three words, it was apparent that this was still a sore point for Otravinicus. 'His name was Solo – Han Solo.' Junk laughed, but Otravinicus didn't get the joke. 'What's so funny?'

'Sorry. I wasn't laughing at you. It's not his real name,' said Junk.

'How do you know?' asked the doctor, frowning.

'Han Solo's a character in a film. Called *Star Wars*.'

'Oh, I see,' said Otravinicus, evidently feeling foolish now. 'Well, it doesn't matter. He agreed to show me the Room of Doors for myself. It would have been the perfect end for my book. In return I was to help him find an island.'

'An island?' said Garvan, who hadn't said anything for a while. 'Why did he want an island?'

'He didn't say. It wasn't a specific island, you understand. I got the impression it was where he wanted to live.'

'So you mean he could still be here?' asked Junk.

'He could, but I have no idea where. He vanished without fulfilling his promise to me. But I would still like to find the Room of Doors. Prove to the world that what I wrote in my book was accurate. Which brings me to what it is you want, young Junk.'

'I'm looking for the man who killed my sister,' said Junk.

'I suspected you might be,' said Otravinicus.

'All I know is he's part of a group called the League of Sharks. Help me find him, and I'll help you find the Room of Doors,' said Junk.

Otravinicus didn't reply for several moments as he considered Junk's proposal. When he spoke, it was to say, 'I've never heard of this League of Sharks.'

'Well, your doorman is one of them,' said Junk. 'Same race anyway. I'm not saying he's part of the group, but he's one of their kind.'

'He's a Pallatan. That's what we call people of his race. You want me to ask him what he knows?'

A short time later and Otravinicus had ordered the doorman up to his apartment. His name was Alsk. The shark-man was strangely obsequious in Otravinicus's presence, all of the previous aggression gone. Otravinicus translated for Junk's benefit.

'He's heard of them but doesn't know anything about them. They're an extremist group. Almost a cult.'

'Ask him if he has any tattoos,' said Junk.

Otravinicus relayed the question to Alsk who shook his head firmly.

'I don't believe him,' said Junk. 'Get him to show us his arm. This one.' Junk tapped his left bicep.

Otravinicus hesitated before asking Alsk the question. Alsk frowned. Clearly he didn't want to oblige.

Because he has something to hide, thought Junk. It was apparent that Otravinicus felt uncomfortable asking and didn't press it. Alsk considered what to do and then stood up. He took off his coat, unbuttoned his jacket and shirt and pulled them down, revealing his left, bare bicep. He showed it to everyone but particularly to Junk. He showed the right one too. Also blank. While he was re-buttoning his shirt Otravinicus asked him something else, which he considered before answering. They spoke and then Otravinicus showed him to the door.

'Well, that was embarrassing,' the doctor said when he returned.

'Sorry,' said Junk.

'He suggested someone else we could ask, though I warn you, it's not in a very good neighbourhood.'

It was only a short journey from Otravinicus's apartment, but they could have been in a different world. The street looked like something out of a Dickens novel. It was dark and wet and the light was almost non-existent. They found a bar with a picture of a walrus outside.

'This is the place,' announced Otravinicus and he entered brazenly. His confidence gave the impression that he had no idea what to expect inside rather than that he was someone who belonged here.

'Maybe you shouldn't come in,' said Junk to Lasel. It was unclear if she understood, but she frowned and followed Otravinicus.

Junk looked to Garvan to share his concern, but the big man seemed oblivious to anything untoward.

'Are you coming?' he said, and held the door open for Junk.

Junk and Garvan went inside. The place was dark and loud and hot. The stink of sweat and alcohol was like a yellow cloud in the air. Garvan coughed and waved a hand in front of his face. The music was so loud it reverberated through their entire bodies from head to toe and back again. Junk could feel his teeth vibrating.

He looked around but couldn't see Otravinicus or Lasel. He did see lots of aggressive, sweaty faces glaring back at him. Without even realizing what he was doing, he leaned back a little, making it clear he was with Garvan, who was easily the biggest guy in here. Though Junk had a feeling size meant nothing in this place. There was a tiny man at the bar. He had a Mohican of blue hair and three eyes; all were looking at Junk. As he got closer he saw that the third eye, on the man's cheek, was a tattoo. Despite his diminutive size, Junk felt he was capable of springing off his bar stool, doing something horrible and disfiguring to Junk and being back on his stool before it had even stopped spinning. He looked away quickly and tried very hard to avoid eye contact with anyone – especially people with three eyes.

Lasel stepped out from a nook in the back and gestured to Junk and Garvan to join her. 'Dusco,' she said, beckoning. *Here.*

The nook contained a round table. Otravinicus was

sitting there with a woman. She was the biggest woman Junk had ever seen. Like Ambeline's killer and Alsk the doorman, she was also of Pallatan descent. She was bald and muscular but strangely feminine nonetheless and her huge slit of a mouth was ringed with red lipstick. Though her shoulders were broad, Olympic-swimmer broad, she had a definite neck that the males of her species seemed to lack. She was wearing a flimsy vest that exposed her powerful and heavily tattooed arms. Junk searched for the mark of the League, but he couldn't see it.

'Junk,' said Otravinicus, 'I'd like to introduce you to Cascér.'

Cascér looked Junk up and down and chuckled. 'Tootu shhnoova,' she said, and made a strange clicking sound with her tongue. Junk had no idea what she had said, but it didn't sound as if she was speaking Jansian.

'What?' he asked, a little nervously.

'You don't want to know,' said Otravinicus.

'What language is that?' Junk asked, his question directed at Cascér. She looked at Otravinicus.

'Trara ju,' he said in her language.

'You speak it?' Junk asked.

'I do,' said Otravinicus. 'It's called H'rtu. It's a Sitan dialect.'

Junk had to trawl through his memory. He remembered Garvan's map. Sita had been the African continent in his time. It was now divided into four separate land masses.

'I have explained to Cascér what you are looking

for,' said Otravinicus. 'She knows all about the League of Sharks.'

Junk couldn't contain his excitement. He looked at Cascér. 'Well?' he asked expectantly.

One of her great fin hands tapped the table and she said nothing. Otravinicus dug into his coat and pulled out some money. He laid it on the table and Cascér snatched it up like a rattlesnake spotting a mouse. She didn't bother to count it, which made Junk fear her all the more for some reason. Then she turned to a morbidly obese man behind the counter and barked at him in H'rtu. A moment later a bottle of green liquid was brought to the table along with five shot glasses.

'Dutu, jay,' said Cascér to Junk.

'She would appreciate it if you poured,' said Otravinicus.

'Sure,' said Junk. He picked up the bottle and tried to pull out the cork. It wouldn't budge. He went red in the face trying, and this proved to be a source of amusement for Cascér. She snatched the bottle from him and pulled out the cork without any effort at all. She smiled and winked at Junk as she handed it back. His hand was shaking a little as he filled the glasses.

'Ja,' said Cascér, waving a hand over the glasses, indicating that everyone should have one.

'Brace yourself,' said Otravinicus quietly to Junk. Cascér sucked back her shot. Garvan did the same, as did Otravinicus. Lasel copied, and even though the drink was strong she forced herself to show no ill effects. When

156

it came to Junk's turn, he followed suit and promptly erupted into a coughing fit. His face turned an alarming shade of blue. Cascér was laughing heartily. All of a sudden she leaned forward and snatched Junk off his feet. Before he knew what was happening, she had installed him squarely on her lap. As the coughing fit subsided, he felt like a little kid visiting Santa's grotto.

'She likes you,' said Otravinicus. 'You might just have to put up with it.'

'This is humiliating,' said Junk out of the corner of his mouth.

Cascér ruffled his hair. 'Na foota bootchek, jay?' she said to Junk, who looked at Otravinicus for a translation.

'She's asking what you want to know,' he replied.

'About the League of Sharks,' said Junk. 'Who are they? How do I find them?'

Otravinicus repeated the questions to Cascér in her tongue and she answered at length.

'She says,' said Otravinicus, translating, 'they are a cult obsessed with their ancestors' reputation as the ultimate predator. Like Alsk said, they are an extremist group. Not representative of her people. She wants to make that clear. Says they're nothing but pirates. Bloodthirsty, I think she's saying. Her language is a little basic. They will kill and maim for pleasure or profit.

'She says the tattoo you describe, the fin and the five stars, is specific to a particular branch that resides in Cul Sita – what would have been South Africa in your day.'

Junk's heart was pounding. This was what he had

been looking for; he was another step closer to Ambeline's killer. He had to get to South Africa. Then something else occurred to him and he looked to Otravinicus.

'The man who killed my sister, he spoke to me. He said, "Fatoocha mammacoola charla."' Will you ask her what it means?'

Otravinicus explained the question to Cascér and she frowned. She said something to Otravinicus and he looked at Junk. 'She wants to know if you're sure that's what he said?' asked Otravinicus.

'I'm sure,' said Junk. He had played those words over and over in his head for three years now. He would never forget them.

'She says it means "Nine Emperors send their regards."'

Junk considered that. 'What does that mean?' he asked.

Otravinicus shook his head. 'She has no idea.'

14

When Junk, Lasel and Garvan got to Dr Otravinicus's apartment the following morning, they were surprised to find Cascér was there already and cooking breakfast. Otravinicus was about half Cascér's size and they made a very odd couple. Though she cooked a mean breakfast. Over food they discussed what to do next.

'I need to get to South Africa,' said Junk. 'I mean Cul Sita.'

'Of course, of course,' said Otravinicus. Cascér stood behind him, massaging his shoulders. She was far too rough, but he merely winced and sucked up the pain. It was too early in their relationship for him to point out her shortcomings. 'Here's what I suggest but it is only a suggestion. If you disagree, I am more than open to an alternative. I think our most direct way to find the League is to return to Garvan's island. If we can find the entrance to the Room of Doors, then all you would have to do is step through the adjacent door that you believe would take to you to Cul Sita.' Otravinicus was making a reference to Junk's suspicion that he should have taken the door on the right when he had been faced with a choice back in the Room of Doors; he felt bad that he had based his decision on nothing more than a childhood rhyme and therefore chance. 'Our alternative is to take a land-ship,' Otravinicus went on. 'Even on the fastest vessel we could find, it is a journey of several weeks.'

Junk considered this and nodded. 'The quicker we get there the better, I say.'

'That's the spirit.' Otravinicus smiled broadly. 'I have already enquired about hiring the fastest ship to take us south. It is moored to the north of here on the coast. We can leave today if that is acceptable.'

'That's perfect, far as I'm concerned,' said Junk with a hearty grin. He beamed at Garvan, who wasn't paying attention, and Lasel, who was frowning. Something was bothering her, but Junk was a teenage boy and was therefore oblivious.

They set off almost immediately, taking a smaller land-ship to the north coast. The journey took less than an hour. They passed the outskirts of a bland, nondescript village by the name of Dissel, which was Lasel's hometown. She sat on one of the open decks seeking out landmarks of her childhood as they rumbled past: a small tor to the west, topped with a crooked tree, where she would sit as a child, finding reasons not to go home. The tree was still there, but she remembered it as being dead and black and twisted. But not now. Now it was caked in blossom. It was alive and vibrant. The grass around it was green and lush and she saw, from a distance, a girl doing handstands against it, just like she used to do. Despite herself, she smiled.

They arrived at the costal town of Turanay, which was a hub for land-ships. Nothing existed in the town that didn't revolve in some way around either the organization, deployment, piloting or maintenance of the ships or the feeding and watering of the thousands of passengers and crew who passed through there each year.

Junk and the others disembarked at a station that housed tracks leading off in every direction. Dozens of ships were docked here, waiting to set off on the next leg of their journey. The place boiled with activity. The air was filled with the clanking of the turning circles moving the next ship to depart into position on its chosen track.

Dr Otravinicus led the way through the bustling station with Cascér by his side. Garvan followed, displaying little interest in his surroundings. Junk came after, marvelling at the ships and the activity around him. Lasel brought up the rear. Her mind was elsewhere, on the crooked tree on top of the tor.

They arrived at a staging platform where they found the ship Otravinicus had hired. It wasn't as huge as the land-ship they had been on before, nor as grand, but it was beautiful. It was called the *Casabia*. Eight masts and made from a dark, almost black, wood.

They stopped at the solitary gangplank and Otravinicus called out, requesting permission to board.

Junk, who was loving all things nautical at that precise moment, thought about old films he had seen where people would have to call out in this way. Old films that were now more than three million years old. He liked how some things hadn't changed.

A figure appeared at the top of the gangplank. He was tall and broad and looked like he could be hit in his vast belly and not even notice. This was the captain of the *Casabia*. His name was Hundrig Shunt. Since Otravinicus had explained the evolution of Jorda's current population, Junk had found himself looking at everyone he met, trying to work out their ancestry. Some were easier than others and Hundrig was very much in that category. His ancestors had clearly been rhinoceroses. Apart from being bipedal and the lack of a facial horn, Hundrig still looked like a rhino.

Junk's grasp of Jansian had improved and he discovered that he understood almost everything the captain said.

'Greetings, Dr Otravinicus. S'good to see you again, sir. Come aboard, one and all. All are welcome.'

Hundrig had what could only be described as a booming whisper. Anything louder and it would have cracked the very ground they walked on. Once on board, introductions were made. Explanations for the journey were given and everyone was shown to their cabin. Once again Junk was expected to share with Garvan, and the first thing he did was look for a convenient balcony to sleep on. Unfortunately there wasn't one, but Junk figured it was a big ship and he would find somewhere to sleep even if it was in the crow's nest. Then it occurred to him that he hadn't noticed whether or not there was a crow's nest on this sort of ship. He resolved to find out later.

The *Casabia* had a crew of ten, who all looked very different from one another. They were big and they were small; they were fat and thin. Their skin was black or grey or white or pink or brown or even, in one case, blue. Junk had been part of many a ship's crew back in his time and the *Casabia* didn't feel that different. Crews tended to be made up of stragglers and people running away from one thing or another or sometimes running to somewhere.

If anything, Otravinicus was even more eager to get going than Junk, and less than twenty minutes after they had boarded the *Casabia* was given its departure berth.

Junk stood on the prow and watched as the ground beneath the ship cranked around and then jolted sideways. Tracks joined up and the magnetic propulsion system got the *Casabia* moving. Slowly at first, but then with each new change of direction the speed increased until the ship reached a massive central turntable. It rotated through two hundred and seventy degrees until it was lined up with the tracks that would take it west-by-south-west.

Hundrig bellowed the order to unfurl the sails, and in the blink of an eye the canvases, each one blood red, dropped into position. The *Casabia* lurched forward, rapidly picking up speed as it thundered out of Turanay station. The suddenness of its forward momentum took Junk by surprise and he yelled joyously as they sped away.

The journey to Garvan's island would take the best part of two days. Junk spent time getting to know the crew. His Jansian was getting better all the time, but, much like crews back in Junk's time, when language let them down, they always found some way to communicate.

The *Casabia*'s crew liked and accepted Junk almost immediately, sensing in him one of their own. A seafarer. In particular he bonded with the captain and with the ship's navigator, an impossibly tall, impossibly thin man called Gaskis. The two of them talked endlessly about the stars. Gaskis was fascinated by Junk's description of the constellations three million years ago. Junk would show him where Orion's Belt or the Plough once were, and in return Gaskis taught Junk the names of the celestial clusters that they were looking at now.

Hundrig took a shine to Junk because of the boy's enthusiasm for all things nautical. The big captain was moved by Junk's story about Ambeline and his search for her killer, and Gaskis explained that Hundrig had lost his wife and young son many years before to disease. Despite the brash exterior, Gaskis said, the captain was a big softie at heart.

Junk, Garvan and Lasel spent time together, sitting up on the foredeck, watching the land or sea go by. Garvan was looking forward to seeing his island again.

He described his home in vivid detail to Lasel, but Junk noticed that he left out the ravenous, flesh-eating Neanderthal birdmen. By this time the three of them were able to switch almost unconsciously between Jansian and English.

'What are you going to do when you find him?' Lasel asked Junk. He knew without her having to clarify who she meant: Ambeline's killer.

Junk shrugged. 'Kill him,' he said, a little too casually. He said it the same way he would talk about making a cup of tea or reading a book.

'How?' asked Garvan.

Junk shook his head. 'I don't know.' He paused. 'Yet.'

'But he's big,' said Garvan. 'Very big,' he added pointlessly, for emphasis.

Junk knew exactly what Garvan meant: *How do you expect to kill someone who could easily flatten you?* 'I was just a kid when I saw him.'

'And what are you now?' asked Lasel. One corner of her mouth twitched, trying to hide the smile that said she was teasing him. Their friendship had reached a stage where she could tease him, but it had got there a little too quickly, so even though they were both comfortable with the actual teasing, they both felt subconsciously uncomfortable with the idea of the teasing. It made for a lot of internal confusion.

At dusk on the first day Garvan went below, leaving Junk and Lasel alone. They sat side by side, their legs dangling over the side of the ship, watching the sun setting. The sky was magical. Streaks of orange, red, pink and gold. It took them a moment to realize that their fingers were touching. They both became aware simultaneously and neither moved. They didn't look at one another or try to move their fingers apart. The proximity made them feel a little light-headed. It was intoxicating. Their hearts galloped. Junk felt his mouth dry up. Lasel was the same.

Slowly Lasel shifted her weight so her body leaned into Junk's. He opened his shoulder, creating a hollow that allowed her to sink subtly into him. The movements were tiny. Anyone watching probably might not even have noticed a change, but to Lasel and Junk they were massive, grand gesticulations. Both blushed.

Lasel started to turn her head towards Junk, but not her eyes. Not yet. As if he could sense her, Junk started to move his eyes to her but not his head. Then, slowly, Junk started to turn his head too and Lasel her eyes. Both were hugely conscious of their own breathing, which sounded deafeningly loud to them but of course was practically inaudible to anyone else.

They both moved to look at one another . . . but instead found themselves facing a plate of dead fish. Both jumped in fright and pulled back. They were so wrapped up in the moment that neither had heard Garvan returning. He had a small plate of mackies that Hortez, the *Casabia*'s cook, had just prepared.

'Mackie?' he said, already chomping on one. 'Fresh.'

Junk and Lasel pulled rapidly apart. Garvan didn't notice anything unusual, assuming they were just making plenty of space for him to sit between them.

'Nice view,' he said with his mouth full.

'I've just got to . . .' Lasel didn't put a huge amount of effort into finishing her sentence. She quickly got to her feet and dashed away.

'Maybe she's gone to get some more,' said Garvan, indicating the plate in his hand, which was now empty. 'We've finished these ones.'

Junk was silent. His head was spinning from the surge of adrenalin. He stared out at the sunset and tried to make sense of what had just happened. Had it been mutual? Had he imagined it?

'What do you think of Lasel?' asked Garvan, as if he could read Junk's mind.

Junk shrugged, a little too forcefully. He shook his head and shrugged again. Put it all together and it looked as if he was having some sort of fit. 'Nothing,' he said. 'I don't know. Not . . . nothing. Why? What do you think?'

'I think she's lovely,' said Garvan.

'What?' This brought Junk to his senses. He turned to look at his friend. What was he saying?

'It can be quite a lonely place, my island,' said Garvan.

'What?' said Junk. Nothing more meaningful came to mind just at that moment.

'It was nice when you were there,' said Garvan. 'I've been alone a long time. I don't want to be alone again.'

'You like Lasel,' said Junk. It was a statement, not a

167

question, and most people would have picked up on the disappointment in Junk's cadence. Garvan did not. Junk knew there and then that Lasel was now off-limits for him. Even though something had happened between them – he was sure of it, and sure she was aware of it too – he had not been the first to vocalize his interest in her. That had been Garvan. Junk would have to put all confusing thoughts about Lasel out of his head. There was a pain in his throat that ran all the way down to the centre of his chest. He didn't know why.

For the rest of the trip Junk avoided Lasel as much as he could. She noticed the change in his attitude and, knowing nothing about Garvan's interest in her, put it down to Junk feeling uncomfortable about what had happened between them. She decided it was best to forget it had ever happened.

Late in the afternoon on day two Junk was up on the top deck with Gaskis when he heard Garvan let out an excited bellow. He looked down to see Garvan on the main deck below jump to his feet and run to the port side. He was big enough to rock the ship but only momentarily.

'Junk!' Garvan shouted. 'JunkJunkJunkJunkJunk!'

Junk had never heard his friend so animated. He went down to see what was wrong.

As Junk reached Garvan, so too did Dr Otravinicus, Cascér and Lasel, all attracted by Garvan's rambunctious hollering.

'What's wrong?' asked Junk. 'What is it?'

'Look,' said Garvan, and he thrust out one of his mammoth arms, pointing into the distance. On the horizon Junk saw an island. It wasn't familiar from this vantage point, but he knew it was Garvan's island. Of course it was. It was the only explanation for Garvan's excitement.

And then, suddenly, Garvan's excitement spilled over and he swept Lasel and Junk up into a powerful embrace. After trying so hard to avoid one another for most of the day, now Junk and Lasel were closer than ever.

'I'm home!' said Garvan.

15

Garvan stood outside his cabin. There was little of it left. The birdmen had trashed it. They had smashed every window, torn off most of the roof, broken down walls and then ripped, shredded and destroyed almost everything inside.

Junk, Lasel, Otravinicus, Cascér, Hundrig and three of the *Casabia*'s crew stood behind Garvan. All could sense his heartbreak. Finally Junk felt as if he had to say something. He stepped up and put a hand on his big friend's arm. He couldn't tell if Garvan even noticed.

'We can fix it,' said Junk. 'I'll help you.' Garvan didn't respond.

'It's getting late,' said Otravinicus after a few more moments of silence. 'We should be getting back to the *Casabia*. We'll go diving first thing. Garvan?' Still no response. '*Garvan?*' His forceful tone jarred Garvan from his thoughts and he turned to look at the doctor. 'Will you be able to show us your fishing spot tomorrow?'

Garvan didn't answer immediately. He just turned back to the remains of his house and looked desperately sad, but after a moment, he nodded. 'Yes,' he said. 'I can show you.' And with that he turned and walked away. The others exchanged awkward looks and then followed him.

The next morning the *Casabia* was anchored in the middle of Garvan's fishing ground and all the crew and passengers were up on deck. It had been decided that Cascér, as the best natural swimmer, would accompany Junk on his dive. Junk was wearing only a pair of shorts. Cascér wasn't even wearing that much. All the crew stared but she didn't seem to care.

'Do you have air?' Junk asked Hundrig in Jansian.

'Air?' answered the captain in his usual restrained bellow.

'Yeah, you know, air tanks? Diving equipment? How do I breathe?'

'Oh, of course,' said Hundrig. 'Lethro's catching it now.' Junk assumed he had misunderstood: *catching* the air? Lethro was another member of the *Casabia*'s crew. Junk looked around for him and was curious to see him on the bow wielding a fishing net. As Junk watched, Lethro, a short, stout man, about as wide as he was tall, let out a triumphant cry and starting hauling in the net.

Moments later, Junk was looking with unrestrained incredulity at a translucent green jellyfish-like creature that was flopping restlessly on the deck.

'Come again?' said Junk.

Otravinicus stepped forward to take charge. 'This is a commust,' he said, pointing at the jellyfish. 'It secretes a viscous substance that forms an airtight and waterproof shell.'

'Right . . .' said Junk, still not getting it.

'The gunk goes over you,' explained Otravinicus. 'You go in the water; the shell protects you, allows you to breathe.'

'Underwater?' asked Junk.

'Correct.'

'For how long?'

Otravinicus had asked Junk about how time was recorded in Junk's era, and Junk had explained seconds, minutes, hours, days, weeks, months and years. 'About twenty minutes,' said Otravinicus.

'OK,' said Junk. It wasn't very long, but back home diving with an air tank would afford him a finite amount of breathing time as well. This wasn't so different. 'How do you get the jelly out?' asked Junk, and almost immediately wished he hadn't. Lethro picked up the commust and threw it to Hundrig, who was standing behind Junk. Hundrig held the creature over Junk's head and popped a large fluid sac on its underside. A viscous yellow substance, that looked a lot like pus but smelled much, much worse, flowed all over Junk, who cried out in shock. It was ice cold on his skin.

'Don't move,' said Hundrig, and Junk didn't move. The liquid oozed slowly down over him. Where separate rivulets met, they joined seamlessly. Soon Junk's entire body was covered in a mould that fitted him perfectly and afforded him full movement.

'Can you hear me?' asked Junk. Otravinicus nodded. His voice was muffled but still audible. Junk touched his ears and realized the jelly had seeped inside and clotted. The same with his nostrils. His entire body was enclosed.

His view of the world was a little blurred as he looked at it through the jelly shell, but after a few moments the substance became clearer and he could see perfectly well. Hundrig burst another of the commust's fluid sacs over Cascér and Junk watched as the liquid contents flowed over and around her, encasing her as it had done him. Seeing it from an observer's point of view, he realized that there was more than mere gravity determining its direction. It was almost as if the material was alive and chose which way to go. It actively sought out more of itself to join with. In less than a minute, Cascér was covered too.

'Now don't lose track of time,' Otravinicus reminded them. 'Twenty minutes.'

'Got it,' said Junk.

As he watched Cascér dive gracefully over the side of the ship, the thought occurred to him that he didn't have a watch and therefore had no way of knowing how long he was under the water. He would just have to guess. And with that he jumped after Cascér.

The water was clear, and the light from above illuminated the world around them to a depth of several metres.

Cascér looked Junk meaningfully in the eye and nodded. He guessed she was trying to tell him something but he wasn't sure what. Then she wrapped one of her big arms around him and drew him into her, squashing his jelly-covered face into her robust jelly-covered breast and started to swim powerfully downwards.

Junk had to twist to turn his head away from Cascér's body so he could see where he was going. He had never moved so fast underwater and it was exhilarating. They sped downwards. The jelly wetsuit was remarkable. Junk sensed no difference in pressure and only the slightest change in the temperature as they descended. Back home when he went diving, the cold stung him through his neoprene more and more the further down he went.

It didn't take them long to reach the seabed, but there had been no green glowing doors on the way. The light at this depth should have been near zero, but Junk noticed that he could still see and realized that his jellied bodysock was bioluminescent. It glowed with a pale blue light that rippled ever so slightly. If he stretched out his hand in front of him, the light from his fingertips illuminated an area a metre or so ahead.

Without warning him, Cascér started swimming with Junk still tucked under her arm. She swam in one direction for about a dozen metres and then up for a similar distance, before going back the way they had come and then down again. She did the same thing three more times, always coming back to the same starting point.

She looked at Junk and shook her head. Junk understood. There was nothing there. He nodded. Cascér pointed upwards with her thumb, suggesting they resurface. Junk had lost track of time but he didn't feel as if his air supply was waning just yet and he wasn't quite ready to go back. He shook his head and gestured that he wanted to look around. Cascér frowned but didn't try to stop him. Junk gestured for her to go back. He wanted to add *if you want* (he didn't want it to seem as if he was ordering her to go) but he couldn't think how to say that through the avenue of rudimentary mime. Cascér didn't seem to take offence. She just nodded once and shot up vertically like a missile. The pale blue light that encased her dimmed rapidly as she went. Soon Junk was alone.

He chose a direction at random and started swimming. He couldn't move as quickly as Cascér but it didn't matter. He loved being back under the water and with a freedom he had never experienced before. He was unencumbered by a mask, breathing apparatus, an air tank strapped to his back and a bulky buoyancy compensator that stifled his movements. He was very nearly able to forget about the film of jelly that covered him. It was almost as if he was down here only in his shorts. It felt wonderful.

At about thirty metres or so he came to the edge of a chasm. There was no way of knowing how deep it went, but he decided to explore just a little. As he went down, his presence startled some of the strange inhabitants living in the nooks and crannies of the chasm's wall. Creatures he had never imagined shot out and zipped through the water around him.

All at this depth were translucent and shared the same bioluminescent qualities as the commust. They were a whole range of different colours and sizes, most of them small. The largest one he saw was some sort of sea snake. It pulsated with a transparent orange glow. Junk remembered that some sea snakes in his time were horribly venomous and he didn't know if that still applied. Nothing he could do about it now. He stayed very still and watched as the snake whirled and danced in front of him. It could have been a show of aggression or attraction. Or possibly it was just lost. However, after about thirty seconds of this, it plunged down further and disappeared from view. It was one of the most beautiful things Junk had ever seen.

Junk made his way to the surface and came up a fair distance from the *Casabia*. He swam slowly on his back to the ship and as he went the protective layer covering him started to disintegrate and wash away. It was gone completely by the time he climbed aboard.

Lasel was waiting for him. 'We were worried,' she said. 'Was everything OK?'

Junk smiled lazily, a feeling of absolute serenity coursing through him. He nodded. 'It was magnificent.'

That evening, as usual, the crew and passengers on board the *Casabia* ate and drank heartily. The food was all caught fresh off the side of the ship, but Junk drew the line at eating the commust which had supplied him with his jelly wetsuit. He felt that would be somehow ungrateful.

Otravinicus flopped down next to Junk. He had been miserable all afternoon, ever since Junk and Cascér had come back up and reported no sign of the door. Otravinicus was not good at hiding his feelings. He was wearing a vest, which exposed his puny little body. His long, thin arms had no muscle definition to them. They were like the arms of a child although considerably longer.

'Why was there no door?' asked Otravinicus. 'I keep asking myself. Either we're in the wrong place or it's closed. Can it open again? Can we open it?'

'I don't know,' said Junk. 'Garvan knows these waters. Knows where he was when he caught me in his net. Cascér and I went straight down from that point – and no door. It must have closed. It's the only explanation.'

'Then we need to find another way,' said Otravinicus.

'I'm open to suggestions.'

Otravinicus shook his head. He had nothing.

Junk changed the subject. Partly because he wanted to think about something else for five minutes but mostly because a series of questions had been niggling away at him. 'Can I ask you . . .' he said, 'about the American? About "Han Solo" . . .' He always wanted to snigger when he said the name. 'Who was he? Where did you meet him? Where did he come from? Why was he here?'

'He came to me in much the same way that you did. Our paths crossed. He knew who I was. Knew I could help him. Knew he had something I wanted. What's the phrase you use? Something about dangling a parrot. He dangled just the right parrot to get my attention.'

'Carrot. You dangle a carrot.'

'Are you sure?' asked Otravinicus with a frown.

'Pretty sure,' said Junk. 'You must have been with him for a fair while. Your English is very good.'

'We were together for several weeks. We went on a journey together.'

'Looking for this island he wanted?' said Junk.

'No, actually that came after. He wanted to go a small town called Ollamah on the southern coast of Jjen.' Junk pictured the map Otravinicus had shown him back in Arrapia but he couldn't recall Jjen. Then he thought about the map Garvan had drawn in the sand and remembered Jjen was roughly where the Arctic was.

'What for?' asked Junk.

'He needed to collect something. A crate.'

'What was in it?'

Otravinicus shrugged. 'He didn't say.' He reached over to grab a copper-coloured bottle from in front of a now comatose crew member. The drink of choice on board was a heavy port-like wine that was almost black in colour. It was called mosshut. Otravinicus poured two glasses, a small one for Junk and a much larger one for himself. He rose unsteadily and picked up his glass. 'Tomorrow is another day, Junk, and tomorrow we will decide what to do next. Right now I'm going to get some sleep.' With that he tottered away. Junk looked at the dark liquid and took a sip. It burned the back of his throat as he drank and filled his belly with a moment of golden fire that delivered a satisfyingly soporific sensation. The world around him danced and swayed and a gentle breeze tickled his bare feet. The captain and Gaskis started singing. Junk's eyelids grew heavy and he drifted off to sleep with a contented smile on his lips.

When he woke several hours later his head felt heavy. He took a deep breath and scratched as he glanced about. Gaskis and a couple of other members of the crew had also fallen asleep on deck.

Junk had spent the previous three nights out here so he wouldn't have to deal with Garvan's snoring, and he was about to turn over on the bench he was on and go back to sleep when a movement caught his eye. Someone was tiptoeing slowly towards him from the far end of the deck. Junk was in the shadow of an overhang and he figured that as long as he didn't move too much, whoever it was wouldn't see him.

Junk realized that he had jumped to the conclusion that whoever it was didn't belong. He couldn't see any detail so it could be a member of the crew, but there was something about the way the figure was moving that caused Junk to fear him. His movements were controlled, wary, and above all silent. Junk knew this crew well enough to know no one aboard did silent with any great conviction. Whoever it was didn't want to be discovered.

Junk remained very still and even lowered his eyelids so that the whites of his eyes wouldn't give him away. The figure was extremely tall and dressed all in black. As he drew nearer, a cloud pulled away from the moon and a blanket of light spread over the deck of the *Casabia*. The black figure was wearing a hooded cloak and his face was lost in shadow. He was broad as well as tall. He crossed silently to a door that led below deck and went in.

Immediately Junk was on his feet. He shook Gaskis, but the lanky navigator just grumbled in his sleep and didn't stir. He tried the other two crew members nearby and they were even more soundly asleep or more likely passed out from too much mosshut.

Junk stood and considered his options. What to do? Who was the intruder? Did he mean them harm? Junk decided he had to assume that he did. Otherwise what was he doing sneaking around the ship in the dead of night?

Junk looked around for a weapon. His toe stubbed an empty mosshut bottle and it started to roll. He moved quickly to block its progress and picked it up. It was heavy. Made of thick glass. He held it by its stout neck and whacked it against the palm of his other hand. He winced in pain. That worked. He followed the black-clad figure inside the ship.

A steep flight of steps led down to the first deck. Junk moved slowly and quietly and listened. He heard nothing but the waves lapping against the sides and the ship creaking. There were lights running the length of the first-deck corridor but they were dim and didn't give off much light. The doorways he passed were thick with shadow and threat.

At the end of the corridor Junk reached another flight of steps, leading down to the next deck, but he stopped. Ahead of him, the door to the bridge was ajar. Had the intruder gone in there or carried on down? Junk wasn't sure what to do. He had to make a decision. The door to the bridge was rarely left open so he moved forward. Just as he reached up to push back the door, he heard a noise behind him. It came from below. Someone was moving around down there.

Junk descended the steps lightly, wary of revealing himself to the intruder. He reached a long straight corridor with eight doors leading off from it. One door was open. The door to Otravinicus's cabin. Junk moved closer.

He paused at the threshold and listened. He heard no sound from within. He reached out slowly and put his hand to the door. He froze. He did hear something. It was a low, guttural murmur. Continuous and rhythmic. Junk slowly pushed the door open.

The moon shone brightly through a porthole. Junk saw the black-clad intruder standing over Otravinicus as he lay asleep. Cascér lay next to him.

The intruder had removed his hood. Junk could see him more clearly now. He was huge, solid, broad-shouldered with a square granite jaw and a heavy brow. His head had been shaved save for two strips of jet-black hair, like parallel Mohicans, that ran from his brow to the base of his skull. The murmuring was coming from him. He had his head bowed and Junk guessed he was praying. He didn't understand the words being spoken, but he didn't need to. The intruder opened his eyes. They were silver and penetrating. He raised his arms and Junk saw something metal glinting in the blue light. A dagger. The intruder held the weapon, two-handed, above his head, ready to bring it down.

'Coorratun,' he said.

'NO!' screamed Junk as he raced into the room. The intruder turned. Otravinicus woke. Cascér leaped out of bed. Junk swung the mosshut bottle with abandon and connected with the intruder's nose, which disintegrated in a spray of blood and mucus, showering one side of Junk's face. The intruder fell hard to the floor and lay gurgling at Junk's feet.

16

It was morning before the man in black regained consciousness. When he did he found himself on the main deck, bound securely to the central mast. Everyone on board was gathered around him. He was sporting two black eyes that made him look like a panda, and the *Casabia*'s medic had splinted his nose. He looked a mess.

Hundrig stood over him and explained who he was, namely the captain of this land-ship. 'You are Uuklyn?' said Hundrig, speaking Jansian.

Lasel, Garvan and Junk stood together. 'Uuklyn?' whispered Junk to Garvan, looking for an explanation.

'A country to the east. Over the border,' replied Garvan.

'And,' continued Hundrig, 'from the look of you, you're a religious man.' He nodded his big head at the intruder's double Mohican.

That's what identifies a religious man here? thought Junk. Not like the priests back in Ireland, that's for sure.

'Why is a religious man stealing on to my ship and attacking my passengers?'

'You can torture me. You can burn the eyes from my skull. I won't tell you a thing.' He made a show of closing his mouth and turned his boxy chin resolutely to the side to illustrate how there was absolutely no chance that they would get any information out of him. A moment later he turned back to Hundrig. 'Other than this . . . I am of an order of monks. We have vowed to protect the Room of Doors. The Room is divine. You are looking for the Room. It is forbidden for mere mortals to set foot inside. No mortal can enter the Room. The wrath of God Almighty would rip the skin from their flesh and the flesh from their bones. Their bones would turn to ash and the ash would be blown away by the breath of God. That is the fate that awaits anyone who dares enter the sacred room. I will not say any more.'

Hundrig scratched his head and looked around, searching out Junk. They exchanged a look and then Hundrig turned back to the intruder. 'For someone who isn't going to say anything, you're kind of chatty. What's your name?'

The intruder shook his head. 'I will say no more.' He paused and then continued: 'Other than to say that I was christened by God himself. He called me Brother and told me I was Rard. Brother Rard. I have had the light of the divine shine down upon me. I am worthy and you are not. I will say no more to you, coorratun.'

That word again. Junk guessed it meant 'infidel' or something like that.

'So you know all about the Room of Doors, do you?' asked Hundrig. Brother Rard said nothing this time. 'Except of course you don't. My little friend here . . .' Hundrig reached out a gargantuan hand and put it on Junk's shoulder. Junk felt as if he was about to be pushed through the deck by the sheer weight of it. The captain gathered Junk close, so he was standing next to him, in front of Brother Rard, and continued: '. . . He's been in your divine Room of Doors, and far as I can tell his skin is still on his flesh and his flesh is still on his bones. Is that about right, Junk?'

'Yes, Captain,' said Junk. 'Skin, bones, flesh, all accounted for.' Junk and Hundrig both looked at Brother Rard. He didn't look happy.

'Blasphemy!' he spat. 'Only a walker may enter the Room of Doors. You are no walker.'

'Walker?' asked Hundrig.

'I will say no more,' said Brother Rard . . . again.

Hundrig looked at the others and shrugged. He couldn't think of anything else to ask. 'Anyone else want to give it a try?'

Dr Otravinicus stepped forward then. 'If I may . . . ?' Hundrig gestured for him to go ahead and he went and sat down. He had been standing for several minutes now and it was a hot morning.

'Brother Rard,' said Otravinicus. Rard did not react. 'Allow me to introduce myself. My name is Otravinicus.

Sznarzel Otravinicus. But I think you know that, don't you? You came to kill me.'

Brother Rard started muttering quickly under his breath, in his own tongue, which Junk didn't understand but it sounded like he was praying again.

Otravinicus ignored the noises the monk was making and spoke over him. 'I am considered by many to be the leading authority on the Room of Doors. Now, I know of the Church's feelings on the subject, but I am unaware of a brotherhood of monks specifically dedicated to the protection of the Room. Tell me, what is the name of your order?'

Brother Rard kept up his muttered prayers for another thirty seconds or so. Then he stopped, took a deep breath and looked up at Otravinicus. 'The day you die will become a sacred day to my order.'

'Well, it's always nice to be remembered,' said Otravinicus gaily.

'We are the Order of the Room of the One True God, Pire. We are the Brotherhood of Pire. Defenders. Protectors. Avengers.'

'Sorry. Never heard of you.'

'Of course not. You are coorratun.' That word again. 'Unworthy.'

'And the head of your order? What's he called?'

'The light, the air, the water, the earth.'

'Catchy,' said Otravinicus, with a smirk designed to rile Brother Rard. It worked.

'Silence! You are not worthy to breathe his name,' shouted Brother Rard.

'I don't know his name.'

'And you never will. Brother Antor is God's chosen son. You are not. You are a parasite crawling on the belly of a worm infecting the faeces of a mongrel dog. He will vomit you into the gutter and you will be washed away with the rest of the filth.'

'My, my, what a lot of anger. You need to learn to relax more. Maybe get a massage. So where do we find this Brother Antor?'

Brother Rard frowned, trying to work out how Otravinicus knew the name of his superior. It took him a moment to remember that he had said it. He admonished himself under his breath.

'I will say no more,' he said.

'Why did you come to kill me?' asked Otravinicus again. Brother Rard looked away and refused to answer. 'It's a reasonable enough question, isn't it?' Again Brother Rard said nothing. 'Did this Brother Antor send you to carry out his dirty work?'

This was too much for Brother Rard and he couldn't hold his silence any longer. 'He did not send me. He did not need to. You are the sworn enemy of the Brotherhood of the One True God, Pire. You are blasphemy in a devil's form and you do not deserve to live. It was Pire, the One True God, who spoke to me, who sent me on my quest. My quest is not yet complete but one day it will be.' He looked deep into Otravinicus's eyes to make sure he didn't miss the point he was trying to make.

While all this had been going on, Lasel crossed to

a bench where the contents of Brother Rard's pockets and his cloak lay. She looked through his few meagre possessions. In a small leather pouch she found some sort of cured meat. The smell caught at the back of her throat. She knew this smell well. She resealed the pouch.

'He's from Murias,' she announced to everyone. Brother Rard looked up sharply, concern etched on his face. How could she know?

Lasel held up the pouch. 'He has cured vettel pig in here. A regional speciality.'

'Murias?' asked Junk.

'East from here. Central Uuklyn,' replied Hundrig.

Junk looked at Otravinicus. 'If they're experts on the Room of Doors, maybe we can get some more answers from this Brother Antor. Maybe he knows how to find it.'

'HA!' Brother Rard laughed. 'He will tell you nothing. His only purpose in life . . . a task given to him by the One True God, Pire, is to guard the key of the doors. This he will do to his very final breath.'

A moment of silence followed, and then Junk said: 'There's a key?'

Brother Rard closed his eyes. He really should keep his mouth shut.

'How far is this Murias?' Junk asked Hundrig.

'Not far,' he said. 'Half a day's journey maybe.'

Junk, Hundrig and Otravinicus looked at each other. 'Sounds like a plan,' said Hundrig. Immediately he started barking orders to his crew and they leaped into action, preparing for the journey to Murias.

*

The *Casabia* sailed north for an hour before coming ashore at a small town called Luta. There was a track station there. Once on land, the *Casabia* headed quickly east through landscape that changed dramatically. The softly undulating green hills nearer the coast became gradually rockier, mountainous. They climbed high above sea level and the air became thinner.

Murias was a region of great towering cliffs and soaring sandstone rock pillars six hundred metres high, rising out of lush woodland.

Otravinicus spent the first part of the journey trying to quiz Brother Rard, but the monk was having none of it. He had finally reached the point where he would say no more. Otravinicus soon gave up and retired to his cabin.

Junk sat near Brother Rard, who had his eyes closed, seemingly in meditation.

'You should not seek the Room, boy,' said the monk suddenly, eyes still closed. 'It is as I described and you will die.'

Junk shook his head. 'The captain wasn't making that up before. I really have been in it. That's how I got here. This isn't my . . . time. My time was three million years ago. I had a sister, you see. She was killed. I was looking for her killer. Ended up following someone through a door from my time. I didn't know where I was going. The Room is, like, so vast you can't even begin to fathom just how big it is. You can't even see

189

all of it. It's so big the edges kind of disappear over the horizon. And the doors are all these green points of light. Thousands of them. Hundreds of thousands maybe. I guess they go everywhere. Everywhere's a lot of places. The planet's what – four and a half billion years old? Well, when I was at school. Little bit older now. That's a lot of places.'

Brother Rard growled in his throat and shook his head. 'That's not what the Room is like at all.'

'You've been in it?' asked Junk.

'No, of course not. I am not divine. It is only for walkers.'

'What are walkers?'

Brother Rard grumbled at Junk's ignorance. 'Envoys of the One True God, Pire.'

'Envoys?' said Junk. 'Like angels, you mean?'

'Envoys,' was all Brother Rard would say.

'Well, I don't think I'm an envoy,' said Junk.

Brother Rard opened his eyes and laughed. It was a short and dismissive laugh. 'No, you most certainly are not.'

Having grown up in Ireland and having had more than one theological conversation with a priest, Junk knew talking to Brother Rard was pointless. His tiny, blinkered view of the world could not comprehend what Junk was saying to him.

'Back in my time,' said Junk, 'there was religion. A lot of religions. A lot of gods.'

'Only one true God,' said Brother Rard.

'Yeah, they all thought they had the one true God as well. Are you going to be in trouble when you get back?' Brother Rard's expression betrayed his concern. 'That's what I figured. You must be cacking yourself. You set out to off the doc, fail, and come back with a bunch of . . . what are we again?'

'Coorratun,' said Brother Rard softly. 'If Pire shows mercy, then Brother Antor will only kill me.'

Junk frowned. He stared at Brother Rard and knew he meant that literally. 'And if Pire doesn't show mercy?' he asked.

A shudder ran down Brother Rard's spine. He bowed his head and continued to pray.

It was early afternoon when the *Casabia* reached the town of Murias. There was some discussion about who would go to the monastery. After all, if Brother Rard was typical of the zealots in the order, it might well be dangerous. Junk made it clear he was going and no one was going to stop him. No one tried to. Garvan said he would go with him and Otravinicus wanted to go too. However, it was pointed out that he was not the order's favourite person – not even in the top ten – or top one million – so it was agreed that it was better if he didn't go Then Hundrig volunteered. Though he had only really been paid to captain the ship, so this was a little beyond the call of duty.

They had a short walk from the *Casabia* to the base of the highest of all the sandstone rock pillars.

It stood separately from any other rock cluster. It was tall and straight. Years of erosion had smoothed all sides and the only way in or out was an elaborate pulley-and-basket system that ran up the south-facing wall.

When they got there Brother Rard explained that the basket could accommodate only two passengers at a time. However, because Garvan and Hundrig were so big, they would have to travel one at a time. Hundrig decided he would go up first, but Brother Rard said that wouldn't work because the gatekeeper at the top – Brother Hath – would not know him and he was not expected so he would not be allowed in. He would be sent straight back down again. Brother Rard said that the only option was for him to go up first and announce them. Then he would send the basket back down. Hundrig wasn't keen on this idea. There was no guarantee that Brother Rard would send the basket down and then their only option would be to sit and wait until someone left the monastery. There was no telling how long that might be.

'I can go up with him,' said Junk. Hundrig didn't like this idea either. Junk was so small and puny. He assumed the rest of Brother Rard's order would be as big as him. 'It's OK,' said Junk. 'I can look after myself.'

Brother Rard wasn't keen on this idea either, but he couldn't think of a reasonable objection so he gave in. He and Junk climbed into the basket. The system was simple. Once in the basket Brother Rard pulled on a lever that released a heavy rock at the top. The rock fell and the basket rose. There was ballast that accompanied the basket for when one needed to descend that had to be hauled up again, ready for next time. It all seemed rather antiquated and inefficient, though it was weighted perfectly and the ascent was smooth and swift.

When they reached the summit, they stepped out of the basket. There was a flat shelf of rock between them and the gates to the monastery. Junk was looking out at the incredible view. It was a bright, clear day and he could see for miles in every direction. There were about a dozen more rock pillars within view. There were buildings on some of the others but none as large or as impressive as the monastery.

The gate was seven metres high and made of solid wood. The walls were made of sandstone and flush to the pillar's edges on three sides, making it seem as if the monastery had grown out of the rock naturally.

It took Junk a little while to realize that Brother Rard hadn't sent the basket back down.

'Is there a problem?' asked Junk.

'It is not permitted for me to invite anyone into the monastery. Only Brother Antor can make this choice,' said Brother Rard.

'You didn't think to mention that when we were down there?' Junk didn't believe Brother Rard.

'Your captain is not a reasonable man because he is godless. I did not think he would understand,' said Brother Rard.

193

'Probably not,' said Junk. 'So get Brother Antor out here and have him give them the OK.'

'Brother Antor does not come running when summoned like a common servant. I must go to him.'

'Well, we have a problem then, because I don't trust you any more than the captain does and I'm not letting you out of my sight.' Junk sounded more confident than he felt and was very aware that he was standing on a ledge that was just a few metres wide. If Brother Rard was so inclined he could easily throw Junk off and there was nothing he could do but fall a very long way and go splat when he reached the ground.

Brother Rard looked hurt. 'But I am a man of God,' he said.

'Try growing up in Ireland and see how far that gets you,' said Junk.

'Ireland?' asked Brother Rard.

'Ah, never mind. It's not there any more,' said Junk. 'Look, please, Brother Rard. I have come a very long way. I don't mean any disrespect to you or your order or your beliefs. I just want to find the man who killed my sister. She was only little and I should have looked after her. I was her knight, you see. Supposed to be anyway. I wasn't a very good one.'

Brother Rard rubbed his chin and considered his options. Finally he nodded. 'I will take you to see Brother Antor,' he said. 'I will accept whatever punishment he thinks is just for disobeying the rules of the monastery and bringing in an outsider without his permission. I believe this is the right thing to do.' He made it sound more noble and courageous than it really was.

Brother Rard turned to the great door and picked up a rock that sat beside it.

'This is the knocking rock,' he said, as if that was a normal thing to say. He used it to rap on the solid door three times. He set the rock down again and then they waited.

After about a minute Junk heard keys being turned and bolts being pulled back on the other side of the door. The sound was heavily muffled and Junk guessed that the door was pretty thick. It swung back slowly and another monk, wearing the exact same type of cloak and black clothing as Brother Rard and sporting the same Mohican hairstyle, stepped forward. He was much older than Rard. His skin was wizened and sagging, his eyes a dull grey rather than the vibrant silver of Brother's Rard's. He was as tall and as broad as the younger monk but his physique had turned mostly to fat. Instead of a solid square lantern jaw, he had two fleshy sacs that hung pendulously below his jaw. The strips of hair on his head were wispy and white.

'Dulluk,' said the monk. 'Tinggwa huum tal tinggwa chul.' He spoke in a language that Junk didn't understand.

'This is the keeper of the gate,' Brother Rard explained to Junk. 'This is Brother Hath.'

'Occootoo,' said Junk. He knew it wasn't the correct greeting. It was like saying *buon giorno* to a German, but it was all he had. Brother Hath glared at him, looking him up and down with a scowl. He and Brother Rard spoke purposefully for several moments. Junk had no idea what was being said, but judging from Brother Hath's combative demeanour and Brother Rard's more conciliatory tone, he assumed that Rard was asking to come in with Junk in tow and Hath was refusing. In the end, Brother Rard must have said something that swayed the argument in his favour, for Brother Hath harrumphed in a manner that was the same in any language and then stepped aside. Brother Rard looked pleased with himself and gestured for Junk to go ahead.

The interior of the monastery was bare and cold, as one would expect from a religious sanctum. There were a few small windows that allowed light in, but the long corridors and rooms they passed through were dominated by shadows. Deep, dark shadows in every corner. Everything appeared stark and unwelcoming. There was no comfort to be found in the Brotherhood of Pire.

Finally they came to a chapel. It was the largest room Junk had yet seen, as high as it was wide. There were a dozen small windows high up along each of the four walls and shafts of light shone through each window, hitting the stone floor. At the far end of the room was an altar. Sitting on top of it was a small cube about the size of a grapefruit. It had a dull bronze finish and was etched with a plethora of lines, squiggles and other markings. Kneeling in front of it, deep in prayer, was another monk.

'Brother Antor,' whispered Brother Rard reverently to Junk.

Hmm, thought Junk, if it isn't the light, the air, the water, the earth himself. He was intrigued to meet this Brother Antor.

17

They stood quietly for several minutes while Brother
Antor finished his prayers. As the silence continued, Junk
was struck by an urge to start giggling. He really had to
struggle not to succumb. A couple of times the beginning
of a chuckle escaped but he was able to turn it into a
muffled cough. Though any noise at all drew frowns
from Brother Rard and Brother Hath, who was loitering
behind them.

Finally Brother Antor finished and stood up. Even
then he did not turn around immediately. He kept his
back to Brother Rard and spoke in a deep, gravelly voice.

'Doonk ka, Dulluk. Dinikanu,' he said. He sounded
cross. Brother Rard answered in a weak, stuttering voice
and his body language was extremely penitent. He
dropped to one knee and bowed at the waist. Brother Rard
spoke to Brother Antor for a long time. Junk understood
none of it but Brother Rard gestured to him occasionally
so Junk knew he was being included in his recounting.
He also heard him refer to 'Otravinicus' more than once.

'What is your name, boy?' said Brother Antor in

Jansian. It took Junk a moment to realize he was talking to him.

'Umm . . . Junk, sir.' There was something about Brother Antor that demanded respect.

Brother Antor turned then and looked down at Junk. He was even bigger than Brother Rard, taller and broader. He reminded Junk of a bodybuilder, ballooned on steroids. He was a little older than Brother Rard but fit and vital. His eyes were not silver, but golden, and they glittered in the low light. He wore the same black clothing as the others. He had the two strips of hair on his head running front to back but he had another strip running left to right. Possibly to signify his rank within the order.

'This is a private order. You are not welcome here.'

'I understand. Brother Rard made that clear. We didn't give him a lot of choice, to be fair,' said Junk. 'Our captain's awfully persuasive. He's outside and would like to talk to you. Brother Rard says he needs your permission to let him in.'

'It is not given, boy.' Brother Antor glared down at Junk. Junk realized at that moment that he was shaking with fear so he held his hands behind his back so no one would see. 'You will leave. You will take your people and go back to your ship and you will leave this place. You will not continue your search for the Room of Doors. Is that clear?'

Something inside Junk changed right then. He was aware of it. Perhaps it was Brother Antor's patronizing tone, the way he was telling Junk what to do. There was to be no debate. The thought occurred to Junk that this Brotherhood of Pire had no more right to the Room of Doors than him. Less maybe. After all, he had been inside it. He knew what it was. They didn't.

'Is that clear?' said Brother Antor again, more forcefully this time.

Junk looked him in the eye and shook his head. 'No,' he said. Brother Rard and Brother Hath gasped audibly. Clearly no one ever said no to Brother Antor.

'We are the Order of the Room of the One True God, Pire,' said Brother Antor through clenched teeth. 'We are the Brotherhood of Pire. Defenders. Protectors. Avengers.'

'Yeah, yeah. I got it,' said Junk. 'Brother Rard told us all that, but who are you to say who can and can't go into the Room of Doors?'

'We are the Order of the Room of the One True God, P—'

Junk cut him off. 'I know. I heard. But you don't even know what the Room is. You've never been in it. I've been in it.'

'Hanisiki,' said Brother Hath from behind them. He bent his head in urgent prayer. Junk guessed 'hanisiki' meant something along the lines of 'blasphemy' or 'lies'.

'You may not enter the Room of Doors,' growled Brother Antor. 'It is not possible. It is a divine place. Only Walkers—'

Junk cut him off again. 'Only Walkers are permitted to enter. Envoys, right? Otherwise they'll get their skin burned off their flesh and their flesh burned off their bones, et cetera, et cetera. Well, I'm not a Walker or an envoy or anything else. I'm just a kid from Murroughtoohy. I'm three million years away from home. You have any idea what that feels like? Of course you don't.' Junk was angry as hell right now. 'Now I'm on a quest to find a murderer and I need the Room of Doors to help me. Brother Rard here says you have a key.'

Brother Rard and Brother Hath both glanced automatically at the bronze box on the altar. Brother Antor growled at their stupidity.

Junk took a step towards the altar. 'So the key's in there, huh?'

Before he could take a second step, Brother Antor roared and pounced on him. He grabbed Junk and slammed him up against the wall, knocking the breath from his lungs.

'For ten thousand years have we been the guardians of the Room of Doors and the key. In that time, many have tried to take it and all have failed. Their bones fill this mountain. If you try to enter the Room of the One True God, Pire, then we will hunt you down and destroy you. Take this message back to your captain: you travel with the coorratun, Otravinicus, which makes you our enemy. You have till sunset to leave Murias, then leave our shores, then leave our waters. I want you on the other side of the world.'

'You can't tell us where we can and can't go,' said Junk defiantly.

Brother Antor's nostrils flared. He dragged Junk

roughly to the altar. There was a small door beneath, which he kicked open with his toe. Junk flinched. Inside was a furnace. A fire raged within. Brother Antor reached down to the base of the plinth and retrieved a metal rod about a metre in length. At one end was a small claw, which he thrust into the furnace.

Junk glanced back at Brother Rard and Brother Hath. To his dismay, Brother Rard had his head bowed as if he couldn't bear to watch what was about to happen. In contrast, Brother Hath was grinning sadistically.

'Don't!' said Junk, trying to pull away from Brother Antor, but his grip was vice-like. 'What are you doing?'

Brother Antor turned and grabbed the front of Junk's shirt. He ripped it open, exposing his chest.

'You say I can't tell you what to do, but I can and I am and you would do well to heed me.' With that, he wrapped the end of his sleeve around the handle of the metal rod and drew it out of the fire. The tips of the claw were bright orange. 'The only reason I am letting you live this day is because you are a child.' And with that he pressed the red-hot claw into the flesh of Junk's chest.

Junk screamed like he had never screamed in his life. He felt the pain in every inch of his body. It spread out from his burning skin and travelled to the tips of his toes and the centre of his brain. The world around him flared into whiteness. He felt as if the bones in his legs had suddenly turned to liquid and they flopped uselessly beneath him. He sagged violently. The only thing keeping him upright was Brother Antor. He was a puppet master manipulating an impotent marionette. Finally Brother Antor pulled the rod away, letting it clatter to the stone floor, and Junk's agony subsided. 'I will not be so tolerant again,' said Brother Antor. With that he hurled Junk halfway across the room, where he landed hard at Brother Rard's feet. Brother Rard helped him to stand and half carried him towards the door.

Junk pulled away from Brother Rard. He would walk himself. He felt angry and humiliated. The excruciating pain emanating from his chest pulsed out to the edges of his body. The room was spinning. He was sure he was about to vomit. His footsteps were shaky and faltering but he was determined not to stumble. Brother Antor's arrogant certitude reminded him of the priests back home. Whatever they thought became the word of God, and no one was allowed to question it. He pulled his shirt together to cover up the wound. Brother Rard laid a gentle hand on his arm but Junk shook it off angrily.

'Don't cover it like that,' said Brother Rard sympathetically. 'The cloth will . . . adhere to the skin and it will not be easy to get off.' Junk let his shirt flop open. Perspiration was pouring down his face and he concentrated on walking. He didn't want to fall down. He wanted to get out of there as quickly as he could.

They didn't speak as they headed back to the huge front gate. Brother Hath was with them and he unlocked the gate. He shot Junk one last sneer as Junk hobbled out.

Brother Rard escorted Junk to the basket and settled

him inside. Brother Rard paused and looked as if he was about to say something but he didn't. His shoulders sagged and he let the basket descend.

On the way down, Junk let himself cry. He was brimming with rage. He stopped before he reached the bottom, where Garvan and Hundrig were waiting. Despite Brother Rard's warning, he covered up the wound before he got out.

'Are you OK?' asked Garvan in English. Junk nodded. 'What happened?'

'I'll tell you back at the ship,' said Junk. They started walking, but Junk was finding it increasingly difficult. He was struggling to remain conscious, but soon lost the fight and crumpled to the ground. Garvan and Hundrig dashed to his side and saw the burn on his chest. They couldn't find words between them so said nothing. Garvan gathered Junk up and carried him back to the ship.

Back on board the *Casabia*, Junk woke in bed to discover a clump of foul-smelling wet grass sitting on his chest. He reached up to remove it but a hand came out of the darkness and stopped him. It was Lasel.

'No,' she said, 'it's buchelous grass. It will help the wound. Go back to sleep.' Junk did as he was told.

Junk slept for a few more hours and woke feeling better. His chest throbbed dully and was stained green by the buchelous grass but its restorative qualities were impressive. The burn had already started to scab over.

He got up slowly and got dressed. He found his clothes washed and neatly folded at the end of his bed. His shirt had been repaired so that the rip was nearly impossible to see.

He went up on deck and found Lasel, Garvan, Otravinicus, Cascér and the crew all together. They had been discussing what to do but hadn't reached any sort of consensus. Otravinicus wanted to attack the monastery in revenge for what had happened to Junk. Though what the doctor really wanted was for Hundrig and his crew to attack. Otravinicus wasn't planning on storming any monasteries himself. Hundrig, like all of them, was outraged by the torture Junk had experienced at the hands of the monks but he was not entertaining any talk of attack.

Junk recounted everything that had happened in the monastery. When he got to the part about the box on the altar that held the key, Garvan sat up a little straighter. Clearly it meant something to him, but he didn't say anything. He let Junk continue. Junk repeated Brother Antor's threats of extreme violence if they didn't leave by sunset.

'Such arrogance!' said Otravinicus forcefully when Junk had finished. 'These people who think their beliefs give them the right to tell us what we can and can't do. They're nothing but terrorists.' He started pacing. He was angry. 'I say we go back there and break down that door and take their damn key.' It was what he had been saying for hours, but his focus had shifted slightly after discovering the existence of the key.

'You haven't seen the place,' said Hundrig. 'It's a fortress. Only one way in or out. It would be impossible, plus there was no storming of monasteries mentioned when you hired us, Doctor. I abhor what they did to Junk but will not put my crew in danger needlessly. I'm sorry, Junk.'

Junk shook his head. 'No, I wouldn't want you to.'

'I'll pay you double,' said Otravinicus.

'We are not mercenaries, Doctor,' said Hundrig. 'We are sailors. There are places where you can hire such people, and if that's what you want I will gladly ferry you there, but nothing more.

'Triple?' said Otravinicus hopefully.

'*Nothing* more.' Hundrig sounded so definite that even Otravinicus finally conceded. 'We'll be ready to set off in an hour. What's our heading?'

Otravinicus was silent for a few moments as he stewed. He was a man who liked getting his own way and didn't react well to being told no. 'North,' he said finally. 'Back to Arrapia.'

'What?' said Junk. 'No. You said we'd go to Cul Sita. You promised.'

'And you promised you could find the Room of Doors for me. There's nothing I want in Cul Sita. The answer lies in that monastery, and getting in there will take planning and research. The best place for that is back in Arrapia.

I'm sorry, Junk. I truly am.' Otravinicus turned to leave but paused. 'Listen,' he said, 'I have paid the captain in advance. The ship is ours until the end of the month. Once I am back home, the captain can take you south until the money runs out. You should reach the waters off Glarn Sita by then. A resourceful lad like you will be able to make it the rest of the way, I'm sure.' He smiled as if that had solved everything.

Junk sat up on the *Casabia*'s prow and looked out at the sun as it started to dip. Garvan came and sat with him.

'Should we go and rebuild my cabin now?'

Junk thought about that. He liked to build things. It cleared his mind. Back home he used to help his father whenever he could. He had helped him build the staircase. Though he was very young, so wasn't actually that much help. He had scratched his name on the underside of one of the treads. He wondered if that was the only evidence now that he had ever been there. Had his mother removed all other traces of him?

'What do you think?' said Garvan.

'No. I'm sorry, Garvan,' said Junk. 'I can't stop yet. Not until I find him. I promise I will help you then.'

Garvan was quiet for a few moments and then he nodded. 'I knew you were going to say that. I will go with you.'

'You don't have to. It'll take you a long way from home.'

'No. Actually it will take me closer to home.'

Junk frowned. He didn't understand. He waited for Garvan to explain but he didn't say any more and Junk was forced to ask, 'How come?'

'How come what?' asked Garvan.

Sometimes it was exasperating talking to Garvan. 'How come that takes you closer to home when your island is half a day that way?' said Junk, pointing.

'I don't come from that island. I just live on it,' said Garvan. 'I was born on a different island. It's called Cantibea. Do you remember when I drew the map in the sand?'

'Of course,' said Junk.

'There was Glarn Sita, Unta Sita, Daté Sita and Cul Sita. Well, in the middle of those is Cantibea. It's quite small in comparison.'

'I see,' said Junk. 'And do you know people there? Any family? Anyone who can help us?'

Garvan nodded. 'My family's there still.' He paused, and Junk could tell there was more to the story so he said nothing and let Garvan come to it in his own time. 'But I can't go back.'

He didn't say any more so Junk had to prompt him. 'Why not?'

'I would have to do something I don't want to do,' said Garvan.

'What?' asked Junk.

'Kill my father.'

'What? Why?'

'Tradition,' said Garvan.

'What sort of crazy tradition is that?'

'Cantibean tradition. It's how one king succeeds another,' said Garvan, and it took Junk a few moments to process that information.

'Wait. Are you saying your father's the king of Cantibea?'

'Yes,' said Garvan.

'And you're supposed to be the next king?'

'Yes,' said Garvan again.

'You're a king?' Junk was incredulous.

'No,' said Garvan. 'Not until I kill my father, and I don't want to do that.'

'Well, no, I can see why you wouldn't.'

'So I left. Now my father will remain king until he dies naturally. Hopefully an old man. Unless one of my brothers hunts me down and kills me. Then he becomes eldest heir and he can kill my father and take his place.'

'How many brothers have you got?' asked Junk.

'Seven,' said Garvan.

'Any of them potentially homicidal?'

'Oh yes, all of them. It's not frowned upon. As I said, it's tradition,' said Garvan. 'I'm the only one who has a problem with it, but then I'm not like everyone else.'

'No,' said Junk. 'No, you're not. But I think that's a good thing. OK, so we won't go anywhere near Cantibea.'

'Hmm,' said Garvan, furrowing his brow. 'Except I think we have to.'

'How come?'

209

'There's a way for me to go home that involves you. I'm just not sure what it is exactly.'

'I don't understand,' said Junk.

'Neither do I,' said Garvan. 'There's a flower, you see, in Cantibea, the nolic flower. It's a tradition to make a tea from its petals. One cup will make you sleep and you dream very intensely.'

'Like you're tripping?' asked Junk.

'Tripping?'

'Never mind. Go on.'

'The dream shows you a path you must follow. Mine showed me I had to leave Cantibea. Showed me the island. Then it showed me you. Except I didn't know it was you then. Didn't look like you. You looked more like a rodent.'

'Gee, thanks,' said Junk.

'At first, in the vision, you spoke but I didn't know what you were saying. Then I did. Just like when I met you. Then I tested you. With the puzzle boxes. You passed. After that I almost died and you chose to save me.'

Junk thought about this for a moment. 'So when we got attacked by those birdmen thingies, you kind of knew that was going to happen?'

'Yes.'

'That was taking an awful big chance. What if I couldn't save you?' asked Junk. 'Or didn't?'

'But you did,' said Garvan.

'So what comes after that?'

'Then we're sitting on a ship next to a tree . . .' Garvan

and Junk both turned to look at a tall, proud tree alongside the ship, 'and I ask you about rebuilding my cabin and you say not yet. Just like now.'

Junk thought about this. It intrigued him. 'And then?'

'And then there's a box. It's a dark gold colour. There are lines all over it.'

'Just like the one they keep the key in,' said Junk, thinking about the box on the altar in the monastery chapel.

Garvan nodded. 'Yes, that's what I thought when you described it. We have to get that box, Junk.'

'But that's impossible.'

'No, it's not,' said a quiet voice from behind them. They turned to see Lasel.

'How long have you been there?' asked Junk.

'Long enough,' she said. 'I know how to get the box.'

'How?'

'Steal it.'

18

Lasel and Junk sprinted through the woods back towards the monastery while Garvan stayed behind to make sure the *Casabia* didn't leave without them. Lasel had told them how she supported herself back in Corraway and the dozens of other places she had lived in since leaving home at the age of seven. She was a thief, plain and simple. There was nothing, she boasted, that she could not steal.

At the base of the rock pillar they stopped to get their breath back. Lasel's plan was a straightforward one: climb up the rear face of the six-hundred-metre rock pillar, cross the roofs of the monastery till they reached the chapel, where she would break in through one of the high windows, steal the box and get back down again.

Six hundred metres had appeared to be very high the first time Junk ascended, in the basket. Now, looking up the north face, the back wall so to speak, even to attempt it appeared to be nothing less than lunacy.

'I don't think this is going to work,' said Junk.

'Course it is,' said Lasel.

'We've got maybe forty-five minutes before the *Casabia* is due to set off.'

'Garvan will hold them up,' said Lasel.

'The rock looks very smooth. Doesn't look like there are many handholds.'

'Don't need them,' said Lasel.

'Look, to be honest, I'm just not sure I'm that good a climber,' said Junk.

'You're not climbing it.'

'I can't let you go up on your own.'

'You're not,' said Lasel. 'We're both going to go.'

'How are we supposed to get up there without climbing?'

'Hauk tines,' said Lasel.

'What now?' asked Junk.

Before they had left the *Casabia*, Lasel had gathered together a few items they would need into an old cloth sack. Now she pulled out two lengths of rope that she had knotted into two loops, like a figure of eight, and two thick leather hoods she had made out of an apron belonging to the *Casabia*'s cook. She pulled on thick leather gloves and gave a second pair to Junk.

'It pays to know your environment,' said Lasel. 'All the rock around here is sandstone. Sandstone is the perfect habitat for hauk tines.'

'And hauk tines are?' asked Junk.

In reply Lasel crossed to some large boulders and

213

moved some smaller rocks until she exposed the entrance to a low cave.

'Tap your finger on the ground like this,' she said, and demonstrated the intensity and rhythm that Junk needed to replicate. She chose a spot about half a metre from the mouth of the cave.

'What's going to come out?' asked Junk nervously.

'Don't stop tapping,' said Lasel. 'Trust me. I know what I'm doing.'

Reluctantly Junk crouched down and started tapping.

'Harder,' instructed Lasel, and Junk did as she said. Lasel moved to the side of the cave mouth, held one of the rope loops in her mouth, the other in her gloved hands, just above the entrance, and waited.

Junk kept tapping, his eyes fixed on the dark hole in front of him. After about twenty seconds or so, the loose gravel around the entrance started to shift. Something was coming out. When it came, it came fast. A hauk tine was about the ugliest creature Junk had ever set eyes on. It was a light sandy colour, blending easily with the surrounding stone, and it was covered in lumps and bumps, looking almost as if it was made from rock itself. It was about the size of a Staffordshire bull terrier and just as muscular. It had a wide, snapping mouth full of sharp, crooked teeth that jutted out at various angles and powerful-looking clawed feet. Its eyes were translucent and white. It was blind and snapped liberally at the air around it as it honed in on Junk's still tapping finger. Lasel threw one of the looped ends of the rope over its head, followed it with the leather hood and pulled. The loop tightened and the hauk tine was plunged into darkness from the hood and instantly ceased its thrashing.

Lasel tossed the hooded creature to one side and moved back to the cave, pulling the other rope from her mouth. 'Keep tapping,' she said to Junk. She dangled the second rope loop in front of the entrance just as another hauk tine came charging out. She repeated the process with the hood and then quickly moved the boulder back over the entrance.

'Come on,' she said, holding both hauk tines by the rope leashes strung around their necks. Both creatures hung at her sides limply.

'What do we do with them?' asked Junk, trailing after Lasel.

When they reached the base of the rock pillar Lasel handed Junk one of the hauk tines.

'Put it by the base,' she said, meaning the base of the rock, 'and pull off its hood. Its natural instinct is to climb. Whatever you do, don't let go.'

'Wait, wait, wait,' said Junk, stopping Lasel just as she was about to unhood her hauk tine. 'Are you saying this thing is going to climb up there, pulling me along with it?'

'They're excellent climbers,' said Lasel. 'Very strong.'

Junk looked up at the pillar of rock towering above him and then down at the lifeless creature in his hand. What Lasel was suggesting did not make any sense, but then again, he had swum underwater covered in gunk from a jellyfish and survived. He took a deep breath and then he and Lasel positioned their hauk tines at the base of the monolith.

'On three?' said Junk.

Lasel shrugged. 'If it makes you feel better.'

'One . . .' Junk left a lengthy gap. 'Two . . .' Then an even longer gap until he couldn't put it off any more. 'Three.' With that, both Junk and Lasel yanked the leather hoods off the heads of the hauk tines and both animals shot up vertically at great speed. Junk screamed at the top of his lungs as he felt his feet leave the ground and he was carried up the side of the pillar. In seconds, he was a hundred metres off the ground. A hundred and fifty. Two hundred. The hauk tines showed no signs of slowing down and their claws had no trouble finding purchase on the sandstone surface. It was as if they didn't even notice the extra weight they were hauling up with them. Their solid little legs pumped furiously as they rose ever higher.

A thought occurred to Junk and he called over to Lasel, who was about level with him.

'What happens when they get to the top?'

'Wait till you're on the roof, and then just let go,' she shouted back.

'How do we get back down?'

'Don't worry,' she called. 'Getting down's easy.'

The hauk tines powered onward and upward. Close to, the rock face wasn't quite as smooth as it seemed from a distance and Junk was being bounced around viciously.

He manoeuvred himself around so his back was to the wall and he looked out over the landscape. It occurred to him that this was a somewhat surreal moment in his life, but it felt wonderful. Just as wonderful as diving down in the ocean unencumbered by scuba gear, like one of the fish. This was as close as he had ever come to feeling like he was flying. He whooped with delight.

As they drew closer to the monastery, Junk and Lasel became silent. The hauk tines reached the walls and without pause continued up on to the sloping black-tiled roof. When they got near the apex, first Lasel and then Junk let go. The hauk tines sped up, surging forward, suddenly relieved of the extra weight of their passengers. They disappeared quickly over the lip at the top. Junk and Lasel both slipped back a little but quickly found purchase and came to a full stop. They lay still for several moments until their hearts stopped pounding.

'That was amazing,' said Junk quietly. Lasel smiled. She liked that he got as much of a rush from such things as she did.

'Come on,' she said. 'Stay low.'

They rose slowly into a crouch and peered over the apex to get their bearings. Junk easily recognized the chapel. It was the highest point in the monastery and its row of small windows just under the eaves made it distinctive.

'There it is,' said Junk, pointing it out to Lasel.

'Follow me,' said Lasel. 'Step where I step.'

Keeping low, they moved quietly across the rooftops, edging their way around to the chapel. As they drew closer they saw that the chapel was separate from the buildings around it, across a gap of three or four metres.

Lasel reached into the cloth sack that she had strung over her back and pulled out a length of rope.

'Tie this end off,' she said to Junk, giving him one end of the rope. He looked around and saw a stubby chimney stack nearby. He wound the rope around it and secured it with a sturdy knot. When he came back to Lasel, she had tied the other end around her waist.

'What's the plan?' asked Junk in a whisper.

'I'm going in through that window,' said Lasel, pointing to one of the small chapel windows directly opposite. Junk glanced down at the ground twenty metres below.

'It's quite a gap,' said Junk. 'Are you sure you can make it?'

Lasel's response was to launch herself from a standing position, sail across the gap and latch on to the eaves of the chapel. In one fluid movement, she twisted round, hooking her toes over a lip on the inside of the eaves so she was dangling upside down. She arched her back until she was facing the window, looking into the chapel. Junk gasped in wonder. She was impressive.

'What can you see?' he called quietly.

Lasel peered into the chapel. As far as she could tell

from her perspective, it was empty. She felt around the window frame. It wasn't designed to open. She assumed none of them were at such a height. She reached into her pocket, took out a knife and proceeded to scrape away at the putty that held the glass in place.

When she was about halfway done, they heard footsteps and both Lasel and Junk froze and held their breath. A black-cloaked monk stepped out of a door directly below Lasel and headed off across the adjacent courtyard. He did not look up. As soon as his footsteps faded into the distance, Lasel got back to work on the putty.

Another minute and the windowpane fell free of its frame. Lasel caught it just before it plummeted to the stone floor below. She tilted it sideways and passed it through the opening, pulling herself in after it. Her toes came away from the eaves and she slithered through so she was half in and half out.

There was a small ledge on the inside, nothing more substantial than a strip of coving, but she was able to rest the pane of glass on it so it was out of harm's way. Now she could get a proper look in the chapel and it was indeed empty. She called softly over her shoulder: 'Take the slack.' Junk braced himself. Lasel let herself drop through the window and dangled in mid-air. She twisted around so she was the right way up and looked back out at Junk. 'Let it out slowly.' Junk nodded and started to feed the rope through his gloved hands.

Lasel descended to the floor of the chapel and untied

the rope from around her waist. Sticking to the shadows as much as she could she hurried to the altar where the bronze box sat unguarded. As Brother Antor had told Junk earlier, many had tried to storm the monastery and all had failed. It was designed to be impregnable and keep rampaging hordes at bay. It was not designed with a single larcenous young woman in mind.

Lasel stood in front of the box and examined it from every angle, bending and twisting her pliant body to get a more complete view. At first the box did indeed appear to be unguarded. That seemed too easy and, from experience, too easy worried her. Then the light caught on something that was almost but not quite invisible to the naked eye. She had to squint and swivel her head slowly from side to side to see that the base the box was sitting on had a length of glass fibre tied to each corner. Glass fibre was thinner than human hair. It was strong enough to support a heavy weight but delicate enough that the tiniest movement would upset its equilibrium and cause it to snap. It ran to the ceiling and she realized that the base was suspended a minute distance above its plinth.

She knelt down to study the plinth and a shallow gully that emerged from under it and ran all the way around the altar. Lasel rubbed the tip of her finger along the gully and smelled a mixture of almonds and something more metallic that caught at the back of her throat. She knew at once what it was: landa-tree oil. Extremely combustible. She wiped her finger on her trousers and stood, considering the altar.

Far from being unguarded, she now saw there was a very elaborate security system around the box. If the glass fibres broke, it would drop down on to the plinth. She could only guess that there was some sort of mechanism within that would shatter a container of landa-tree oil, which would flow out, quickly filling the surrounding gullies, and be lit by a flame from the furnace that would send up a wall of fire. She would be burned to a crisp in seconds.

Tricky, she thought, but not impossible. She hopped up on to the altar, careful not to disturb the glass fibres. Then she reached down and ever so gently picked up the box. Instantly the fine balance was disturbed, the glass fibres broke, the base dropped, the flame was ignited and a maze of fire whooshed to life, completely surrounding her. The heat was far more intense than she had anticipated. She could feel her eyeballs drying out and shut her eyes tightly. Her throat was instantly scorching and dry. She gasped and inhaled a pocket of air so hot that it singed her insides. The smell of the burning oil was far more acute now and the nutty, metallic odour bubbled in her nose, making her feel nauseous.

She tossed the box into her cloth sack and took as much of a run-up as she could, opening her eyes only as much as was absolutely necessary. The wall of fire burned violently for a distance of three metres in every direction around her. She skipped across the altar and launched herself off, arms spread wide, legs straight, feet together, toes pointed, propelling herself over the tips of the flames. She could feel her clothes charring as she went. She flew in a perfect arc, landed outside the fire wall, rolled and was on her feet, patting down her smouldering torso and legs. Without pause, she started running for the rope.

At that very moment, the monks of the Brotherhood of Pire were eating their supper. It consisted of a variety of root vegetables, all equally bland and unappetizing. It was the same meal they had twice a day, every day. It came as a relief to most when the alarm was raised.

The monks flooded into the courtyard outside the chapel. Brother Antor was first and caught sight of Junk and Lasel racing away across the rooftops. He barked orders to some of his brothers to extinguish the fire in the chapel and the rest to follow him.

Junk and Lasel darted over the rooftops towards the south side of the monastery and the front entrance. They clambered down so they were outside the robust gate. Lasel dipped into her cloth sack and retrieved a small flask that she had purloined from the *Casabia*'s armoury. It contained an explosive charge. She pushed a small amount into the lock and fed in a short fuse.

Inside, Brother Antor and a dozen of his fellow monks rampaged along the corridor towards the gate. As he approached he bellowed at Brother Hath to open up. Brother Hath quickly started pulling back bolts and turning keys.

Outside, Lasel and Junk could hear the locks being unfastened. The fuse seemed to burn down agonizingly slowly.

'This only works if they don't turn that key,' Lasel said to Junk, pointing to the lock with the explosive wedged into it.

Inside, Brother Hath reached to turn the last key, but hesitated as he saw wisps of smoke snaking out of it. Brother Antor arrived.

'Dan dun do?' he cried. Brother Hath pointed out the smoke and Brother Antor knew exactly what it meant. He moved quickly to turn the key, but just at that moment the fuse burned down and the explosive sparked briefly to life.

Outside, the effect was distinctly underwhelming. A short fizzing sound and then nothing.

'What happened?' asked Junk.

Lasel turned and smiled. 'Done,' she said.

'Done?'

'Fused the lock. They can't turn the key. Can't turn the key, can't open the door.' She turned to see that the sun had almost set. They would have to hurry. They jumped in the basket and started to descend.

Brother Antor raced back along the corridor and took a side door into the nearest courtyard, from where he scrambled up on to the roof. He climbed over and jumped down so he was outside the gate. He ran over to the basket and pulley system and looked down. He saw Lasel and Junk were on the ground already and running towards the forest. They had cut the ropes of the pulley so the basket couldn't be hauled back up. It would take them hours to repair it. They would have a hell of a head start but no matter. He dropped to his knees on the edge of the shelf and started to pray. Brother Antor would go after them and retrieve the box. Then he would kill every last person on board their land-ship.

19

Lasel and Junk returned just as the *Casabia* was about to depart so their absence wasn't even noted. They waited until they had put some distance between themselves and Murias before revealing their acquisition to Otravinicus and Hundrig. The captain was furious. He knew that such an action would incur the wrath of the Brotherhood and he and his crew would be held no less accountable than Junk and Lasel.

'I'm sorry, Captain,' said Junk. 'I had no choice. I hope you understand that.'

'Understanding and condoning are two very different things,' said Hundrig. 'Your rash behaviour has endangered my crew. Religious types are unpredictable. Sometimes they turn the other cheek, scuttle into a corner and pray up a storm and sometimes they come looking for you, all brimming with the wrath of God and righteousness. You'd better hope they're up there right now praising and begging forgiveness. Though if that Brother Rard was anything to go by, I somehow doubt it.'

'Captain, if I may,' said Otravinicus, 'what's done is done but this . . .' he ran a finger across the cold surface of the box and his eyes glittered with avarice, 'this is older than the Brotherhood. They have no more right to it than anyone else.'

'I'm not sure they would agree,' said Hundrig.

'We have a contract, you and I,' said Otravinicus. 'You agreed to transport us where we need to go, and until the money I've paid you runs out I expect you to honour that agreement. Are you a man of your word?'

Hundrig growled in his throat. Junk thought Otravinicus's words were harsh, even hypocritical. After all, the doctor had given his word to Junk and then gone back on it when things didn't work out to his liking.

'I will keep to our contract.' Hundrig said the words through clenched teeth.

'Excellent,' said Otravinicus. 'Then take us back to Mr Fiske's island.'

'No,' said Junk. Otravinicus and Hundrig turned to him.

'No?' asked Otravinicus. 'Then where?'

'I've been thinking about it,' said Junk. 'I don't know exactly where the door I came through is. The ocean's deep there. I might have been ten metres down or a hundred. It's too big an area to search. What if the key has to be right where the door is to work?'

'So what do you suggest?' asked Hundrig.

'There's the other door. The one I entered in my time. If I could take a look at your charts, Captain, I think I could work out exactly where that one was when I went diving. Plus it's closer to here than Garvan's island.'

Otravinicus considered this and nodded. It made sense, and all he really wanted was the Room of Doors. He didn't care how he got to it. 'Good, good,' he said, picking up the bronze box from the table. 'You work out where we're going and I'm going to spend some time seeing if I can get this open.' He left the room.

Junk looked at Hundrig. 'I really am sorry if what I've done causes you problems, Captain,' said Junk. 'It wasn't my intention.'

Hundrig sighed, then nodded sagely. 'I know, Junk. I know.'

Hundrig called Gaskis in and the three of them pored over the *Casabia*'s navigational charts. Back when he was working on the *Pandora* with Timur, the crazy Russian, Junk had plotted the exact spot where the *Pegasus* had sunk. Though all the land masses had changed and any reference points that they used were now a totally different system and scale, it was possible to use the current charts to pinpoint the last resting place of the *Pegasus*.

The country that was called Uuklyn now was basically Greece and a little bit of Albania and a smidgen of Macedonia. Borders and names had changed, coastlines had moved, but there were some reference points that were consistent and that was what Junk used to plot their position. In Junk's time, Murias was on the northwestern edge of the plain of Thessaly in central Greece, and Corfu, where Junk had been diving with Timur, was due west of their current position.

According to the charts, the island that had been Corfu was now much smaller. He assumed the rest of the island had been submerged, which meant the part still showing would be what was the highest point in Junk's time. That would be Mount Pantokrator. Using the summit of that as a reference point, he could work out exactly where the *Pegasus* lay. From there he could estimate the distance he had travelled from the wreck to reach the green door and he was confident he could get within a metre. They had their coordinates.

Otravinicus had been sitting for the best part of two hours trying to unlock the bronze box. He was having zero luck. He had tried everything. The box was covered in depressions and gullies, but none of them seemed to be the lid. On top of that there were no hinges that Otravinicus could detect or a catch or any obvious way of opening the thing up. His last attempt involved beating it with a chisel but that had no effect either. He was also unable to mark the box in any way. Whatever it was made from appeared to be indestructible. During his final frenzied assault he managed to slice open the palm of his hand, and he threw the box across the deck in frustration and went off to see to his wound.

Garvan had been sitting close by, watching quietly. He got up and crossed to where the box lay. He stood over it and looked down at it. Turning his head first one way and then the other, getting an overview of it. Then he bent down and picked the box up.

He returned to his seat and, holding the box by four of its corners, turned it slowly around in his hands. He did this for several minutes. Just looking.

Then he heard Otravinicus returning.

'I'm afraid to report that it has stumped me,' he heard the doctor saying. 'Damn near sliced off my hand trying to get the stupid thing open.' Otravinicus and Junk stepped up on to the deck. 'Maybe it's broken, I don't know. Maybe it's not meant to open.'

'So how do we get the key out?' asked Junk.

Otravinicus looked around for the box. It took him a moment to notice Garvan was holding it.

'May I have that, please?' He held out his hand and Garvan gave it to him. 'We're going to need some sort of drill, I think,' said Otravinicus. 'I've asked the captain – they don't have the correct tools on board so we're going to have to find a port somewhere.'

'There's no need to break it,' said Garvan.

'You've come across a box like this before, have you?' asked Otravinicus with a sarcastic sneer.

'No,' said Garvan.

'I thought not. Leave this to me, Mr Fiske. I will get into this box if it's the last thing I do.'

'Sure,' said Garvan with a shrug. As Otravinicus turned and started to walk away Garvan called after him, 'It's just, you don't need to break it is all. It's a puzzle box.'

Otravinicus stopped and looked back. 'What do you mean?'

'Garvan makes puzzle boxes,' said Junk by way of explanation. He took the box from Otravinicus and held it out to Garvan. 'Can you solve it?'

'Yes,' said Garvan, but didn't move to take the box. Junk waited but nothing happened.

'Will you?' asked Junk.

'OK,' said Garvan. Now he took the box and placed his big fingers precisely at different points on its surface. Then he twisted both wrists, simultaneously pushing forward then back, twisting again, and suddenly the box opened up like a flower in bloom.

The six faces spread out to produce a cruciform. The interior was even more intricately and beautifully decorated than the exterior. However, it was empty. There was no key inside. There was nothing.

'I don't . . .' Otravinicus didn't even try to hide his disappointment. 'I don't understand. There's no key.'

'Yes, there is,' said Garvan. Otravinicus looked at him hopefully. Garvan went on. 'It is the key. The box. The box is the key. These lines –' he picked up the open box and turned it over and back again – 'they're not random. You see, it's a map.'

Otravinicus frowned as he stared at the box. He saw only meaningless lines and shapes. He shook his head. 'I don't see a map.'

Garvan shrugged, as if to say *that's not my fault*.

'A map of what?' asked Otravinicus.

'The Room of Doors, I suppose,' said Garvan. 'Junk said there were thousands of doorways . . . well, I think this tells you how to navigate them.'

'Can you read it?' asked Junk.

'No,' said Garvan. Then, after a lengthy pause, 'Not yet.'

'But you'll be able to?' asked Otravinicus hungrily.

'Given time.'

'Well, why don't we leave you to study it? See if you can make head or tail of it,' said Junk.

'Head or tail?' asked Garvan with his face screwed up, trying to figure that one out. The box had neither.

'Never mind,' said Junk. 'Just a saying.' He led Otravinicus away. The latter left a little reluctantly, eager to find out the secrets of the box.

Some time later and the *Casabia* was anchored above the last resting place of the *Pegasus*. Or at least where Junk hoped it was. Lethro had already netted half a dozen commusts and was busy cutting out their fluid sacs before returning them to the sea. It turned out that commusts could just regrow fluid sacs quickly and easily and therefore there was a constant supply.

Garvan was still puzzling over the box. He had spent most of his time just staring at it and Otravinicus was becoming increasingly impatient. His irritation was in turn irritating Cascér, so she decided to dive overboard to reconnoitre below. Hundrig popped one of the commust

fluid sacs over her, and as soon as it covered her she was
gone.

'We should get ready to go down too,' said Otravinicus.

'But Garvan's not worked out the box yet,' said Junk.

'Clearly,' said Otravinicus, glaring over to where
Garvan was sitting. 'He's done little else but stare at it. I
fear if we wait for Mr Fiske, we will be waiting for a very
long time.'

'But until we know how it works, how are we
supposed to use it to open a doorway?' asked Junk.

'For all we know, Junk, the box may merely need to be
in the vicinity of a doorway for it to make itself visible. It's
a worth a try. If it does nothing, we've lost nothing.'

Junk considered this and shrugged. 'I suppose so.'

Junk left Otravinicus and crossed over to Garvan. He sat
down next to him.

'How's it going?'

'I'm getting there,' Garvan said, without taking his
eyes away from the key.

'What happens next?' asked Junk. 'In your dream
vision thing, I mean. After we got the box.'

'Well,' said Garvan, 'it's a bit unclear.'

'Unclear?'

'It's not an exact science. The dream is open to
interpretation sometimes. The next part was a bit fuzzy.'

'OK,' said Junk, 'what's your interpretation of what
happens next?'

'We get into the Room of Doors, something happens – I'm not sure what, but we have to go our separate ways.'

'What? Why?' Junk didn't like this idea. He liked having Garvan around.

'It's OK – it's not forever. We find each other again.'

'OK . . .' Junk was glad of that but still not happy about losing his friend to begin with. 'How long?'

'That I'm not sure about. It could be a day or a week or a year or ten years.'

'What? Ten years?!'

'All I mean is I don't know how long. The dream wasn't that specific. The thing is, you look the same when I see you next, but you still look like a rodent in the dream so it's hard to gauge how old you are and how much time has passed.'

'I don't think that's right,' said Junk. 'I think we should stay together.'

'It's not up to us. The path is already set,' said Garvan.

'I don't believe that,' said Junk. Garvan shrugged. 'So where does getting you back home without you having to kill your dad come in?'

'Oh, there's lots to do between now and then. It starts raining snakes at one point. Then there's the man with no face, and the volcano. And you have to understand, I've not seen every moment of what happens between now and when we get back to Cantibea. It's more like highlights. And much of it, like I said, is down to interpretation.'

'So it might not be literally raining snakes is what you're saying?'

'Maybe, maybe not.'

'There's a lot to get your head round,' said Junk, letting out a grand sigh. 'Can I –' Junk was about to ask to borrow the box but Garvan had folded it up, locking it into its cuboid form, and was holding it out to him, as if he knew already what Junk was about to say.

'We should really wait until I've deciphered it,' said Garvan. Junk was about to say Otravinicus was pushing to go now, but he didn't need to. Garvan said it for him. 'But Dr Otravinicus doesn't want to wait. His impatience could cause problems, you know.'

'Yeah, I know,' said Junk. 'You're right, but he's paying for all this so he figures he's in charge. I suppose he is.'

Garvan shrugged ambiguously. 'I'll work on the map some more later. Pretty sure I'm almost there.'

'Set yony,' they heard Lethro calling. *She's back.*

Junk and Garvan moved to the portside along with everyone else and saw Cascér treading water. She shook her head: no door. Junk felt that shake of the head in the pit of his stomach. He had to be right or everything would have been for nothing.

Junk stood on deck wearing nothing but a pair of trunks as Hundrig sliced open another of the commust fluid sacs and the viscous contents covered him. Then Junk picked up the box and turned to dive overboard.

'Wait.' It was Otravinicus. 'I want to come too.' Junk was itching to get in the water, but he could hardly say no so he waited as Otravinicus stripped off his clothes, folded them neatly and set them down out of harm's way. Then Hundrig took another fluid sac and doused Otravinicus. Once the doctor was ready, he jumped into the water without waiting for Junk. Junk dived in after him.

Cascér took a hold of both Junk and Otravinicus and they swam straight down to the seabed. Junk looked around, hoping to spot some landmark that he remembered, but there was nothing. So much time had passed that the *Pegasus* had of course disintegrated entirely. The seabed had shifted a thousand times and nothing was the same.

They stopped by a series of markers that had been lowered from the *Casabia*, plotting the last resting place of the Pegasus based on Junk's calculations. One of the markers signified the stateroom Junk had been in when he first saw the green light.

He swam to the marker and took a moment to imagine himself back on board the *Pegasus* all those weeks ago. He remembered seeing the green light seeping in through the hole in the hull. He got his bearings. The door had been about twenty metres away. He swam to where he thought was the right point. Cascér and Otravinicus stood to the side and watched.

Junk held the bronze box up in his hand and, reaching forward with it, passed through where he thought the door had been. Nothing happened. He frowned. Otravinicus swam over next to Junk. He snatched the box from him, much to Junk's annoyance, and waved it around in front of him. Nothing.

Cascér looked on, unimpressed. Her mind wandered

and suddenly an odd sensation came over her. The skin at the back of her broad neck pimpled. Had she had any body hair, some of it probably would have stood on end. She turned to look behind her, feeling that they were not alone, but there was nothing but flat seabed for thirty metres and then a low wall of rock. She stared in that direction, certain something or someone was out there.

Junk held out his hand to Otravinicus, asking mutely for the box. Otravinicus ignored him and Junk reached over and pulled it from him. Immediately Otravinicus tried to snatch it back, but Junk just pushed the little man away. He held the box in his hands and felt the surface for dimples. The commust gel coating his fingers seemed to know what he was doing and responded accordingly by becoming thinner. Maybe Junk was just imagining it, but he felt that his skin was touching the cool metallic surface. He found an indentation on the front elevation, another on the bottom, two more on the back and one side. He pressed them simultaneously. Nothing.

Cascér was still looking back at the rock wall. She turned and started edging over in that direction. Something was unsettling her. What was out there? Then, in a flash, she got her answer. The seabed at her feet erupted and a huge fish lurched up at her. She had to move quickly to avoid it, throwing herself backwards. The fish, a type of shark, was five metres in length, muscular and powerful, rippling with energy and menace. Its skin was jet black and as smooth as marble. It had a mouth full of razor-sharp teeth, three tight rows of them, and its jaws pumped non-stop, furiously snapping at Cascér. She closed her fists into one and, wielding them like club, brought them down hard on the monster's snout, driving it into the ground and kicking up a twister of silt. She turned and swam away as fast as she could. The shark shrugged off the blow and went after her.

Cascér reached Junk and Otravinicus and spun them round. Their eyes grew wide as they saw the immense gnashing mouth coming at them. Cascér pulled them out of reach just in time. The fish swam past at such a speed that it had to make a huge turning circle. Then it started heading back for another attack.

Otravinicus looked at Junk and stabbed his finger at the box. His meaning was clear: OPEN THE DAMN DOOR. There was no way they could outrun the shark and get back to the ship.

Junk looked at the box in his hands. How did it open? He thought back to what Garvan had done on the *Casabia*. That was different. He had opened the box, and Junk wanted the box to open the door now. He remembered the puzzle boxes that Garvan had made for him back in his cabin. Corners. Corners were always important. He pressed each corner in turn. Nothing.

Cascér pulled him to the side just as the fish pounced again. Caught in a vortex, they spun around and Junk lost hold of the box.

It took him a moment to get his bearings. He saw

the box on the seabed beneath him and picked it up. He started pressing combinations of corners, two at a time and then when that garnered no result, combinations of three.

Out of the corner of his eye he noticed Otravinicus was flailing wildly. The shark had left a gash in his jellied bodysuit and water was pouring in. He was about to drown if he didn't get eaten first.

Junk turned to see the shark coming back for another attack. It was seconds away. He focused on the box. It was a key, and keys open doors. One finger on the top back right corner, thumb on the bottom front right, little finger on the bottom back right. The same with the left hand and then the corners moved. Suddenly light flooded along the fissures on the box's surface, like lava flowing through tiny rock gullies. Junk looked up to see a shimmering green door floating in front of them. There was no time to admire it. Otravinicus pushed Junk out of the way and powered through. Cascér grabbed Junk and pulled him in with her.

Junk and Cascér landed hard on the green-black metallic floor. Junk looked back to see the shark rushing through the door after them. Cascér saw it at the same time and they rolled in opposite directions. The fish landed with a resounding thwack on the ground and started thrashing about in violent panic as it was suddenly, inexplicably (to the fish anyway) not in the sea any longer. It thrashed around so much that it moved itself towards another door, directly opposite. As it got closer, the pull the doors exerted latched on to the shark, and in the blink of an eye it was sucked through and vanished. Sent to who knows where.

20

ALABAMA, 1922

It was a hot July morning. The sun was only just starting to rise but the air was already thick and the June bugs were chattering up a storm. Hobie Somerset sang to himself as he walked through the old forest. He sang a song his mother used to sing to him when he was a child.

'Shut up, boy,' said one of the men dressed all in white walking behind him. There were four of them. All wore the white ceremonial robes of the Ku Klux Klan. All carried shotguns; one carried a lynching rope too.

They reached the old gnarled tree in the middle of the forest. Many a man like Hobie had lost his life here for no other reason than the colour of his skin.

'You wanna cry and beg for your life, boy?' said one of the white robes. 'Cos now's the time.' He lifted his hood to spit out a slug of chewing tobacco and Hobie looked into the eyes of a schoolteacher he had known most of his life.

It wasn't a surprise to Hobie. He knew all these men. They were all about the same age, had all been born and raised within twenty miles of here.

'I wouldn't mind praying, if that's OK,' said Hobie.

'Sure. Why not?' said the schoolteacher. 'Just be quick about it.'

Hobie nodded and looked to the sky. 'Dear Lord,' he said aloud, 'I respect your wisdom, and whatever reason you've chosen for this thing to happen to me today, I know it's a good reason. Go easy on these men, Lord. They're dumb as a bucket of pigswill and they don't know any better.' At that, one of the men slammed the butt of his shotgun into Hobie's stomach and he doubled up in pain, but he was smiling. It had been worth it.

'Come on, let's get this over with.'

The rope was thrown over the old lynching branch and looped around Hobie's neck. The four men in robes all took a hold of the other end of the rope and were about to pull on it when a rectangle of green light appeared above them and a scared and confused five-metre-long shark from three million years in the future dropped down on them. It thrashed and bit and tore the men to shreds.

Hobie Somerset looked on with an open mouth. It's not every day a shark drops from the sky to save your life, especially not in the middle of Alabama.

When it was over, the four men were no more and the shark had quietened down due to overexertion and having been out of the water for too long.

Hobie looked to the sky. 'That was very impressive. Thank you,' he said.

He took the rope from around his neck and set off for home.

21

The Brotherhood of the One True God, Pire, had no purpose in life other than to protect the key, and after hundreds of years of protecting it successfully they had become complacent. That was the only way Brother Antor could explain how they had lost the box so easily. That and Brother Rard's abject stupidity at bringing the boy into the monastery.

No.

No, it was wrong to blame Brother Rard. The blame must lie squarely with Brother Antor himself. Passing the buck was the refuge of a coward. Brother Antor knew he was not that. Over the years, he had done everything he thought was right with Brother Rard, but clearly it was not enough. He glanced at the young monk. He would have to punish him of course and severely. Though what Brother Rard wouldn't understand was that Brother Antor would really be punishing himself. Whatever he did to Brother Rard – burn his flesh, blind his eyes, break his feet – he would really be doing to himself. Not literally, but it would hurt just as much. Though not as much.

The forty-seven monks who resided in the monastery of the One True God, Pire, now stood on a stony beach gazing out at the *Casabia*, anchored a mile offshore. The tide lapped around their booted feet. They were all armed with a collection of staffs, swords and bows.

Brother Antor marched into the water and the others followed. They kept walking until the sea was over their heads.

The colour had returned to Otravinicus's skin thanks to Cascér. He tapped her meaty thigh as an indicator that he would very much like to get up now. She unfurled her long limbs and Otravinicus scuttled free.

He stood on the spot and turned slowly, looking all around at the thousands of rectangles of green light glistening in the blackness.

'It's so beautiful,' he said. A tear bloomed in the corner of his eye and ran down his face. He looked over at Junk, who was also gazing up at all the doors. The last time he had been here he hadn't had time to stop and appreciate the Room's inherent beauty. 'You did it, Junk. You did it.'

They heard Cascér swear in H'rtu behind them and they turned to see her looking down at her arms. The protective commust fluid was starting to dissolve.

'Navoora *Casabia* chachin zuc harutuk,' she said.

Otravinicus looked at Junk. 'She says that you need to go back to the *Casabia* and bring us down some more fluid sacs before yours dissolves too. Otherwise we won't be able to swim back up.' Junk looked at his torso. His covering was still intact.

'OK,' he said. 'I'll be as quick as I can.' He started back for the door they had come through.

Otravinicus stepped into his path. 'Why don't you leave that here?' He pointed to the box in Junk's hand. Junk's gut instinct told him that was a bad idea.

'Probably best I take it with me,' said Junk. 'I mean if the door closes while I'm on the other side, I won't be able to get back in, will I?'

Otravinicus glowered but couldn't argue with that logic. 'I suppose so,' he said, turning away. 'Just don't be long.'

'Sure,' said Junk. He dropped the box into the netting bag slung around him and jumped back through the door.

Junk was spat out on to the seabed and saw the markers they had lowered from the *Casabia* to indicate the last resting place of the *Pegasus*. He got his bearings and started for the surface.

After a few moments the hull of the *Casabia* came into view and Junk powered upwards through the water towards a ladder on the port side. The bottom fifth of the ladder was submerged. Junk reached out for it. He could see blue sky above now. What happened next happened quickly. A dark shape fell from the boat. As it plunged towards the water and Junk, it grew larger and more distinct. However, Junk only had time to acknowledge it was coming but not get out of its way. It turned out to be a monk. A member of the Brotherhood of the One True God, Pire. His name had been Brother Guge, but Junk had never met him and never would. He was dead before he hit the water. A metal hook with a perpendicular wooden handle was embedded in his ear.

Dead Brother Guge hit the water hard and sank rapidly. He collided violently with Junk, knocking the air out of his lungs. Brother Guge's velocity forced Junk back down. The impact ripped part of the commust suit and the seawater flooded in. Brother Guge continued to sink and Junk went with him. The seawater found its way into Junk's mouth and he started to splutter. With a surge of panic, he realized he might drown.

Junk pushed up against Brother Guge's body and shifted the dead man's weight to one side, causing him to roll off. Dead Brother Guge continued his descent as Junk turned and clawed his way to the surface.

As Junk emerged into the air and filled his lungs, coughing up the saltwater, he was instantly aware of a commotion coming from the *Casabia*. He could hear the sounds of battle.

Another body fell from above and splashed into a watery grave. In the split second before he sank Junk saw the face of Hortez, the ship's cook. He was as dead as Brother Guge.

Junk grabbed hold of a rung on the ladder and started to climb. The higher he got, the louder the sounds of fighting became. As he reached the top he peered cautiously over the side of the ship. The monks of the Order of the One True God, Pire, had boarded the vessel. Straight away he saw that Hundrig and his crew were heavily outnumbered. There looked to be about fifty monks versus the nine remaining crew members and Lasel and Garvan. Hundrig and some of the bigger members of the crew were fighting three or four at once. Garvan was holding six monks off with apparent ease. He didn't appear to notice any of the blows he received.

Lasel was no fighter, but she was quick and agile and used that to her advantage. As Junk pulled himself up on to the deck, a pair of monks were coming at her from opposite directions. The one on the left swung his sword. The one on the right was armed with what looked like a medieval mace: a crudely formed metal sphere atop a long wooden handle. This he let fly, launching it at Lasel. She jumped up, planting a foot firmly on the mace-wielding monk's chest and pushing off. She twisted balletically as she went, arching her back. The mace went over her and the sword passed under her. The momentum of the two monks' swings made them lose their balance. The sword cut the throat of the mace-wielder and the mace mashed the face of the swordsman. Each fell into a heap on the ground and Lasel landed firmly between them.

Junk ran across to her, keeping low and zigzagging to avoid the weapons caning the air. Lasel spotted him and came to meet him.

Another of the monks, a powerfully large man, stumbled into Junk's path, crashing down on to one knee and roaring in pain as he did so. He steadied himself and looked up into Junk's eyes. Junk froze. The monk's gaze was pulled down to the box held in the netting bag hanging at Junk's side. He made a grab for it, but as he did so Lasel landed on his back and drove him face first into the deck. He was left dazed and spitting out teeth.

Lasel seized Junk by the hand and hauled him across to a cluster of packing crates. She pulled him behind the crates, out of sight.

'They're here for you and for that,' she said, pointing to the box.

'Of course they are,' said Junk. 'Listen, it works. We've found the Room of Doors. Otravinicus and Cascér are down there now.'

There was an almighty crash and Hundrig landed hard on his back next to them. He was bloodied and bruised but still raring to go. He was about to scramble back to his feet when he spotted Lasel and Junk.

'Junk! When did you get back?'

'Just now,' said Junk. 'We've found the Room of Doors! It's where I said. We can all get in there. The monks won't follow – they think they'll die if they go in. But we need more commust sacs.'

Hundrig nodded towards the top deck at the stern. 'Whole bag of them up there. Get Garvan and go.'

'No,' said Junk. 'All of us should go. This is my fault.'

'I won't argue with that, but you're a sailor, Junk. You know I can't abandon the *Casabia*. Nor would any of my crew. This is our home. Go now. There's no time.'

'But, Captain—'

'Don't fret about us. We're tough old birds. A few God-botherers can't stop us. I'll see you again, Junk.' Hundrig put a fatherly hand on Junk's head.

'I've got an idea,' said Junk. 'Get ready to set sail. I can get them off the ship.'

'Junk, no . . .'

But Junk didn't give Hundrig time to finish. He jumped up and grabbed Lasel by the hand. The two of them sprinted across the deck, heading for the steps leading up to the top deck. They went via Garvan, who was busy punching as many monks as he could.

'Junk, you're back.'

'Come on,' said Junk. 'We're going. Got us a plan. Can you swim?'

'Course I can,' said Garvan, following Junk and Lasel to the top deck. 'I lived on an island. Who lives on an island and can't swim?' Garvan paused to punch a few more monks before carrying on.

It was quiet on the top deck, the battle being confined to the main deck. They found the bag of fluid sacs. It took two to coat Garvan. Once all three were covered, Garvan and Lasel gathered together the remaining sacs and all their clothes, as well as those belonging to Otravinicus and Cascér, sealed them in a waterproof sack and slipped silently overboard and started swimming downwards, following the markers as Junk had instructed.

Junk gave them as much time as he thought they needed and then jumped up on to the balustrade surrounding the top deck.

'BROTHER ANTOR!' he roared at top of his lungs. Little by little, the battle beneath him stopped and all eyes turned to Junk. Brother Antor stepped forward and Junk held the box aloft. 'Is this what you're looking for?'

'Return what you have stolen and I shall spare your wretched life,' said Brother Antor. He was lying.

'Sure,' said Junk. 'Come and get it.' And with that he dived off the starboard side of the ship.

Brother Antor ran to the rail and saw Junk enter the water with barely a splash. He didn't hesitate. He jumped in after him. The rest of the monks, those still standing, jumped in too, following their leader.

In seconds the *Casabia* was peaceful again. The crew stood around, unsure what to do now.

'Let's get her under way,' shouted Hundrig. 'Toss the stragglers overboard.'

The crew threw the unconscious monks into the water and the anchor was pulled in. The blood-red sails unfurled and the *Casabia* set off.

Junk powered through the water, going deeper and deeper. He was sure the monks would not follow him for long. After all, none of them were wearing the protective fluid. He glanced over his shoulder and was horrified to see that the brothers were still coming, and what was more, they were gaining. They were protected by their zealotry.

Ahead, two pale blue shapes started to materialize out of the darkness: Lasel and Garvan.

As Junk got closer, Lasel and Garvan spotted him coming, and saw the monks right behind him. Junk waved, pointing them in the direction of the green door. They turned and swam quickly.

The door was ahead of them and first Lasel and then Garvan reached it and went through.

Junk looked behind him, straight into the determined eyes of Brother Antor. He was not going to give up, and Junk wasn't sure he could get to the door before Brother Antor got to him. Junk put everything else out of his mind and surged onwards.

Some of the monks started to drop back, unable to hold their breath any longer or stand the cold. But not Brother Antor. The power of his faith drove him on. In the distance he saw the doorway of green light. The entrance to the Room of Doors. He had never seen one before. He realized Junk was going to get there before him and then the key would be lost forever. He couldn't let that happen. He increased his speed.

Junk focused on the door now. Only a few more metres. He was just about to make it when he felt fingertips on his heel. Brother Antor was that close. Junk pushed forward, reaching out ahead of him. His fingers touched the light of the door and he felt the pull of the door's force. He was being drawn inside.

But then Brother Antor got a hand around Junk's ankle and pulled. He was more powerful than Junk, and Junk was jerked back, away from the door. Panic crashed through him. Brother Antor increased his hold on Junk.

He reached for the netting bag and ripped it free. Then he dug his fingers into the fluid covering Junk's face and tore it apart. The icy seawater burned as it hit Junk's skin and his first instinct was to open his mouth. It took all of his willpower to resist.

Brother Antor was on the seabed now. He bent his knees and pushed off with force, aiming for the surface, the netting bag containing the box in his hands. Junk watched him go and then looked at the door. He could make it. He looked to Brother Antor, rising in the water. If he went after the monk, Junk would die. His hands were clamped over his nose and mouth to stop himself inhaling. His oxygen-starved lungs were starting to send urgent demands to his brain for resupply, but there was only one real choice. Junk kicked off the seabed and swam with all his strength after Brother Antor.

Brother Antor didn't see him coming. Truth be told he had forgotten all about him, dismissed him as a problem no longer, and all his focus had turned to reaching the surface. So when Junk caught up with him and whipped around him without warning, snatching the netting bag from his grasp, Brother Antor, who had been holding his breath for much longer than Junk, gave in to instinct. He opened his mouth to protest and the ocean roiled into him. Junk turned and started swimming back down to the door as fast as he could. His skull felt as if it was about to implode.

He didn't look back to see Brother Antor convulsing violently as he drowned. When his body stopped thrashing, he drifted downwards. A dark shadow cut through the water, cloaked in a flurry of bubbles. It was Brother Rard. He grabbed Brother Antor's motionless body by his hood and kicked up towards the surface.

Junk shot into the Room of Doors and collapsed, filling his lungs with air. He was panting hard from exertion. His vision was blurred, his brain pounding. He looked behind him at the door, wondering whether any monks would follow him through, but no one came.

Garvan stood over him and helped him to his feet. 'This place is big,' he said, always a master of understatement.

A short time later, once everyone had dried off and dressed, they gathered to decide what to do next. Junk knew where he was going.

'First time I went through, I went along that way.' He pointed. 'Thirty-nine doors down, took me up there.' He looked up at the row upon row of doors stretching above them. From ground level the narrow ledges were invisible so the doors looked as if they were hovering in mid-air. 'Then eighteen along. Two doors side by side. I had to guess which one the Pallatan I was following had gone through. I took the one on the left. Took me to your island, Garvan. The Pallatan must have gone through the other one. If I'm right, the other door should lead to Cul Sita. That's where I'm going. Anyone's welcome to come with me.'

'Now hold on there,' said Dr Otravinicus. 'Look around you for a moment. Look at all these . . . wonderful possibilities.'

'I'm not sure that's a good idea,' said Junk. 'I mean, you don't know where any of them go. Wouldn't it be better to wait till Garvan's had a chance to decipher the box?'

'And how long will that be?' Otravinicus looked to Garvan.

Garvan shrugged. 'I don't know. Think I've almost got it.'

'You think?' said Otravinicus, a tone of disdain clear in his voice. 'Here's what I suggest: Junk, you go wherever you need to go. Your friends –' He looked at Lasel and Garvan – 'can go with you or wherever they want to go, but the box stays with me.'

'It's not yours,' said Lasel. 'It was me and Junk that got it.'

'It was you and Junk who *stole* it. It doesn't belong to you any more than it does anyone else. I am a scientist, I am the recognized authority on the Room of Doors, therefore it makes sense for me to keep it.'

'OK, how about this?' said Junk, trying to sound reasonable. 'We decide where each of us wants to go – majority keeps the box. Sound fair?'

'I'm going with you,' said Garvan.

'Me too,' said Lasel. 'That's a majority. Box stays with us.'

'OK.' Otravinicus nodded sourly, looking from Junk

to Garvan to Lasel and back. Nodding continuously as he pondered the best way to handle this. He plastered a plastic smile on his lips. 'Well, fair enough,' he said, throwing his hands up in a gesture of capitulation, 'majority wins. Looks like we're all going to Cul Sita. Thirty-eight along, nineteen back, right?'

'Thirty-*nine* along, *eighteen* back,' Junk said, looking up in the general direction of the relevant door. The moment Junk's attention was elsewhere, Otravinicus snatched the box out of his hands and ran for the doorway nearest to Cascér.

'Come on,' he called to her gleefully.

'NO! Stop!' Junk started after him, as did Lasel, but it was no good. They wouldn't catch him in time.

As Otravinicus ran past Cascér he grabbed her hand and leaped for the doorway. The portal started to pull him in and Otravinicus was a split second away from disappearing. Except Cascér didn't move. She stayed right where she was and yanked Otravinicus back. He looked at her, blinking, not sure why she wasn't moving. Then Cascér grabbed the box from his grasp, planted her big hand over his face and pushed him backwards through the doorway. The opening sucked him through and he was gone.

Junk and Lasel skidded to a halt, open-mouthed with shock. Cascér held out the box to Junk.

'Chikka na radoo,' she said by way of explanation.

22

A rectangle of emerald green light opened on a clear day. The sky was bright blue and the sun hung low in the sky. Junk came tumbling out of the door and found himself falling. The door was floating about four or five metres off the ground. There was a fleeting feeling of weightlessness as he was initially ejected and then he fell. Beneath him was a hillside, pitched at a steep sixty-degree angle. He landed hard on parched brown grass which did little to break his fall and then gravity, proving it really wasn't on Junk's side today, started him sliding.

His speed increased quickly and he scrabbled in an attempt to grab a clod of earth or a tussock of grass to slow his descent, but he only succeeded in upsetting his trajectory and he started spinning and rolling as well.

As the world hurtled around him, he became aware that the hillside was about to end abruptly in what, from his revolving perspective, looked like a very high cliff-top. He thrust his heels down, looking for purchase. He clawed at the ground, using his fingernails to dig into the rough, stone-strewn earth that ripped and bit back at him until his hands were bloody, but little by little he slowed until he came to a stop with only his legs dangling over the cliff edge. He lay there panting for a few seconds. Then he pulled himself up and glanced over the precipice to see a staggering drop of maybe a thousand metres. He whimpered in triumph and fear and moved away from the edge.

He turned in time to see Lasel being spat out of the door. Like him she fell, hit the ground and started rolling, her speed increasing. Junk didn't think. He started powering up the hill towards her. When he got close he launched himself on top of her, hoping that the force of his ascent would counteract the speed of her descent. It didn't. The pair of them, locked together in an embrace of tangled limbs, tumbled down the hillside, both digging their heels into the gritty sod. Working together, they were able to stop themselves a little further away from the edge than Junk had been able to do alone. They were knotted in one another's arms and their faces were intimately close.

'Thank you,' said Lasel.

'No problem,' said Junk. 'There's a bloody big drop down there. Wasn't easy to stop.' They each became aware of their breath on the other's face. Lasel's breath smelled sweet. Junk found he liked being this close to her and his immediate instinct was not to move away.

However, the moment was broken by the arrival of Cascér as she was spat out of the door, hit the ground and started rolling. Junk and Lasel disengaged themselves from one another, jumped up and started running to intercept her. Both leaped on top of her, but it was like trying to stop a boulder by throwing two pillows at it. They just got caught up in her momentum and all three started sliding down the hillside towards the edge. Cascér wrapped her arms around Lasel and Junk and smashed her heels down hard into the ground. Huge clumps of soil were churned up in their path until all three came to a stop, on their backs, looking up at the clear sky.

'Atcha fanany muunt,' said Cascér. Neither Junk or Lasel understood and it was probably just as well.

The three of them took a deep, cleansing breath and got to their feet. Then they stopped and exchanged wide-eyed looks of horror. All had simultaneously had the same terrifying thought: Garvan. They turned to see their giant friend coming through the doorway just as they had. He fell just as they did. He hit the ground, but not as they did. Garvan landed squarely and firmly on his own two feet, with a ground-shaking solidity, and started walking casually down to meet them. It was as if he had just hopped off a low wall.

'Maybe you should go through first in future,' said Junk. 'You can be official catcher.'

Garvan shrugged.

They moved cautiously to the cliff edge and looked out at their location.

Far below was a bustling coastal city. The sea that stretched out ahead of them was a rich turquoise colour.

'Do you know where we are?' asked Junk.

Lasel nodded. 'That's Wotashi – biggest city in Cul Sita.'

'Cul Sita,' said Junk. 'Home of the League of Sharks.' He had made it.

Wotashi, as it turned out, was the headquarters of the League. They were easy to find. Everyone knew exactly where they were. They lived in a shanty town on the western outskirts of the city. The area, known locally as Cuca, which translated as 'the bloody streets', was a no-go area. It was a hive of wretchedness, home to murderers, thieves, junkies and the League of Sharks.

They met an old man called Stook, a street vendor selling greasy parcels of unidentifiable meat wrapped in a hard unidentifiable coating that tasted like cheese, albeit crunchy cheese. They were hungry so they bought some. Junk and Lasel couldn't manage more than a bite each without wanting to throw up. Cascér and Garvan however ate a dozen between them.

Stook told them all about Cuca and the League. He said everyone in Wotashi knew never to wander into Cuca. You would come out without your money or you might never come out at all. Stook, who was small and wrinkled with the blackest of black skin, grinned, showing his pink toothless gums, as he explained that the residents of Cuca, however, knew never to wander into the League's territory. They occupied a compound on the far side of Cuca where the shanty met the desert.

When they left the old man Cascér said that she would head into Cuca and take a look around. Lasel and Cascér had discovered that they had a language in common. Both had spent some time in Hooskar, a country in Cul Tayana. Though neither of them spoke Hooskarian fluently, they both spoke it well enough to make themselves understood. Garvan, who spoke fluent H'rtu, wasn't communicating with anyone until he had figured out how the box worked, so he was of no help.

'I don't think that's a good idea,' said Junk to Cascér, and Lasel translated. 'You heard what the old man said.'

Cascér smiled and explained that she had spent most of her life in shanty towns just like Cuca. She would fit in and pass unseen whereas Junk, Lasel and Garvan would look like outsiders. Junk didn't feel comfortable with Cascér taking such a risk on his account. When Lasel translated this for her, Cascér laughed heartily and pinched Junk's cheek.

'Toota shhnoova,' she winked.

Junk blushed.

While Garvan remained behind to continue working on the box, Junk and Lasel accompanied Cascér to the edge of Wotashi, where the buildings became more run-down and there were fewer people on the dirty, dusty streets.

As they said their goodbyes, they didn't notice that they were being watched. A Pallatan sat in the dark interior of a one-room building that was little more than a shack. His name was Itchil Rumanow and he was a big man bearing the symbol of the League of Sharks on his left arm. His head was malformed, the top of his skull flatter than in most of his kind. The shack was a makeshift diner. Rumanow had just finished eating and was taking his time, sipping a fermented curdled yoghurt drink that was a local favourite. Cascér's shapely looks caught his eye and he liked what he saw. He barely glanced at Junk and Lasel as they left Cascér and she carried on towards Cuca. Rumanow threw some money down and left.

Cascér knew how to walk through places like Cuca so that she didn't provoke the interest of strangers. She had never stopped to consider what it was before. Too much eye contact and you invite attention, not enough and you look like you're hiding and therefore invite attention. It was looking without looking.

Cuca was full of thieves and junkies, just as they had been warned, but it was also home to families. Children played in the streets. Streets that were littered with garbage, broken glass and excrement. The children laughed and shouted, just like children everywhere. Huge mounds of refuse were all about them. There was no rubbish collection in Cuca. The children played in and around the detritus that was home to skinny dogs, bloated rats and scavenging birds. Cascér had grown up in a place much like this. She saw a very young Pallatan girl, a toddler, playing with some other children of several different races. The Pallatan girl was wearing a bright dress that stood out against the squalor. Cascér smiled as she looked at the girl and thought back to her own childhood. She remembered playing in the streets with her brothers and friends when she probably wasn't much older.

She walked on for a little way, looking out for the League's compound, but she didn't need to look too hard. The shanty town ended abruptly in a towering wall constructed from a mishmash of building materials; seemingly anything that could be scavenged had been used. Blocks of ragged stone made up the base. On top of that were sections made of weathered wood next to panels of rusting metal alongside blocks of untarnished falakite. Despite its random appearance, it was solid and secure. So secure in fact that there didn't seem to be a way in. She walked around the perimeter. On the far side, Cascér found herself looking out at endless desert: rocky, dry and uninviting. She carried on until she was back where she had started. It was bigger than she initially assumed from looking at the front. It took her more than ten minutes to walk all the way around. She hadn't come across anything that resembled a door.

Just to the right of where she had begun was a ramshackle outbuilding that had long been abandoned. Most of its roof was gone and it looked as if a good breeze might sweep the rest away, but Cascér thumped its walls and they appeared solid enough. She glanced around and couldn't see anyone paying her any attention so she scrambled up on to the old shack. The moment she did this, everyone within view stopped what they were doing and looked in horror.

Who was this idiot? they were thinking. Doesn't she know who's behind that wall? Adults grabbed their children and quietly moved them inside, locking doors and closing window shutters as they went. Had Cascér looked around she would have noticed how the surrounding streets had suddenly emptied of life.

Cascér wasn't looking behind her however. She stood on the corner of the shack's wall and got her balance. The old building shifted a little beneath her but it felt sturdy enough. She reached up to her full height and could almost touch the top of the compound's wall. Bending at the knees she launched herself upwards and her fingertips snagged on to the lip of the wall. Coarse wood bit into the skin of her left hand. Smooth falakite felt cold under her right. She found it hard to get much of a grip on the falakite and she could feel her fingers slipping back. Straining her upper arm muscles, she started to pull herself up.

'What do you think you're doing?' The voice came from down at ground level behind her. A gruff male voice speaking H'rtu.

Cascér stopped what she was doing and turned to look at the speaker. It was Rumanow. He had followed her. Cascér didn't answer.

Rumanow hammered on the wall. 'Get out here,' he bellowed. 'Got a snooper.' He looked back up at Cascér and grinned. He waved his big hand at her. 'Why don't you come down here, girlie?'

Cascér could hear movement on the other side of the wall. Heavy footsteps, clanking metal, animal growls. Nothing appealing. She lowered herself down and then dropped the last little bit, finding her balance on the rickety roof of the outbuilding.

On the other side of the wall she could hear great locks being pulled aside and the mounting rumble of a vast gate starting to open.

She jumped off the outbuilding and landed firmly on the dusty ground in front of Rumanow. She rose slowly to her full height. Rumanow was considerably taller than her. His hand shot out and grabbed her chin. The suddenness of the action startled her.

'So what were you doing?' he asked. He looked her up and down. The slit that was his mouth stretched, showing dozens of small sharp teeth in blood-red gums. It was a smile. Sadistic and sinister. 'I think you maybe should come inside with me and my friends.'

There was a low metallic groan and the creaking of rusted wheels as part of the wall started to open outwards. It was a door made up of an entire section of the outer wall, which was why Cascér hadn't notice it before. She heard excited animal noises coming from behind it, impatient whines, claws scraping at the dirt in eagerness. She didn't want to see what was on the other side of it. She looked at Rumanow, holding his gaze. He smirked. He could see her fear. Then Cascér brought her foot up with as much force as she could muster, right between Rumanow's legs. The attack was so unexpected that Rumanow hardly made any noise. He croaked a little as he crumpled to the ground, his silver-grey skin turning purple. Cascér didn't look back as she ran.

The huge door opened fully and a dozen League members strode out. Several of them had dog-like animals straining on thick chains, snarling and snapping at the world. They were called yadis and looked like a cross between a large hyena and a more muscular hauk tine. Their mangy striped pelts were a dirty mustard colour. Their jaws were full of crooked jutting fangs dripping with saliva. The League members were all Pallatans, all male, all big, powerfully built, bald and heavily tattooed. One had a fish tattoo on the crown of his head. He was the Pallatan that Junk had followed through the first doorway, way back when he was diving the wreck of the *Pegasus*.

The Pallatans stood over Rumanow, who was still incapacitated on the ground. The crowd parted as one of their group made his way through the others. He reached Rumanow and looked down. Rumanow caught his breath and looked up into the scarred face of his superior. His name was Jacid Mestrowe and he was the man who had killed Ambeline.

'What are you doing?' Mestrowe looked irritated.

'Spy,' was all that Rumanow could manage. That and a small jerk of his head, indicating the direction Cascér had gone.

Mestrowe growled in the back of his throat, as if Rumanow had interrupted him in the middle of something he would much rather get back to, and looked at his lieutenant, an even more scarred individual than himself. His name was Koba Orrant. His broad silver face was criss-crossed with old scars, and in place of a left arm, from the elbow down, he bore a trident.

'Go,' said Mestrowe. Orrant gave a silent signal to several of the League members in possession of the animals and they set off at a brisk pace, the dogs pulling them forward. They fanned out, heading in different directions to cover more ground.

Cascér ran as fast as she could, trying not to look back but unable to resist. She stumbled and tripped as she powered through the desolate, labyrinthine streets of the shanty town. She didn't know where she was going, and too many streets she turned into were dead ends. She kept having to double back. She could hear the League members and their snarling animals coming after her. The Pallatans' thundering boots shook the fragile buildings around her. She was becoming increasingly scared now and she hated that.

Another dead end. She turned and went back. She was lost. Unsure which way she had come to begin with. The sound of her pursuers closed in on her from every direction.

She turned a corner and her eyes grew wide as she recognized where she was. This was where she had seen the little Pallatan girl in the colourful dress. She thought back, retracing her steps. She knew how to get out. She ran along the street and turned left. She slid to a stop as she found three League members coming towards her, their yadis barking and biting at the air. They saw her. Sight of their quarry thrilled the beasts and spittle flew free.

'HERE!" shouted one of the League members, one whose entire face had been tattooed. Cascér turned and ran the other way. But facing her were more League members with more frenzied animals, boxing her in.

She saw a gap between shacks and ran, throwing herself at it. She forced her way through somehow. The gap was a lot narrower than she was, but she refused to let such a trifling detail stop her. She pushed with all her might, squeezing through. Behind her the hounds were snapping at the opening, spraying foam up the edges of the shacks, desperate to be let loose. One by one they were unleashed and they pounded after her. The three beasts jostled for pole position, holding each other up just enough. Jagged hooks of metal and splinters of wood jutting out of the shacks on either side cut into Cascér until she stumbled out on the other side. Her body and face were streaked with bloody gashes. She grabbed a barrel overflowing with garbage and slammed it down at the exit she had just come out of. She heard the yadis slam into the other side. Felt their strong bodies pushing against it. She used a length of wood to jam the barrel in place and then she continued running.

She turned a corner and her heart sank. She found herself looking at the League's compound. It was the last place she wanted to be. She had managed to come full circle. She considered her options quickly and decided that the desert was her best hope. She hurried onward, and as she passed the gate that led inside the compound she saw Rumanow leaning back against the wall, still in pain from her assault. He saw Cascér at the exact same moment she saw him. He clambered to his feet. Cascér didn't slow down.

'SHE'S HERE!' shouted Rumanow. 'I'VE GOT HER!' As soon as Cascér got close enough she kicked out at Rumanow, aiming between his legs once more. She didn't even slow down as he dissolved to the ground. This time he was crying.

Just a few short strides past the compound the ground turned from dirt to rocky sand. Before her was the vast stretch of desert. Her lungs were burning and her muscles screaming. She needed to stop, but she knew she couldn't. She was totally exposed out here. There was nowhere to hide.

Back at the gates to the compound, the other League members had found Rumanow sobbing on the ground. Mestrowe lifted his head up.

'Where?' he asked. Rumanow could only look in the right direction.

Mestrowe let his head drop abruptly and led the others to the edge of the desert. The sun glared and he squinted as he looked out. It was hard to see anything in all the nothingness, but the longer he stared, the more his vision became accustomed to the situation and that was when he made out Cascér's fleeing shape.

'Orrant,' was all he said. The man with the trident arm nodded to three of the Pallatans who had yadis. They let the animals off their chains and they raced out into the desert. Mestrowe didn't care to see the outcome. The dogs would do what dogs do and then they'd come back. He headed back into the compound.

The three beasts darted over the sharp sandy-coloured ground. The saliva spilling from their jaws hit the dusty earth, leaving wet, black patches. They could smell their prey and gained on her quickly.

Cascér knew they were coming. She could hear their crazed snarls getting louder as her pursuers approached. Her strength was leaving her as quickly as the beasts were closing in on her. She looked over her shoulder. She could see them now. The animals were the colour of the sand and rocks. She could see their shadows more than them. She knew she had only seconds left. When they reached her, they would rip her to shreds. There was nowhere to hide, nowhere to go. Nothing she could do. She stopped running and turned. She caught her breath a little and wiped away the sweat that was stinging her eyes. Then she scanned the ground around her and found two jagged rocks that she could hold comfortably in her hands. She waited.

The three beasts honed in on her. The strongest, most vicious of the pack, was a dozen strides ahead of the other two and he attacked first. He leaped into the air, fangs bared, claws spread. He wanted nothing more than to taste first blood. Cascér brought one of the rocks up hard and fast and struck him across the top of his snout. He tasted first blood, but it was his own. He hit the ground, yowling with pain and shock. This turn of events gave the other two a moment's pause and they pulled up short. Cascér started running at them. Then the beasts stopped thinking and let instinct take over. They attacked. They bit and scratched and tore at her. Cascér beat them with the rocks.

23

Lasel and Junk paced the floor of the hotel room they had booked into. Cascér had been gone for hours and they knew something was wrong. Nothing could divert Garvan's attention from the box, so they didn't include him in their discussion about what to do. They had decided that, dangerous or not, they would have to venture into Cuca. Someone must know what had become of Cascér. They told Garvan they were leaving, but he didn't acknowledge them. They opened the door and gasped. Standing in front of them was Cascér.

She staggered into the room. Her clothes were ragged and she was covered in blood, her own as well as that of the dogs. She made her way over to one of the beds and fell on to it. Her hands and arms were covered in cuts and scratches, claw marks painted her skin.

'Jesus, what happened?' said Junk.

Cascér explained as best she could in Hooskarian, and Lasel translated. She described the League's compound and how she was spotted. She recounted the yadi attack and Lasel and Junk turned pale. Then she reached into her mouth and picked out a clump of fur from between her teeth. Junk and Lasel realized the fight wasn't as one-sided as they first thought. The dogs survived, said Cascér, and limped off with their tails between their legs. Apart from one whose tail was out in the desert somewhere.

'We need to get a doctor,' said Junk, but Cascér shook her head when Lasel translated. She assured them she would be OK and just wanted a bath. She got up and headed to the bathroom. She paused in the doorway.

'He's there,' she said in Hooskarian. 'The man with the scarred face. The man you're looking for.' She went in and locked the door behind her.

The next morning, Cascér announced that she was leaving. Junk couldn't blame her after what had happened, but she assured him that wasn't the reason.

'Then why?' asked Lasel.

'It's a fortress. You would need an army to defeat them.' She paused. 'And I know where you can find such an army.' Once Lasel had translated for Junk they both looked expectantly at Cascér. 'You must go to Tremmelleer. It is an island east of Payana and it's the only place to find Twrisks.'

'Twrisks? What are Twrisks?'

'The only army that could ever defeat the League.' Cascér looked deeply troubled as she spoke. 'What I'm telling you to do is the worst crime that could be carried out on a Pallatan. I'm betraying my own race by telling you this. And that is why I have to leave.'

271

'I don't understand,' said Junk. 'What sort of army are they?'

'The very worst,' said Cascér through Lasel. With that, Cascér left. She said that she hoped their paths would cross again one day but she couldn't stay any longer.

'Who on earth are they?' said Junk when she was gone. Lasel knew no more than he did. 'How long will it take us to get to this Tremmelleer?'

'By land-ship? Weeks.'

'I'm not keen on that idea then. It's taken me a very long time to get here. I don't want to set off on a new trajectory, not now I'm so close.'

'Sometimes . . .' said Garvan suddenly. It was the first thing he'd said in hours. '. . . the final step is the hardest to achieve.'

Lasel and Junk stared at him. Garvan stared back.

'So you think we should go to Tremmelleer?'

'I don't know.' Garvan shrugged. He blinked a couple of times and then turned his attention back to the box.

'Who are they? I mean, how do we get them to fight for us?' asked Junk. 'We can't pay them.'

'There's always a way of getting money,' said Lasel matter-of-factly.

'All right,' said Junk, 'but even if we could get enough money together, it'd take us weeks to get there, weeks to get back, and on the way back we'd have to find a way of transporting an army.' He shook his head. It all sounded so impossible. Though the truth was, he wanted this to be over now.

'It might work if Garvan ever figures out how to use the box,' said Lasel. This was the final straw for Garvan. He roared his frustration and got up, kicking the table. The table disintegrated.

'I can't do it,' he said through clenched teeth. 'I don't understand it. I always work things like this out. I've never failed before.' His cheeks looked flushed. 'I always understand everything I want to understand.'

'Come on,' said Junk. 'No one understands absolutely everything.'

'No, of course not,' agreed Garvan. 'Just the things I want to understand. There's plenty I don't understand, but I have no interest in those things.'

'Why don't you go and get some fresh air or something?' suggested Junk.

'How would fresh air help me decipher this?' asked Garvan. 'Air isn't a factor in the map. Unless it is.' He thought about it for a moment. 'No, it's not.'

'It clears your head sometimes,' said Junk. 'Gives you perspective. Maybe helps you think of something you've not tried so far.'

'I've tried everything,' said Garvan.

'Not everything,' said Lasel. 'Not the right thing.'

Garvan couldn't argue with that, so he went off for a walk. He promised to breathe regularly while he was out.

When he had left, Lasel went to have a bath and Junk was left alone. He picked up the box from the remnants of the destroyed table and crossed to a smaller table by the window. Garvan had left it opened out in its cruciform configuration. Junk traced the many interconnecting lines with the tip of his finger. He picked it up and turned it over. The hinged edges bent both ways and it all clicked together with a reassuring snap.

When he tried to open it up again he discovered, to his surprise, that the edges that had been hinged a moment before now separated and those that had been unconnected previously were now hinged. He tried to pull one of the sides free from the rest but it wouldn't budge. The six square faces that made up the cuboid could change their configuration but always needed to be connected on at least one edge.

Junk went to return the box to the formation that Garvan had left it in, when something cut him. He pulled back quickly and sucked the blood from a razor-thin line on the pad of his forefinger. At first he couldn't see what had inflicted the injury. He tilted the box slowly in all directions and then he noticed that there was another layer inside. It was made of glass fibre and was so thin that it was virtually invisible. On closer examination, he discovered that each face of the cube had a second transparent face. That meant there were twelve faces and not six.

Junk tapped one of the 'glass' faces gently with his fingernail. Because it was so thin, he assumed it was extremely delicate. But he was wrong. It made a tinging noise as he tapped it, so he tapped it harder, and harder again. It felt solid despite its insubstantiality.

He opened out all twelve faces and then started to slot them together. Almost as if they were designed to find their mate, they snapped into place with ease until Junk had made a twelve-sided polyhedron. If he'd known anything about geometry he would have been able to identify it as a rhombic dodecahedron. However, he didn't, so he didn't identify it as anything. As the last side slotted into place, the light that had glimmered when he had depressed the corners in order to open the doorway that had taken them to the Room of Doors bloomed to life. It flooded through the grooves and fissures on the solid sides and continued along the translucent faces as black lines.

Junk held it in his hands, marvelling at what was happening. The lines of illumination crept around the twelve-sided shape until they all met up, and suddenly it pulsed and a vast multidimensional map was projected all around the room, all around Junk. It was like being in a planetarium. He revolved slowly, gazing in wonder at lines and circles that floated all around him. It was like being surrounded by a map of the London Underground, though not as colourful but with many more train lines.

He set the dodecahedron down on the floor so his hands were free and reached out, trying to touch the light projection. To his astonishment, when his finger brushed through one of the many circles it reacted to his touch. It turned green and a green beam shot out from it, seeking out another circle. The one it found was at the heart of the projection.

The door to the bathroom opened and Lasel stepped out wearing a towel. She gasped at the sight that greeted her.

'What did you do?' she asked.

'Think I might have figured out how the map works,' said Junk. 'Look, you press one of these.' He touched another circle, which did the same as the first one. It turned green and connected via a beam of light to the circle in the centre. 'I think the circles are the doors wherever they are. And this one . . .' He pointed to the middle of the projection. '. . . This, I think, is the Room of Doors itself. All lines go there.'

At that moment, Garvan returned. 'I did breathing,' he announced as he entered. Then he saw the projection and stopped. His jaw bobbed slackly.

'What did you do? You solved it!' He looked down at the dodecahedron and pointed. 'It has more sides. Where did they come from?' His questions were all rhetorical. He stepped further into the room and stood next to Junk and Lasel so the projection enveloped him too. The three of them stared in awe, turning on the spot.

Garvan reached out and prodded the circle at the heart of the projection, the one Junk thought represented the Room of Doors. The moment he touched it, bright beams of light shot out from it and joined together to create a doorway just like the one they had passed through to reach the Room of Doors. Once it was complete, it started moving towards them, picking up speed. They had only a split second to panic, not long enough to react or move, and then it flashed past them and suddenly they weren't in the Wotashi hotel room any more. They were in the Room of Doors itself.

They were in a different part to where they had been before. It felt as if they were in the centre of the Room now, whereas before they were out on the periphery. Everything looked much the same here: thousands of green doors shimmering in the metallic darkness. However, there was a raised platform in front of them. A feature they had not seen before. Junk looked down and nudged Lasel. The dodecahedron was sitting on the ground with them, and though it was still humming with life and illumination, the projection had vanished. Junk picked it up and tucked it under his arm protectively.

'I'm just wearing a towel,' Lasel pointed out to the others. Junk waved her concern away. They would return to the hotel soon. He stepped up on to the platform and Garvan and then Lasel followed.

In the middle of the stage was a column about a metre and a half high. There was an impression on the top that looked like it was made for the dodecahedron. Junk felt sure he was doing the right thing when he slotted the quietly humming shape into the hole. It fitted perfectly and the moment it snapped into place the box exploded with light and the projection that had filled the hotel room returned but expanded a thousand-fold or more. It lit up the entire Room, marking each and every door that stood before them.

'Wow,' said Junk.

'Chul,' said Lasel, which was her equivalent.

'If you could decipher this, Garvan,' said Junk, 'we could go anywhere. We could go to Tremmelleer just like that.'

'Tremmelleer,' boomed a mighty disembodied voice, making all three of them jump. It continued in English. 'Temporal information required.'

'Who's that?' asked Junk.

'Temporal information required,' came the reply.

'You speak English.'

'I speak every language. Temporal information required.'

'Criptik Jansian?' asked Garvan. *Do you speak Jansian?*

'Maro. Criptiktar vara criptik.' *Yes. I speak every language.* Taking this as a challenge, Garvan repeated the question in every language he spoke, and every time the disembodied voice answered him in the corresponding tongue.

'I think we can take his word for it,' said Junk. 'Who are you?' he called out.

'I am the Gatekeeper,' came the reply.

'Are you real?' shouted Junk. 'Can we see you?'

'I am all around you. You are looking at me.'

'You're the Room?' said Junk.

'I am the Gatekeeper. Temporal information required.'

'Temporal?' Junk considered what this meant. 'Time. You want a date?' He looked at Garvan and Lasel. 'He's asking for a point in history. Err . . .' Junk thought about it and then said, 'Present day.'

A line in the projection flowed quickly out from where they were standing and made its way to a door seven levels up and a couple of dozen doors along. 'Location: Tremmelleer. Present day,' boomed the voice.

'Can I change my mind?' said Junk. Instantly the line receded to where they were. 'Tremmelleer. One hundred years ago.' Another line shot out from their location and made its way to a different door, this time nine levels up and twenty-eight along. 'Wait a second. How does your . . . dating stuff work?' Junk wasn't sure how else to term it.

'I am aware of all calendar systems.'

'Murroughtoohy, 23 March 2004.' Again a stream of green light shot out from the column and raced to a specific doorway.

'What's that date?' asked Lasel.

'The day Ambeline was born.' Junk surprised himself picking that day out of all the dates he could have picked. For years he'd thought of it as the worst day of his life, but now he realized that there was a part of him that wanted to go back and start all over again and be a better big brother this time, be a better knight. Of course that wouldn't stop scarface killing her. Maybe he should go back to that night, the night he came to their house, then lie in wait and kill him before he ever got inside. 'How precise can I be with the time I want to go to?'

'To the second,' came the Gatekeeper's reply.

'That's impossible,' said Garvan. 'You'd have to have trillions of doors to cover every second in history.'

Lasel looked around. 'Maybe there are trillions. Haven't you noticed that no matter where we are, we never see a wall? Maybe the Room just goes on forever.'

'Or it's more likely,' said Garvan, 'that the Gatekeeper controls which door takes you where and when.'

'If that's the case, why not just have one door then?' asked Lasel. Garvan furrowed his brow. He didn't have an answer. 'And how come he wasn't here when we went through before?'

'I don't know,' said Garvan. 'I know as much about it as you do. Junk?'

Junk hadn't been listening. His mind was still thinking about the night Ambeline died. He didn't know why scarface did what he did. He knew the League of Sharks were mercenaries. What if he had just been hired to kill Ambeline? That sounded daft. Who would hire anyone to kill a little girl? He could always ask him then. Scarface would be on his own and Junk would have the element of surprise. It would be perfect. 'Murroughtoohy, 14 December 2010, 2 a.m.' Ambeline had come into his bed just past midnight that night, and he was certain at least two or three hours had passed before scarface came.

Junk waited but nothing happened. 'Murroughtoohy, 14 December 2010, two a.m.' he said again but still nothing happened. He, Lasel and Garvan exchanged puzzled looks. 'What's wrong?' Junk called out.

'That date is forbidden,' came the disembodied Gatekeeper's reply.

'Why?' asked Junk, but the Gatekeeper didn't say anything else.

'Listen,' said Lasel, 'can we go back to the hotel now? I'm wearing a towel.'

Reluctantly Junk agreed. They asked the Gatekeeper to return them to Wotashi, and in the blink of an eye the gargantuan Room of Doors vanished and was replaced with their hotel room.

After Lasel dressed, she headed out to get some food to bring back to the hotel for them all. Junk paced the room. Why was going back to the time and place his sister died forbidden? Was there something larger and more sinister at play here? Was the Room of Doors part of a grander conspiracy? He knew how ridiculous such thoughts sounded, but then he was talking about a room that connected every point in history for the entire planet and perhaps beyond for all he knew. Maybe the entire universe. The whole thing was fantastical. He shook his head to clear it and focused on what needed to be done next. He had come a long way and the finishing line was within view.

'I'm going to go to Tremmelleer first thing in the morning,' he said to Garvan. 'If there's an army there capable of defeating the League of Sharks, then Tremmelleer is where I need to be. I'm going to go alone though.'

'Why?' asked Garvan.

'There's no need for you and Lasel to be exposed to any more unnecessary danger.'

Garvan snorted derisively and shook his head. 'We've come this far with you, Junk. We'll go to Tremmelleer too.'

Lasel was walking back with the provisions and not paying attention to her environment. Her mind was elsewhere, thinking about the Room of Doors and what was to come next. She didn't notice that she was being watched. A shadow stepped out into her path. Rumanow.

'I know you,' said Rumanow in H'rtu, which Lasel didn't speak. 'I saw you with *her*.' His hand shot out and grabbed Lasel by the throat. She dropped the bag as he lifted her off the ground. 'Who are you?'

Lasel didn't understand what he was saying. She squirmed and struggled and shouted for help but Rumanow was too strong for her.

Up in the hotel, Junk and Garvan heard Lasel's cries and ran to the window in time to see Rumanow carrying her away, heading in the direction of the shanty town.

'Oh no,' said Junk. His mind was racing, trying to work out what to do. He made the decision quickly and didn't question it in case he managed to talk himself out of it. 'Use the Room,' he said to Garvan. 'Go to Tremmelleer, try and get help'. Junk moved to leave.

'We should think about this,' said Garvan.

Junk shook his head. 'No time.'

'What are you going to do?'

Junk shrugged. 'Distract them until you can get there.'

'What if the Twrisks won't come?' Junk didn't have an answer. At least not one he fancied articulating. He left.

Garvan turned to the box and started to open it out.

24

Junk ran out of the hotel and raced through the dark streets of Wotashi, heading west towards Cuca. Wotashi was not a lively town at the best of times, but after nightfall it almost completely shut down. Junk didn't see another soul. Everything was quiet and closed up for the night. He couldn't see the Pallatan who had carried Lasel off or hear her shouting any more.

As soon as he reached the outskirts of the shanty town, it was as though he was in a different place altogether. As he drew closer, he heard laughter and music and loud voices. There were bonfires on every street corner. The residents of Cuca were sitting outside their rickety two-room homes eating and drinking, talking with their neighbours. Children of all ages were playing in the streets. It was like a party was being held in every one of its narrow, dirty alleyways.

The bonfires cast long shadows and Junk was careful to stick to the darkness. He was quite sure he wouldn't pass for a local if anyone noticed him. It wasn't easy. The shacks were pushed up against one another and there wasn't much space that wasn't occupied.

But Junk kept his head down and moved briskly.

The closer he got to the League's territory, the quieter it became. Finally he reached the high patchwork outer wall. He saw the dilapidated outbuilding that Cascér had scaled, but she was considerably taller than him and even if he got up on to the roof, he wasn't sure he could then make it to the top of the wall. He stood staring up at the towering slab before him, trying to work out how to breach it. Cascér had said it was the same all the way around. Getting over it was going to be quite some task.

Then he had a flash of inspiration. What if he went under it? Maybe it was designed with people the size of Pallatans in mind. Would someone as small as Junk even be considered a threat by the League? He dropped down on his hands and knees and started scraping away the dirt at the base, hoping that they hadn't planted the foundations too deeply. He was in luck. The boulders that made up the bottom strata of the wall were only buried a metre and a half down. The dirt here was dry and it only took Junk about ten minutes to dig a small passageway beneath the wall.

He slid under, arching his back and pushing his way through. Loose soil rained down on him, getting into his eyes and mouth. He came up inside the compound and was careful to stay low, looking around to get the lie of the land. It was dark here so he was hidden from view. However, the first thing he noticed was that there was no one around. There were twenty or so single-storey buildings in small groups of three or four on either side of a crooked path. Everything was quiet and still. Then, just as he was about to carry on, he registered movement out of the corner of his eye and he froze. He turned to see a yadi – he recognized it from Cascér's description – come padding around the corner. It stopped and looked in Junk's direction. Its fur was patchy, there was crusted blood on its snout and one ear had been bitten almost in half. A flap of cartilage clung on stubbornly. If this was one of the beasts that Cascér fought with, then she had possibly come off the better.

After a few moments of seeming to stare straight at Junk, the animal walked on. Junk watched as it entered a small barn just beyond the single-storey buildings. He moved quietly to the barn and peered inside. There were a dozen similar animals. Most appeared to be asleep or on the brink of nodding off. Junk reached out and pushed the door shut. There was a bolt on the outside, and he slid it across quietly.

Then he stood up and looked around. Where was everyone and, more importantly, where was Lasel?

The buildings inside the compound were much the same as those outside: poorly constructed shacks. There was another group, a dozen or more, dotted around an open-air exercise yard. As Junk drew closer, he heard low voices murmuring and one dominant voice. Junk rounded one of the shacks and found himself looking out over the entire assembled League of Sharks standing in a broad circle under the stars. There were about twenty-five Pallatan men, all branded with the League's symbol: the shark's fin and five stars. Most sported numerous other tattoos as well, on their bodies and hairless heads. Junk was reminded of Russian gangsters he had seen (and made sure to avoid) in the waterfront bars of Arkhangelsk in northern Russia, when he had been working on a trawler in the White Sea. Their criminal history and life story was written on their bodies through tattooed symbols, such as cupolas signifying prison sentences and a ship expressing a desire for freedom, among dozens of others.

Junk moved around the back of one of the shacks in order to get a better view. The sight that greeted him filled him with horror. A metal stand that looked like a gallows stood in the centre of the yard. It was five or so metres high, and hanging by her ankles from an arm at the top was Lasel. Two of the Pallatans were swinging her back and forth, making her spin. Junk recognized one of them immediately. He was the one with a fish tattoo on the top of his head. The one Junk had followed into the Room of Doors. The other was Rumanow. Most of the rest looked on, muttering to one another, their eyes following the swinging girl. One of the Pallatans was standing in front of Lasel with his back to Junk. He was the one speaking. He spoke Jansian. His voice rode over everything else.

'My patience wears thin, girl,' he said. 'Where is she? Tell me now.' Junk knew he meant Cascér.

Rumanow spoke: 'Let me ask her, Jacid. I will get her to talk.' Then the man in front of Lasel turned and Junk saw his face. He recognized him at once. It was scarface.

The man who killed his sister. The man he had come here looking for. And now he had a name. Half a name anyway: Jacid.

'Mestrowe,' said another man, this one with a trident in place of his left lower arm. Junk had a full name for his quarry now: Jacid Mestrowe. 'Rumanow's right. We can't just stay here all night. She's not said a word.'

Junk formulated a quick plan in his head. He needed to distract the Pallatans, set Lasel free and get them both back to the hole under the outer wall before anyone realized. The first thing he noticed was that the rope around Lasel's ankles was secured to the base of the metal stand with a type of hitch knot: easy to tie and, more importantly, easy to untie.

A few metres to his left was a barrel-shaped brazier burning brightly. It was one of many dotted around the exercise yard. Staying low and out of sight, Junk crept close to the brazier until he was able to get his hand underneath. Slowly he pulled it towards one of the shacks and carefully he tipped it back so it was resting precariously against the front of the shack, rocking gently from side to side. The coals inside shifted with each movement so that the rocking gradually increased. Junk crept back into the shadows and moved away as fast as he dared.

Lasel felt ill. She had been hanging upside down for too long and the constant spinning and swinging wasn't helping. She felt sure she was about to throw up and was determined to direct it at one of her captors. Rumanow was closest.

Mestrowe stopped her swinging. It was a relief. 'For the last time, tell me who you are, girl. I'm growing impatient.'

Lasel was raised high enough off the ground so that she was face to face with him. 'You were seen with the woman. Where is she?' Lasel said nothing. 'Who else are you with?' Lasel said nothing. 'What is it you want with us?' Lasel said nothing. 'Speak or I will leave you to their mercy.' He gestured over his shoulder at the grinning hordes of the League of Sharks. 'And they have none,' he added, a little redundantly.

Lasel opened her mouth to speak, but as she did so something caught her attention and she looked up to see one of the shacks was ablaze. Half of the Pallatans rushed to put out the fire, but it spread quickly and more and more of the League went to help until Lasel was left alone.

Junk moved fast. He sprinted out into the open, across the exercise yard, coming up behind Lasel. He ducked his face in front of hers so she knew it was him. Instinctively she started to speak but he put a hand over her mouth to stop her. She quickly got the message.

Junk grabbed the end of rope trailing from the knot and pulled. It should have unravelled easily, but it didn't. It seemed that although it looked like a type of hitch knot, it wasn't. It was a type Junk had not seen before. Pulling the rope only tightened the knot. Junk cursed under his breath and set about trying to undo the knot. He kept one eye on the Pallatans, who were all still occupied with the fire.

Junk's heart was pounding and his fingers felt fat and clumsy. The sweat dripped from his brow, stinging his eyes and blurring his vision. Everything he did to the knot only made it stronger and more secure. So he stopped. He realized he needed to think clearly. He took a breath, wiped the sweat off his face and studied the knot. It took him a few seconds to see how it had been tied and therefore how to untie it. He looked up at Lasel and smiled. Then he noticed that scarface had turned away from the burning shack and was staring straight at him. For a moment it was as if scarface couldn't believe what his one good eye was seeing. He barked to his comrades in H'rtu and started striding back towards Junk and Lasel. Junk felt the panic rising in him again and he tried to focus on undoing the knot. Two fingers under the bight, pull back and out and the rope unravelled. Scarface and some of the other Pallatans were halfway across the exercise yard as Junk lowered Lasel to the ground.

A throb of elation ran through Junk for a split second until he realized that the rope was still tied securely around her ankles and she was unable to move. Junk had no choice but to scramble to his feet and throw Lasel over his shoulder. He started running.

They didn't get very far before they were surrounded by the League.

*

After all this time, Junk finally found himself face to face with the man who killed his sister. Unfortunately it wasn't quite how Junk would have liked this meeting to take place. He and Lasel were both now strung up by their ankles back to back. Junk was looking into Jacid Mestrowe's one good eye upside down.

'I don't know you,' said Mestrowe in Jansian. 'Who are you, boy?' Junk didn't answer. He was scared, very scared, and he didn't want to sound weak in front of Mestrowe. He managed to hide his fear by clenching his jaw tight shut. It gave him a resolute look.

Rumanow pitched forward and backhanded Junk, sending him spinning wildly. 'He asked you a question, you scust. You better answer. I saw you both with her.' Mestrowe reached out to stop Junk's unfettered spinning.

'What do you want with us?' said Mestrowe, calmly and quietly. Junk still didn't answer. Suddenly Mestrowe's hand shot out and clamped around Lasel's throat. He started to squeeze. He could crush her windpipe like a dry leaf if he chose.

'No,' shouted Junk.

'Who are you?' Mestrowe asked again. Lasel's face was starting to turn purple.

'Murroughtoohy,' said Junk.

Mestrowe stared at Junk. He didn't relax his grip on Lasel, who looked as if she was about to lose consciousness. Her tongue was ballooning out from between her teeth. Her eyes were all white.

291

'Please stop,' said Junk. Mestrowe carried on for another few seconds and then pulled his hand away. Instantly, Lasel gulped down as much oxygen as she could take in at one go. She started coughing violently, every angry exhalation shaking her whole body.

Mestrowe pushed her aside, ignoring the sound, and looked blankly at Junk. 'What is Murroughtoohy? Is that supposed to mean something?'

'You went through the Room of Doors . . .' Junk noticed Mestrowe react to the mention of the Room. 'You went three million years back to a place on the west coast of Ireland. You took a little girl from her bed.' Mestrowe frowned as he thought back. 'That was my sister. I chased you but you went over the cliff.' Mestrowe shrugged. It meant nothing. Junk forgot about his predicament briefly. Anger mushroomed inside him. How dare Mestrowe not remember something that had changed Junk's life so completely. 'How can you not remember it?'

Mestrowe grabbed Junk's face and brought it close to his. 'Watch your tone with me, boy,' he said. 'I've killed lots of sisters and brothers and mothers, fathers, husbands, wives, sons and daughters. Why would I remember one out of so many? And I don't remember you.' Mestrowe pushed Junk away and he swung back and forth, rotating first one way and then the other.

'Fatoocha mammacoola charla,' said Junk to Mestrowe's back as he started to walk away. Mestrowe stopped and turned. He caught Junk and stopped him swinging. Now there was a look of dawning recognition on his face.

'That's what you said to me that night,' said Junk. 'I've never forgotten those words. Do you remember me now?'

Mestrowe didn't answer straight away. When he did he said, 'No.' Junk felt crestfallen. 'But I remember the girl.'

'Fatoocha mammacoola charla,' said Junk again. 'The Nine Emperors send their regards. Tell me who the Nine Emperors are.'

'This has haunted you, hasn't it, boy?' said Mestrowe.

Junk tried not to respond but despite himself he nodded.

Mestrowe grinned. 'Good.' He laughed. 'Let it stay that way.'

Junk thrashed, straining at the ropes binding him. 'Why did you kill my sister?' he shouted.

Mestrowe laughed heartily to see his distress. 'You'll never know, boy. Though let me tell you, she died screaming.'

'NO! NO! NO!' Mestrowe's words had the desired effect, turning Junk apoplectic with rage. He whipped back and forth, struggling to get free. Laughing, Mestrowe pushed him away and Junk swung towards Rumanow who, laughing too, swung him towards Orrant, who swung him to Fish-Head. All the Pallatans were laughing now and stamping their feet.

'Stop it,' shouted Lasel. 'Stop!'

Mestrowe stopped laughing. He grabbed hold of Junk and stopped him swinging. The atmosphere ran cold.

'Cut their throats. Let them bleed out,' said Mestrowe to Rumanow. 'Then dump their bodies in the desert. The scavengers can have them.'

Junk and Lasel looked on with wild, staring eyes as Rumanow drew out a long blade and started advancing on them as Mestrowe strode away.

Junk and Lasel swung next to each other, powerless. Junk raced through the distant corners of his mind for something, a way out.

'This is your last chance,' he shouted. 'Free us or die.'

Mestrowe stopped and turned, looking furious but only for a moment. Then his face exploded into a huge grin and he started choking with laughter. All the Pallatans joined in. Tears were streaming down Mestrowe's face as he held his arms wide. 'How?' he said. 'How do you intend to kill us?'

'Free us or die,' he said again.

'Maybe I should keep you around for the entertainment value,' said Mestrowe through his laughter. He stopped laughing abruptly. 'But no,' he said. 'Kill them.' Once again he turned to leave, but as he did so the dazzling glow of a doorway of green light appeared on the far side of the exercise yard. Everyone turned. Junk breathed a sigh of relief: the cavalry was here.

There was movement and someone stepped out of the doorway. Junk frowned. It was not what he had been expecting. Standing in the green glow was a short, stocky creature, not quite half a metre high and about as wide as he was tall. He looked like a moving boulder with stubby little legs. His skin was a milky pale colour and he was dressed in rags. His head was small, his face smaller still. His eyes and mouth (no nose) were squished into the middle of his face, framed by an expanse of featureless white skin.

'What's that?' said one of the Pallatans with an amused sneer.

More movement now and more of the little creatures stepped through the portal. About two dozen or so.

Orrant got to his feet. He was breathing heavily and had a worried look on his face. 'We need to go,' he said mostly to himself and turned, breaking into a run. The other Pallatans looked after Orrant and laughed. They exchanged puzzled looks. Who would be afraid of such creatures?

The tiny men who had come through the doorway were hard to tell apart. All were pretty much the same height, build and colouring, and all dressed alike. They fanned out, each moving towards one of the Pallatans, with a docile mouth and twinkling eyes. They looked and moved in a dreamlike fashion. Like they were sleepwalking through bubblegum.

'What do you want, titch?' said one of the Pallatans.

In response, the little man standing in front of him smiled serenely and held out his hand. The Pallatan was about to take it when, in the blink of an eye, the little man pounced into the air and latched on to him. In that instant, they all attacked. They were like people who have been in the desert for too long and have spotted an oasis. Despite the vast difference in size and strength, the Pallatans instinctively backed away as the little men kept coming.

One of them ran at Rumanow, who kicked out at him, catching him square in the chest. The Pallatan's foot embedded itself in the small man's torso as if it was hollow and he hopped around comically, trying to shake off the tiny body attached to him. Finally he sat on the ground and pulled it off. Only then did he notice that its face was gone. There was a gap in the middle of its head where the face had been. Rumanow paused for a moment, trying to work out what had happened. Then he felt something on his back and twisted, trying to see what was there.

What was there was a milk-white snake-like creature, about four inches long, bearing the face of the little man who had attacked him at the front of its slimy, fat little tuberous body. It slithered swiftly up Rumanow's torso towards his head. Panicking now, the Pallatan was trying to grab it or brush it off, but the creature moved too rapidly. It reached his ear and dived in, burrowing inside. Rumanow grabbed his head and started screaming.

Junk had been watching, transfixed by what was happening to Rumanow, who was directly in front of him. He looked on with horror now. Then he became aware of more screams. Screams from all around the compound. All the Pallatans were being attacked. Some were fighting back; most had already lost. Some were on the ground, wrestling with their small round assailants. Others were thrashing about, trying to shake off the fat white worms. Others, like Rumanow, were just sitting there, silent and dazed, staring blankly in front of them.

Jacid Mestrowe was sitting on top of one of the little men, pummelling him with his big fists. Suddenly the little man's body collapsed in on itself and Mestrowe's fists went straight through his calcified chest cavity. Mestrowe looked down at the creature, looked into his eyes, and for a moment the Pallatan thought he had won.

Then he watched in horror and disbelief as the creature strained and twisted its face and ripped it back, separating it from the middle of its own head. The face vanished from view for a moment and then reappeared, gliding up Mestrowe's arm on a larval body.

Mestrowe hurled himself backwards and started flailing about on the ground, trying to shake the creature off. He paused for a moment, having lost track of its progress. He looked down at his sleeve. A trail of pus was leading up his arm and he followed it over his back to the opposite shoulder. He twisted his head to look and there was the creature. It winked at him before launching itself at the side of his head. Mestrowe felt it penetrate his ear. He tried to grab it but it slipped between his fingers.

Mestrowe froze. He could feel it moving about inside his head. The creature followed the Pallatan's ear canal until, burrowing deeper, it drilled into his brain. Mestrowe grabbed his head in both hands and rolled around the floor, screaming in agony, bucking and jerking. Inside him, the creature reached his brain stem and wound itself around it, fixing his position with tiny barbs that grew out of his underbelly.

Junk and Lasel stared, taking in the astonishing sight. All the Pallatans were calming down now. One by one they developed the same sleepy expression on their faces. The screaming around the compound gradually petered out until a hush descended over the area. All was still.

A new shadow appeared in the door of green light. Garvan stepped into the compound and moved through the detritus of the little people's discarded bodies. He made his way to Junk and Lasel.

'What happened?' asked Junk. 'What are they?'

'These are Twrisks,' said Garvan.

'What have they done to the Pallatans?' asked Lasel. 'Have they killed them?'

Garvan shook his head. 'Quite the opposite. Twrisks are "gelda". I'm not sure what the translation is in English. They live inside the host. Attach themselves to their brain stem, and then it's like the host has a pilot. Their problem was that the only species they're compatible with are Pallatans, but there aren't any Pallatans on Tremmelleer so they build these funny little bodies . . .' he glanced around at all the discarded desiccated carcasses scattered over the floor, '. . . but it's only half a life. They jumped at the chance to come here.'

*

298

The battle was over now and the Pallatans had lost. The Twrisks had each found a host body. Some chose to share a host with a mate. Garvan helped Lasel and Junk down.

'I don't understand,' said Junk. 'How come they live somewhere with no Pallatans if they need Pallatans?'

'They were exiled there a long time ago and they can't travel very easily or very far. These bodies they build for themselves are functional but basic.' Garvan picked up a discarded leg and handed it to Junk. On examination, Junk saw that it was hollow. It appeared to be made out of animal hair, mud and some sort of shiny discharge.

'So the Twrisks are just the little wormy things?'

'That's right,' said Garvan. 'The rest is like a shell to a crab.'

'Wow,' said Lasel. 'Who exiled them?'

'Pallatans, of course,' said Garvan. 'Wouldn't you?'

Junk sought out Jacid Mestrowe and stood over him. Mestrowe sat on the floor, shivering and cupping his right ear.

'K-k-kill me,' he pleaded to Junk, and a flash of pain inflicted by the Twrisk inside him shot through his body. 'Don't be like that,' said Mestrowe, but the inflection in his voice was different. It was the Twrisk inside him speaking through him, using Mestrowe's own vocal cords, tongue and mouth. Mestrowe rose to his feet clumsily and looked at Garvan.

'You were as good as your word,' said the Twrisk, using Mestrowe's mouth.

'Is that you, Payo?' asked Garvan.

'It is,' said Mestrowe's mouth.

Garvan turned to Junk and Lasel. 'Payo was one of the first Twrisks I met when I got to Tremmelleer. Payo, these are the friends I told you about – Junk and Lasel.'

'I'm happy to meet you,' said Payo–Mestrowe. 'Garvan told us about your journey. Sounds epic. So I picked the bad guy, huh? What do you want to do with him?'

'Well, my plan had always been to kill him, but he seems to want that to happen now so I think leaving him how he is would be a worse punishment.'

'No,' barked Mestrowe, but Payo inflicted pain on him somehow and he pulsed and then was quiet.

'But I'd like to ask a favour of you, Payo. I want you to come with me to take him back home. I need to show my mother I wasn't lying, that I didn't kill my sister; he did. Would you mind? After that, I'll take you to Tremmelleer or wherever you want to go.'

'No problem,' said Payo–Mestrowe.

'No,' said Mestrowe, and then he flinched in pain again.

'It takes a while to break them in,' said Payo–Mestrowe. 'I'll happily come with you. I've been stuck on Tremmelleer for such a long time it'd be good to see somewhere else.'

The Pallatan–Twrisks explored the compound. Garvan had promised to return them to Tremmelleer if that was where they wanted to go, but only about half a dozen took him up on the offer. The rest decided to stay put and explore the world in their new bodies.

Junk returned to the hotel room and found Lasel was there already. She looked sad.

'What's wrong?' asked Junk.

'You'll be leaving soon,' she said. 'Going home.'

'That's right,' said Junk.

'Your home's a long way from here.'

'Not that far. Only about six thousand miles . . . and three million years.' They both smiled.

'Will I ever see you again?' asked Lasel.

Junk frowned, considering for the first time that he would have to part ways with Lasel, and Garvan too. 'You could come with me.' Junk didn't want to leave Lasel, but was trying not to sound too desperate. Unfortunately he overcompensated, and to Lasel it sounded like he really didn't care one way or the other.

She shook her head. 'I don't belong there.'

'I guess not,' said Junk. He really wanted to say the exact right thing, the thing that would make her come with him, but his mind was blank. 'What will you do now?'

Lasel shrugged. 'I don't know. See where life takes me. It's how I've lived since I was seven years old. It's worked out so far.' She gave him a thin smile.

Junk wondered what would happen if he told her how he felt. He wished Garvan hadn't made his feelings towards Lasel known. Would his friendship with Garvan survive? Would she laugh in Junk's face? Or worse, be embarrassed? He decided it was far better to say nothing and if Lasel felt anything at all for him, then maybe he would pick up on a hint from her.

A doorway of green light materialized in the middle of the room and Garvan stepped through, holding the box in its dodecahedron form. The doorway closed after him.

'That's all the Pallatan–Twrisks that wanted to go back returned to Tremmelleer,' said Garvan. 'What are you two talking about?'

'Nothing,' said Junk and Lasel together, which sounded suspicious. 'Just about me going home,' added Junk.

'Oh, you're not going home yet,' said Garvan casually.

'Err, yeah, Garvan, I am. I have to, mate. I haven't seen my mum and my dad for years. I've done what I came here to do.'

'Oh, I understand that,' said Garvan. 'It's just you don't go. Not yet.'

'What? Why not?'

'I don't know. It wasn't in the dream.' Garvan shrugged and headed into the bathroom, closing the door after him. Junk and Lasel only had time to exchange a quick look of mutual puzzlement and then the door to the bathroom opened again and Garvan stuck his head out. 'It might have something to do with what Mestrowe tells you.'

'What do you mean? What does he tell me?'

'I don't know,' said Garvan. 'That wasn't part of the dream either.'

Junk headed out of the hotel and went back to the compound. All the remaining Pallatan–Twrisk hybrids were awake. Twrisks didn't need to sleep. Pallatans did, but the Twrisks could put their bodies into sleep mode any time they wanted and twenty minutes would recharge them. Pallatans who learned to embrace their passenger could live long and fulfilling lives. Those that didn't would also live long lives but would lose their Pallatan mind along the way. It would retreat to some dark, dank corner of their psyche and stay there shivering for the rest of their days. The Twrisk would have full control but it would be a lonely existence. Twrisks preferred the company.

Junk found Payo–Mestrowe in the compound's kitchen sampling all sorts of different types of food.

'Junk,' said Payo when he saw him approaching, 'would you like some blue stuff?' He offered Junk a tub with a blue-tinged dip inside. 'What's it called?'

Junk shrugged, but realized almost immediately that Payo wasn't talking to him. He was talking to Mestrowe. It was quite disconcerting.

'Yarud,' said Mestrowe.

'Would you like some yarud?' said Payo to Junk. Junk shook his head. Payo dipped Mestrowe's finger into the tub and scooped out a glob, which he ate, nodding appreciatively.

'I don't know how this works but can I ask *him* a question?' Junk felt it was clear he was referring to Mestrowe.

'Course,' said Payo, through another mouthful of yarud. 'Ask away.'

Junk took a deep breath and settled himself before speaking. His mind had been working overtime since Garvan had said that Mestrowe was going to tell him something. He had thought of every possibility and had convinced himself that he was going to explain who the Nine Emperors were and why they had sent their regards. 'Is there something you have to tell me?' He and Payo both waited for a response, but none came.

'Well, answer him,' said Payo.

There was an almost imperceptible change in the expression on the Pallatan–Twrisk's face, as if Mestrowe was now the more dominant.

'Your sister . . .' said Mestrowe, and Junk tensed. His fists clenched, ready to strike out if Mestrowe said anything despicable. 'I wasn't hired to kill her. I was hired to obtain her.'

The words raced around inside Junk's head, waving their arms about and making as much noise as possible. He found it hard to process what Mestrowe had said. Mestrowe could see it on Junk's face and so he clarified.

'She's not dead. At least, not the last time I saw her. I delivered her alive and well.'

'Delivered her? Delivered her to who?' said Junk. He was shaking. Not ready to believe what he was hearing, but wanting, for all the world, for it to be true.

'To the Nine Emperors, of course,' said Mestrowe.

'Why?' asked Junk.

'I don't know. That's what they paid me to do, so that's what I did.'

Junk walked slowly back to the hotel. His mind was raging but gradually his thoughts were beginning to settle. For over three years he had thought his sister was dead, and his objective had been clean and unwavering: to find her killer. It was what he needed to do to go home and he so wanted to be able to go home, but he knew now that that wasn't going to happen. Not yet.

Garvan and Lasel looked at him expectantly when he returned. They were eager to hear what Mestrowe had said.

'You were right,' Junk said to Garvan. 'I'm not going home yet. My sister's still alive. I'm going to go and find her.'

TO BE CONTINUED . . .

JANSIAN GLOSSARY

A

a	the
ai	hey
ambe	anyone
ante	anywhere
arrat	inside
artch	snap/break

B

ba	you
barrat	outside
Bosck dei Varm	Room of Doors
brask	appointment

C

car	like
carrollotu	we would like to
casca(ba)	call (you)
chiva	let's go/come on
chul	wow
chuva tapar	I don't go
coorratun	heretic/infidel/unworthy
cootun	bastard or similar
criptik	language/speech/say
criptiktar/criptik te	I speak/you speak
criptik tapar	I don't speak your language
cul	south

D

daté	west
dattakar	thief
dinta took	what a tale/story
dint	what
dusca	where (are we)
dusco	here

E

et	his/him

F

fal	ten
fal-gi	eleven

G

galm	from
glarn	north
gusk	leave

H

harru	look/see
hupta	problem
hyka	day

I

inta vol	on my island
its	hear

J

jard	aboard
jorda	ground; also the name of the planet
junta	police

K

kimmer	stay/wait here/remain
krimpta criptik te?	how many languages do you speak?

L

lanatar	do you have
lugh	note

M

maro	yes
mosshut	a port-like wine
mullatapar	I don't understand

N

nenga	not/no
nusca (ba)?	who are (you)?

O

occootoo	hello
oot	about

P

palar	I can
papakar ...	how do I ...
penca	usually
puttum	climb (up)

R

rooth	choice

S

salli	money
set	her
solip	roof
song	make
sonta	with
sonti	without

T

ta	me
tamatay	I'm alone
tankata	follow me
tapar	I don't
ta pody ti cluka	your friend needs to wake
ta pody ti veta chet	your friend is asleep
tarra dei omm	ticket office
ti	is
tumpah plugh	open his mouth
tunk	stop
tunty	little
tuug	now

U

unta	east
utta	why

V

vara	every
vestum	help
vontra	doctor

Y

yony	back/return

Z

zebla	welcome

H'RTU GLOSSARY

A

Atcha fanany muunt	██████████████

C

chachin	get some/get more
chikka na radoo	he was an irritating little man

D

dutu	pour

F

Fatoocha mammacoola charla	Nine Emperors send their regards

H

harutuk	quickly

J

ja	cheers
jay	little man

N

na foota bootchek	now what do you want to know?
navoora	return/go back

T

tootu shhnoova	delicious/a tasty snack
trara ju	he's asking about your language

Z

zuc	sacs/bags

ACKNOWLEDGEMENTS

I would like to thank Roisin Heycock, my fabulous editor, and everyone at Quercus. A really outstanding team. A huge thanks to Talya Baker for once again saving me from my own mistakes.

Thank you to Eugenie Furniss and Liane-Louise Smith at Furniss-Lawton for all their advice and hard work on my behalf. And Lucinda Prain and Rob Kraitt at Casarotto-Ramsay for guiding the other half of my working life for me.

Thank you to Zhiqiao Zheng, Priti Barua, Ingela Holland, Garret Cummings and Alexina Ashcroft for their translation skills.

Thanks also to Jason Cramer, whose drawings turned my camembert-fuelled dreams about goat doctors and elephant men into something tangible and kickstarted this book.

And a very special thanks to George Arton, my good friend who is still bemoaning the fact I forgot to name-check him in my last book even though I added his name for the paperback – though I don't think he's noticed that yet because I don't think he's actually read the book.

And last but by no means least, thank you to my amazing children, who make me very proud, Joseph, Grace and Gabriel, to the world's greatest dog, Harper, our new addition, Dok the python, and to my beautiful, wonderful, patient wife, Lisa.

THE NINE EMPERORS

Watch out for the next instalment
of Junk's adventure

COMING AUGUST 2014

www.quercusbooks.co.uk

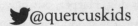@quercuskids